11-28

#9

Teardrop
Lane

Center Point
Large Print

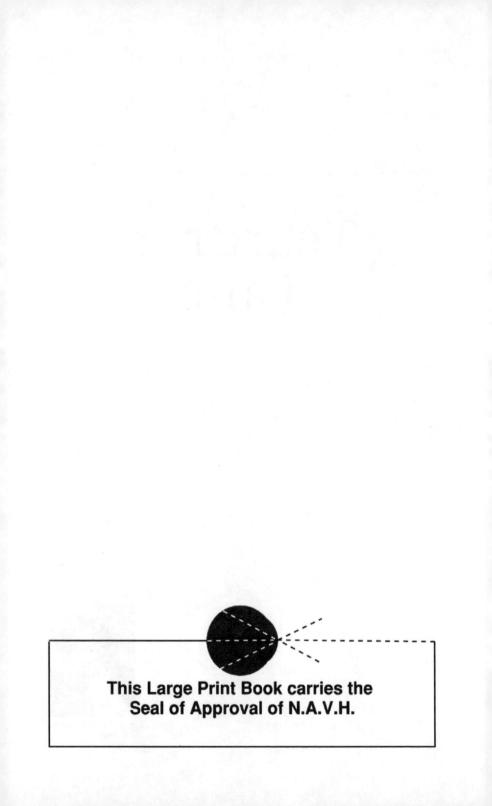

**This Large Print Book carries the
Seal of Approval of N.A.V.H.**

#9

Teardrop Lane

An Eternity Springs Novel

EMILY MARCH

CENTER POINT LARGE PRINT
THORNDIKE, MAINE

This Center Point Large Print edition is published
in the year 2015 by arrangement with Ballantine Books,
an imprint of Random House,
a division of Penguin Random House LLC.

The text of this Large Print edition is unabridged.
In other aspects, this book may vary
from the original edition.
Printed in the United States of America
on permanent paper.
Set in 16-point Times New Roman type.

ISBN: 978-1-62899-591-6

Library of Congress Cataloging-in-Publication Data

March, Emily.
 Teardrop Lane : an Eternity Springs novel / Emily March. — Center
Point Large Print edition.
 pages cm
 Summary: "Town physician Rose Anderson has given up on dreams of
a family until she meets artist Hunt Cicero, who has just become
guardian to his sister's children and needs Rose and her warm maternal
instincts to complete his patchwork family"—Provided by publisher.
 ISBN 978-1-62899-591-6 (library binding : alk. paper)
 1. Women physicians—Fiction. 2. Large type books. I. Title.
 PS3604.A9787T43 2015
 813′.6—dc23
                                                    2015010046

For Kate Collins, Junessa Viloria,
and Gina Wachtel.
For all you've done to bring
Eternity Springs to life,
my most sincere thanks.

One

January
Galveston, Texas

The throbbing beat of U2 blasted from speakers mounted on the metal rafters of the old warehouse as Cicero extended the long metal blowpipe into the crucible and gathered glass. Heat from the furnace burning at two thousand degrees hit like a fist, but he didn't notice. The image of the sculpture drawn in pencil on the top sheet of his sketch-pad filled his mind.

A long strand of hair, black as midnight, slipped from the leather cord tied at the nape of his neck and fell forward across his face, absorbing the bead of sweat that dribbled across the chiseled ridge of his cheekbone. Cicero ignored the moisture, just as he disregarded the visitors who entered his studio as he dipped the gather of molten glass in rock crystals of color.

Wondering why Gabi Romano had shown up with his friend and her lover, Flynn Brogan, in tow, when she was supposed to be in Italy serving as an apprentice to the master glass artist, Alessandro Bovér, could wait. The image burning in his brain took precedence over everything.

As he closed his lips around the end of the pipe

and blew life into his work with a first puff of air, Gabi pulled her long, dark hair into a ponytail and stepped into the role of gaffer. Wordlessly, he accepted her assistance and blocked out everything but the work, losing himself in the seductive and compelling fog of creativity. For a stretch of time unmarked, the two worked in a silent and practiced ballet of motion, molding the glass, applying heat, shaping and blending and blowing.

Hunter Cicero played with fire for a living and he was very, very good at it.

The graceful figure in his mind gradually took shape in the glass. He vaguely noted when his own apprentice, Mitch Frazier, sauntered through the door and stopped in surprise upon seeing Flynn leaning against the wall, his arms casually folded. Mitch's gaze swept from Flynn, toward the workbench where Cicero sat, and then to Gabi as she confidently extended the blowpipe into the furnace to reheat the glass. Mitch observed the work for a full two minutes before nodding with approval. He stepped forward and seamlessly joined the creative effort.

The trio spent another forty minutes at work before Cicero decided the piece had taken final form. With a well-placed tap from a pair of metal jacks, he separated his sculpture from the punty, and it fell into Gabi's gloved hands. He set the punty aside while his gaffer placed the work into the annealing oven to slowly cool to room temperature. Rising from his workbench, he grabbed a bottle of water from the fridge and drained it in one long draw.

He switched off the music and spoke to Mitch first. "You were late."

"Sorry, Boss." Mitch pulled the rubber band from his long Rastafarian braids, which allowed them to swing freely down past his shoulder blades. "I stayed out late last night and overslept."

"Use your alarm next time. Better yet, save the late nights for weekends. I don't want you here when you're tired. You'll be careless and have an accident, and your mother will kill me."

The woman would do it, too. Cicero had barely made it off Bella Vita Isle alive after he'd convinced his apprentice to accompany him to Galveston to help establish a hand-blown-glass studio that catered to the tourist trade.

Cicero finally turned his gaze on Gabi, who stood twirling a long, dark curl around her finger, the light in her clear blue eyes timid. She offered him a tentative smile, and he scowled at her. The woman was too smart to be nervous; seeing her here did not make him happy.

"Did you get lost on your way back to Italy?"

Gabi visibly braced herself. "No, Cicero. I'm not sure I'm going back."

Her statement came as no real surprise. Cicero wasn't stupid. Obviously, she and Flynn had reconciled, and she'd decided to cut her yearlong apprenticeship short—by nine months. Was she about to bail on the Eternity Springs project, too?

Maybe, he thought, his stomach sinking. If she and Flynn were together, why wouldn't she? The man had more money than Midas. Mindful of his not insubstantial investment in the small Colorado mountain town, and the stack of bills piling up on his desk, Cicero felt his temper rise.

"What's wrong with you, Legs? Working in Alessandro's studio is the opportunity of a lifetime, one that countless other artists would kill for. What about all that talk you spouted about your dream and your passion? You're going to throw it all away?"

"I don't intend to throw anything away," she replied, her chin coming up. "I said I wasn't sure that I was returning to Italy. Cicero, last summer you came to me with a business proposal. Now I'm coming to you to propose a modification to that plan. Will you sit down and discuss it with me?"

Annoyed at the flash of relief over her assurance, he allowed his frown to deepen and shot a glance toward Flynn. "Are you part of her scheme?"

Flynn lifted his hands, palms out. "I'm an interested bystander, here to support you both."

Honesty glimmered in his friend's eyes, so Cicero hooked his thumb toward the small room off the studio where an old, gray metal desk and two ratty chairs sat piled high with paper. To Mitch, he said, "I need you to shift the Valentine's Day goblets for Beachcomber's Gifts to the top of your work list."

"Really?" Surprise glinted in the young man's brown eyes. "I delivered a dozen of them last week."

"Yeah, well, yesterday a seven-year-old went on a rampage in the shop."

"Oh, mon!" Mitch exclaimed, the Caribbean strong in his voice. "Kids are such a . . ." His words trailed off when he noted the pain in Cicero's expression. "Wait. Was it—?"

"Keenan." His seven-year-old menace of a nephew.

Mitch winced. "I'll get right on 'em, boss. No worries."

"No worries," Cicero repeated in a mutter, as he followed Gabi and Flynn into his office. He cleared a stack of manila folders off a chair so Gabi could sit, then opened the small refrigerator and pulled out bottles of water. He tossed one to Flynn, another to Gabi, and took one for himself before clearing off the chair behind the desk and taking a seat. He twisted the lid off his water bottle, drained half of it in one drink, then said, "Bottom line it, Romano. What do you want?"

"First I'd like to explain why I want what I want. You see—"

Cicero interrupted. "It's the middle of a workday and I have an appointment at two. I don't have time for explanations. Cut to the chase, Gabriella."

"Okay. Well."

She wiped her palms on her jeans and despite himself, Cicero was tempted to smile. Ordinarily, Gabriella Romano was one of the most self-assured women he'd ever met. The only other time he'd seen her like this she'd been working up the nerve to ask him to teach her to blow glass.

"Spit it out."

She nodded, then spoke in a rush. "Instead of returning to Italy to finish out my apprenticeship, I want to divide my time between Texas and Colorado. Here in Galveston I'll work and learn with you and Mitch like I did on Bella Vita. I'll use my time in Eternity Springs to concentrate on getting the retail shop ready to open in time for the upcoming tourist season."

Cicero took another long sip from his water bottle while he considered her idea. His initial reaction was annoyance. He'd called in a favor to get her the spot in Alessandro's studio. He didn't like to see her bail. Scowling, he asked, "What does Alessandro say about that? You came home for Christmas, not for the Fourth of July. I trust you let him know your plane didn't go down on your return flight?"

"Of course. I called him. He's fine with the idea. He thinks you can teach me everything I'll need to know because"—she paused, grimaced, and muttered—"this is more humiliating to repeat to you than I had anticipated."

She inhaled deeply, exhaled in a rush, then said, "Alessandro tells me I'll never be an artist, so I can learn everything I need to know from you."

Ouch.

Cicero pursed his lips. "I can't decide if that's more an insult to me or to you."

"Me, definitely," she replied, a whine in her voice. "He thinks you're the Second Coming of Chihuly, while I'm competent and enthusiastic, a hard worker, entertaining company and lovely to look at, but I don't have fire for the fire."

Sounded like Alessandro realized he wasn't getting in her pants. Cicero had told him from the beginning not to expect a conquest.

He sat back in his chair and gave her a thorough once-over. Except for her obvious nervousness, she looked great. Her time in Italy had agreed with her, though he suspected that Flynn had more to do with her sparkle than anything. Had he been wrong in his judgment of her passion for glass?

"Do you agree with his assessment?"

"Absolutely not!" Gabi made no attempt to hide her annoyance. "I have plenty of fire. But I also have family. I missed them."

He shouldn't be surprised. By the end of her first week in his studio on the island, Cicero had known that Gabi came from a tight-knit clan. She talked about them incessantly. As someone who'd grown up in the foster care system, he'd been both attracted to and repelled by the way the Romanos appeared to live in one another's pockets.

"I was homesick," Gabi continued. "Last year was—difficult."

Flynn rested a supportive hand on Gabi's shoulder, and said, "*Difficult* is an understatement. Gabi's scars aren't as visible as mine, but—"

"Last year was a bitch for you both," Cicero interrupted. "I get that."

It had been one of the factors behind his decision to approach Alessandro on Gabi's behalf. In May, Gabi had been aboard Flynn's sailing yacht in the Caribbean when it was set upon by pirates. She had taken one man's life that day; Flynn had killed two. The fallout from the event had wounded Gabi's heart, and all but destroyed Flynn, but they had fought their way back to health and now, apparently, to each other.

"You've been a great friend to both of us, Cicero," Gabi said, her tone heartfelt. "Flynn and I both recognize and treasure that. And the opportunity you gave me—it's been magical."

"So magical that you're ready to throw it aside?"

"Not at all. I'm not saying that at all. If you don't get on board with this idea, then I'll go back to Italy."

"*We* will go," Flynn said. "I can work anywhere."

Gabi flashed Flynn a quick, intimate smile, then returned an imploring gaze to Cicero. "But I'd rather we be in Eternity Springs. It's where my heart is whole and where my fire is free to burn. Alessandro is a fine teacher, Cicero, but so are you. Maybe he's right and I'll never produce gallery-quality work. But it's also possible that he's wrong. Maybe if I'm home and happy and surrounded by loved ones, I'll be able to create something spectacular. Eternity Springs is a special place. Just ask Sage Rafferty. She'll be the first to say that living in Eternity Springs inspires her work."

Sage Rafferty owned the town's art gallery and had made a name for herself in the art world for her boldly colored, whimsical paintings. She'd spoken enthusiastically about her hometown and its influence on her work in an interview he'd read in an art scene magazine recently. Cicero knew better than to dismiss the power of inner peace for an artist. Wasn't the lack of it showing in his work these days?

And yet, his obligations to Jayne caused him to miss so much studio time lately that he didn't see how he could commit to teaching Gabi anything.

"My hours here aren't regular. It'll take you eight years to learn from me what Alessandro would teach you in eight months."

"I can't believe I'm saying this, but you underestimate yourself, Cicero."

That coaxed a grin from him. Underestimating himself had never been an issue of his.

"Cute, Romano."

"You also have more patience with your apprentices, and that makes it easier to learn."

"You lose a point there. I'm not patient at all."

"I didn't say you had an abundance of patience. I said you had more than Alessandro." She leaned forward in her chair, her blue eyes gleaming earnestly. "I know this plan slows down my progress, but it also allows me to be around to watch my nieces and nephew grow. I didn't realize how much that mattered to me until I left home. They change so fast, especially that first year. I don't want to miss it."

"So you're giving up your opportunity for kids? Somebody else's kids, at that?"

"This from the man who traded the aquamarine of the Caribbean for Gulf of Mexico gray in order to be nearer to his sister and her children?"

Cicero's gaze shifted to the stack of invoices on his desk. Houston Oncology. MD Anderson Cancer Center. Physician's Services.

"The two situations are completely different."

Gabi's eyes softened with sympathy. "How is Jayne doing?"

"Good," he replied, trying to believe it. "She's good." Then, to ward off any further questions about his sister, he added, "You can watch kids grow by viewing pictures on the Internet. You don't have to be in the same town."

"But I *want* to be in the same town. I recognize that it's a trade-off. Life is a series of trade-offs. I can be passionate about glass and passionate about people, too. I'm searching for the right balance between the two. I know you understand that. You would never have left Bella Vita otherwise."

No, balance had nothing to do with his return to the United States, though he did understand the concept.

"I can be of help to you here in Texas, Cicero. My training in Italy was intense. I'm good enough now for tourist work. You can shift things like Valentine's Day goblets to me, and free Mitch up to help you with your work."

Cicero sat back in his chair. "You have it all figured out, don't you?"

"I've put a lot of thought into it, and—oh." She snapped her fingers. "I forgot to mention one other applicable point. The remodel schedule. I know you've had trouble with the contractor you hired. Harold Benton does fabulous work but as he's gotten older, he's really slowed down. With someone on hand to encourage him, you'll get better, faster results. Especially if that someone is me. He owes me."

"Why?"

She pursed her lips. "Let's just say that when I worked as a sheriff's deputy, I used my discretionary power in his favor."

"Always handy to have the law in one's corner, I guess." Cicero picked up a pen and drummed the tip against the desktop. Gabi, her arguments made, sat back in her seat and waited quietly, though judging by the nervous tapping of her toes, less than patiently. Flynn's attention drifted to the studio where Mitch removed a gather of glass from the furnace.

Cicero surveyed the clutter on his desktop and mentally shifted his money around. No matter how many ways he shuffled, he always came up short. Times had certainly changed since last summer when he committed to the Colorado studio. As someone lucky enough to have had only rare dealings with the medical industry prior to this, he'd been woefully naïve about the financial costs of exceptional treatment. In hindsight, he should have never jumped into the Eternity Springs expansion so fast.

Getting the Eternity Springs store stocked and open for the tourist season could be a godsend to his cash flow. He'd already sunk a pretty penny into purchasing the old church property and starting the remodel. Most of the materials were paid for. He still had some credit left. Maybe once Harold Benton finished up the loft apartment where he'd planned to stay during his visits, he could rent it out. Get someplace cheap to live. He didn't need much. Maybe—

Maybe he could think of something more self-

serving than to agree to Gabi's proposition, but he'd have to try damned hard.

Murano. Venice. Italy. The three years he'd spent there had molded him into the artist he was today. That training showed in every piece he produced. She simply didn't know yet how important this time was to her art.

He tossed his pen onto the desk. "Gabi, I don't agree with Alessandro. I've seen pictures of the work you've been producing, and I believe you do have the talent to be an exceptional glass artist. I would be doing you a disservice if I agreed to this. Alessandro is—"

"Not as good as you," she interrupted. "He might have more experience and a flashier reputation and a studio in the most famous glass city in the world, but Alessandro isn't as good as you are. He will never inspire me the way you do."

The vehemence in her tone, along with the declaration itself, took him aback. What had Alessandro been thinking to say the woman lacked fire? *Flynn Brogan is a lucky man.* Then, just to goad her, he arched a brow toward Flynn. "You let your woman say such things to another man?"

"*Let* me!" Gabi exclaimed.

Flynn laughed. "Gabriella Romano is very much her own woman, as you well know. It's one of the reasons why we both love her."

"True enough." He gave her a wolfish once-over and added, "I should never have yielded the field to you, Brogan."

Flynn's expression oozed self-satisfaction. "Doesn't matter. You never stood a chance with her."

"Confident of yourself, aren't you?"

"Excuse me. I'm sitting right here!"

Both men ignored that.

Cicero recognized the instant when Flynn's gaze went from amused to serious. He propped a hip on the corner of Cicero's desk, and his voice resonated with sincerity as he said, "I'm confident in her. As so should you be. Our Gabi is loyal and honest and insightful. She has excellent instincts. She is passionate about her work and passionate about her world. Listen to her. Trust her. Believe in her."

Cicero absently fanned the corner of the stack of invoices on his desk, and in an uncommon moment of openness replied, "I'm afraid I've lost the ability to believe in much of anything."

Gabi reached out and covered his hand with hers. "In that case, you need to get to Colorado as quickly as possible. I know it sounds corny, but you can believe in the magic of Eternity Springs."

"It changed my life," Flynn agreed. "It can change yours, too."

"I don't need magic. I need a miracle."

Gabi's smile went as bright as the furnace.

"Hey, we do miracles, too. Just ask my sister-in-law, Hope."

Before Cicero could respond to that, a colorful whirlwind of noise and motion burst through the studio's front door.

"Uncle Skunk!" Seven-year-old Keenan exclaimed. "Where are you, Uncle Skunk?"

"Hey, Uncle Hunk," called nine-year-old Misty. "Wait until you hear what happened at school!"

The sister of his heart, Jayne Prochaska, carried two-year-old Daisy in her arms and offered him an apologetic smile. "Junior? I'm so sorry, but Amy isn't answering her phone and I need to run into Houston. Could you watch the kids for a little bit?"

"Unc Nooner!" Five-year-old Galen exclaimed. "Do you have any candy?"

"Uncle Nooner?" Flynn repeated, his brows arched and his lips twitching. "Man, am I going to have fun with that."

Cicero opened his mouth, then shut it. What could he possibly say? Some things that came from a four-year-old's mouth simply went beyond explanation. He closed his eyes briefly, shook his head, then grasped the lifeline Gabi had offered. "I'll agree to your proposal on one condition."

Warily, she asked, "What's that?"

"Babysitting."

She narrowed her eyes warily. "How much babysitting?"

21

"I won't abuse you. Much."

Gabi made a theatrical grimace, though he could tell her heart was singing. "All right, we have a deal, *Uncle Hunk.*"

Two

February
Eternity Springs, Colorado

Rose Anderson removed her stethoscope from her ears and patted the silver-haired gentleman on his knee. "Your heart sounds just fine, Mr. Henderson."

"It's not my heart that's paining me, Doctor," he grumbled. "I told you I broke my ankle!"

"I think it's sprained, but the EMT will be here to transport you to the clinic any moment now for an X ray. Dr. Coulson will fix you right up."

"Dr. Coulson! What about you? You're my doctor."

Inwardly, Rose sighed. "I'm not on call tonight."

"Then why are you wearing your white coat?"

Rose searched for patience. She wasn't going to discuss details about her upcoming laundry day with Gilbert Henderson. "Dr. Coulson will take excellent care of you. There's no need for concern."

The septuagenarian scowled. "He's not as pretty

to look at as you. His bosom doesn't brush up against me when he examines me."

"For this we can all be grateful," Rose deadpanned.

"You're a prize to look at, Doctor Rose. The Irish is stamped across you. I've always taken a shine to redheaded, green-eyed girls. Bet you burn in the summertime if you're not careful. How come you're not married?"

The question could have made Rose angry, but she'd grown accustomed to it being asked. She didn't hear it as often since moving to Eternity Springs—one of the pluses to small-town living. People ferreted out what they wanted to know about you quickly, and once they did, word got around even faster. Her friends, acquaintances, and patients knew her story by now.

Unfortunately, Mr. Henderson had a bit of dementia going on.

Ignoring the query, she said, "I know the ankle is tender now, but unless Dr. Coulson finds something on the X ray, I predict that you'll be back to dancing in a couple of weeks."

Her patient crooked his finger for her to bend closer, then he all but bellowed into her ear. "What about *S-E-X?* It is Valentine's Day, after all."

Yes, my personal Halloween. Rose patted his knee and told herself that she didn't care that this senior citizen had a more active love life than she did.

"Talk to Dr. Coulson about that."

Thankfully, the EMTs showed up and assisted Gilbert Henderson from the Angel's Rest activities center. As Rose tucked her stethoscope back into her bag, Celeste Blessing glided up beside her. Celeste was Eternity Springs's angel investor, the person whose idea—and whose financial stake— had created Angel's Rest Healing Center and Spa, and spurred the economic revitalization of this little mountain town. An active and interested Judi Dench look-alike, Celeste had uncanny instincts, which she used to the benefit of those she befriended. And Celeste made friends with everybody. Rose adored her.

Celeste's blue eyes showed a glimmer of concern as she asked, "Is Gilbert okay?"

"Gilbert is the Energizer Bunny of Eternity Springs's seventies set, and he'll be just fine if he stays off that ankle for a few days."

"Good. I'd hate for anything to cast a damper on our first official Angel's Rest Valentine's Day Dance. It's been wonderful so far. And just look at our honorary king and queen. Have you ever seen a more romantic pair?"

Rose followed the path of Celeste's gaze to where Flynn Brogan and Gabi Romano swayed to Elvis singing "Can't Help Falling in Love," wrapped in each other's arms, lost in each other's gazes. "They are . . . sweet."

Sickeningly so.

"We've had some fabulously romantic marriage proposals here in Eternity Springs already," Celeste continued, "but I will say I'm partial to how Flynn proposed. The way he reengineered that motorboat into an iceboat so he could take her sailing on Hummingbird Lake in order to pop the question shows not only a brilliant mind for design but also a truly romantic nature."

Rose's disdain melted a bit. She didn't give a whit for romance, but a brilliant mind had always turned her on.

Of course, that was what had led her into trouble more than once, wasn't it?

"They make a nice couple," Rose observed, trying to show some interest in the local lovebirds. She liked Gabi. In fact, she liked all the women in her sister's group of friends, and she considered them her friends too. But ever since she'd come to town, the single women had been dropping like flies—i.e., getting married. They were all so blissfully happy with their handsome husbands and darling kids. While they never intentionally excluded her, she was invariably the fifth wheel, the old maid, the auntie. Sometimes it simply grew old. And now, Gabriella Romano had joined the ranks. Another confederate bites the dust.

"Has Gabi said when the wedding will be?"

"I think they're still negotiating. Gabi wants to plan a wedding—with a capital *W*. She does love

25

all the froufrou and lace. Flynn, on the other hand, would like to elope."

"I'm sure they'll work it out," Rose said, zipping up her physician's bag. She lived in the garret apartment of Cavanaugh House, the Victorian mansion at the heart of the Angel's Rest grounds. She wanted to get home to a hot bath, glass of cabernet, and the postapocalyptic novel she was reading. Exactly why she particularly enjoyed that genre of book, she couldn't say, but she read every one that came out. She liked how the protagonists rose from the ashes, and built new worlds for themselves. Maybe because she identified with the premise. Wasn't the life she was presently living postapocalyptic in its own way?

"I'll be at home if you have any other accidents, Celeste," Rose told her, thinking she might snag a brownie off the refreshment table on her way out. "Just give me a call."

"Oh, Rose," Celeste protested. "Won't you stay and enjoy the dance with us? Not everyone here has a date, you know. We particularly designated it as a singles-welcome event."

Rose's gaze found the newly engaged couple once again, and then trailed over to where her sister danced with her husband, their expressions unfortunately sappy for a couple who should have moved beyond that dreamy-eyed stage by now. "Thanks, but I need to—oh, no."

She switched back into doctor mode the instant

she spied the bloodstained boy dash into the room. She took half a step forward, then stopped and reassessed. Not blood. Food coloring? Or paint? Probably paint.

The kid was maybe seven or eight years old, and he wore red-stained jeans, a red-stained Oregon Ducks jersey, and a panicked expression. The reason for the panic became immediately obvious.

A man burst through the door in hot pursuit. Hair dark as sin flowed nearly to his shoulders and framed a face that belonged on a Hollywood movie poster advertising the latest too-handsome-to-be-human vampire flick. Dark brown eyes gleamed above sharp cheekbones and a blade of a nose. His lips drew back over straight white teeth in a tight, predatory smile.

"Get back here, you little hoodlum," he hissed, his path taking him toward Rose. "I swear, I'm going to string you up by your shoelaces and make you listen to show tunes for two hours straight!"

The boy stopped in the middle of the hall, glanced wildly around for an escape, then darted straight for Rose. He hit her legs with enough force that she swayed and took an inadvertent step backward.

"Save me!" the boy cried out.

"From what?" she wondered aloud. Then, meeting the stranger's grim gaze, she asked, "Show tunes?"

Mile-wide shoulders shrugged and a deep voice rumbled. "They're torture."

"You like to threaten little boys with torture?"

"Doctor"—his gaze lowered to the name embroidered on her lab coat, then dropped a little more and lingered on her breast—"*R. Anderson.* In the last two days, I've been stabbed with a Tinkertoy, beaten over the head with a Wii controller, drenched with fox urine, and bitten twice. So yeah, whatever nonviolent defense mechanism works."

Then, to the boy, he added, "Keenan, stop. You are too young to feel up the pretty doctor."

Rose's mouth gaped, but before she could comment, the stranger continued, "Let go of her leg and come with me, you little vampire."

"No!"

"I'll give you cake."

"Okay." Keenan's face brightened, showing Rose that bribery worked with this child, too.

The hands wrapped around her legs released her, and the stranger moved like lightning to wrap his big hand around the little boy's wrist. Keenan pulled against him, pointing toward the door. The stranger said, "Sorry for the interruption, ladies. Doctor, if you'll send the cleaning bill for your coat to me, I'll be glad to pay for it."

He'd taken two steps away when Rose said, "Wait!"

He pulled up. Rose focused on the boy. "The

room is full of people. Why did you run to me?"

"You're a doctor. Doctors save people." The boy yanked from the stranger's grasp and darted for the door.

The man met Rose's gaze, and his lips twisted in a bitter smile. "Poor kid still believes in fairy tales."

The beautiful stranger turned away and followed the boy. Rose watched him go, his confident, long-legged strides eating up the distance. When she realized that her gaze lingered on the way his butt filled out his jeans, she snorted in self-disgust.

"Who in the world was that?"

"Why, he's the newest member of Eternity Springs's Chamber of Commerce, Hunter Cicero. Cicero is a brilliant glass artist, our Gabriella's mentor. He moved here from Texas ten days ago."

"Oh, Sage has talked about him." *And how totally pretentious to go by one name,* she thought as she slipped off her lab coat and inspected the paint stains. "His little boy is darling, with that white-blond hair and blue eyes. Not much family resemblance, there."

"Keenan isn't Cicero's son. He's his nephew. Keenan, his brother, and sisters are visiting Eternity Springs for a few days while their guardians ski over at Wolf Creek. They are staying at one of our cottages here at Angel's Rest. The poor little dears lost their mother last month. Cancer."

As always, a knot formed in Rose's stomach at the mention of the word. Then, because this was winter in a small town where gossip ruled as a main form of entertainment, and because she needed a distraction from black thoughts, she indulged her curiosity. "Why guardians? Where is their father?"

"Fathers, plural," Celeste corrected. "According to Misty, the nine-year-old who is quite the chatterbox when you can coax her out of her book, all four of the children have different fathers, three of whom have never been part of their lives. The mother must have been quite the free spirit."

"That's a charitable term, Celeste," Rose observed. "Personally, I'd go for irresponsible."

Celeste didn't argue. "The woman did marry the youngest child's father, but tragically, he passed before little Daisy was born. His sister and her husband are the children's guardians."

So they're orphans. "Poor kids."

"Yes, they are heartbroken and afraid. And, a handful for whoever is supervising them. Keenan and his siblings are spending the evening in the Little Angels center."

"Aha. That's where the red paint came from. Looks like craft time got out of hand."

"Yes," Celeste said, with a sigh. "I should probably go check on things. Thanks for your assistance with Gilbert, dear."

"Glad to help."

Rose's gaze followed Celeste toward the door, which led to a set of rooms currently serving as Angel's Rest's day care center. She hoped young Keenan hadn't created too much chaos. Those rooms had to be just as crowded as the dance, she knew.

The Eternity Springs baby population was booming, so much so that her sister had agreed to see pediatric patients in the clinic one day a week until the town could recruit a new specialist. Although Sage was trained as a pediatric surgeon, she'd found that her second career as an artist and gallery owner suited her better than medicine. Of course, she loved her role as wife and mother best of all.

Rose was happy for her sister. Admittedly, envy reared its little green head upon occasion, but for the most part, Rose was content. She liked her life. She loved being a small-town doctor, adored her role of doting aunt to Sage's son, little Colton Alexander, a.k.a. Racer. She valued her independence. She still had dreams of seeing one of the medical thrillers she'd written on bookshelves someday, but that wasn't a happiness deal breaker.

Sure she had regrets, but who went through life without any regrets? Nobody she knew. As a rule, she was a positive thinker. Right now she was thinking positively about red wine, a book, and a bath.

Rose loved to read, and she'd started a new, postapocalyptic book last night. The author had done an excellent job of world building, and she was anxious to immerse herself in the story.

With any luck, she would discover that in the new world rising from ashes of the old, Valentine's Day didn't exist.

Thirty-two hours, Cicero told himself. The Parnells were due here to pick up the pest quartet in thirty-two hours. He could handle things that long. They'd be asleep for eight of those hours, too, so really, he only had twenty-four to contend with. He could survive twenty-four more hours.

Maybe.

Possibly.

A crash sounded from the room off the studio where the monsters were supposed to be parked in front of the TV watching cartoons. Cicero closed his eyes and muttered, "I'm toast."

"You should take them outside," Gabi suggested as she placed the vase they'd just completed into the annealer and closed the door. "Let them run off some energy."

The thought of going through the significant effort to get everybody suited up into snow gear exhausted him. "Maybe you could—"

"Not on your life. You promised me when I took charge of them this morning that I'd fulfilled my babysitting duty for this visit."

32

"You're fired."

"Empty threat, boss," she shot back. "I'm the only gaffer in at least a hundred miles. So, what do you want me to work on while you are out with the little cherubs?"

"See what sort of start you can make on the teardrops for the Danbury Homes light fixture order."

He no sooner finished than a second crash occurred, followed by a howl. He pivoted and strode into the storage room currently serving as his studio's child care center. His gaze searched for the reason for the wails—no blood. LEGO bricks lay strewn across the room, five-year-old Galen looked smug, and Keenan appeared ready to start swinging.

"He broke my bridge!"

"All right, you hoodlums. Everybody into their cold weather gear. It's time to go sledding—oh." His Daisy lay curled up in one corner fast asleep. "How does she sleep with all the racket?"

"It's like this all the time," Misty said, not looking up from her book. "She's used to it."

Keenan and Galen jumped to their feet and grabbed for their coats.

Misty turned another page. "I'll stay inside with her, Uncle Hunk."

"Hunt," he stressed. "You have to stop saying that."

She looked up from her book and managed to

stare down her pretty little nose at him. "You stop calling me a worm."

"I'm going to clean your clock!" Keenan said to his brother.

"What clock?" Galen replied, his little brow knitted in confusion.

"Not *a* worm," Cicero answered Misty, "just worm. As in *book*worm. It's a term of endearment."

"Whatever." She shrugged and went back to reading. "Daisy will sleep for an hour. Go play with the boys. We'll be fine."

Cicero hesitated. Before Jayne died, he'd noticed how often she'd dumped responsibility for Daisy off on her older daughter. It had reminded him of how he'd been forced to watch after Jayne and two younger children during his five months in the Weber household. As a ten-year-old, he'd placed the blame squarely on seven-year-old Jayne's shoulders rather than where it belonged— on those of his foster parents. When he couldn't sign up for Pee Wee football because he had to babysit, he'd resented Jayne. When he had to change diapers, he'd held Jayne responsible. When Penny Weber required him to take the younger kids to the park and push the baby in the kiddie swing rather than join the other kids his age in a pickup baseball game, he'd bitterly faulted Jayne. After all, to his mind, the Webers could do no wrong. They'd rescued him and Jayne from three months in hell at the Radmacher house.

Even all these years later, just thinking that name made Cicero's stomach roll.

He turned his attention back to Misty. He couldn't do anything about how her mother had treated her, and he had next-to-no influence over what the Parnells did, but he could darn well make sure that *he* didn't ask too much of her.

"I changed my mind. Since there are clocks needing to be cleaned, you boys can have a snowball fight instead of sledding. Misty, we'll be in the side yard. The minute your sister starts to stir, you shout at me."

She nodded without looking up.

He added, "Later, we'll make a visit to the library."

Interest glowed in the gaze that flickered up.

Gotcha.

Misty was a changed girl since her mother had gotten sick. Where before she'd been vivacious and open, after Jayne's diagnosis, she had withdrawn into herself. Now she regularly escaped into fictional worlds where wizards ruled the day. Cicero wasn't too concerned about it. In fact, her reaction seemed healthy to him. Because Jayne had moved her brood from Oregon to Houston after learning of her illness, the girl effectively had lost her home, her friends, and her mother. She needed a chance to grieve. In time, she'd bounce back. If that didn't happen, then he'd suggest to Amy that Misty see a counselor. What was one more doctor bill at this point?

He helped Galen into his snow gear and shooed them outside, grabbing his own coat as he called over his shoulder to inform Gabi of the plan. Outside, sunshine sparkled off the three inches of new snow that had fallen overnight. His breath fogged on the crisp mountain air, and as he watched his sister's sons take immediate delight in tracking up the pristine yard, he realized he'd needed a break, himself.

He was tired. Bone-deep, ass-dragging weary. Beginning with Jayne's sudden death in early January, life had been one challenge after another. Hell, life had been a series of challenges since he'd learned about her cancer last May.

The snowball to the face caught him by surprise. "Take that, Uncle Skunk."

Slowly, he wiped the cold, wet snow from his cheek as he stared at the culprit who giggled maniacally in response.

Damn, but wasn't that a nice sound?

In retrospect, he should have expected the attack. He'd have done the same thing at Keenan's age. Narrowing his eyes, he spoke in a deep, threatening tone. "Keenan Brian Gresham. Prepare for defeat. You are going down."

"No way." Keenan turned and ran, his brother trailing after him as usual.

The property where Cicero lived and worked

had once been the town's Episcopal church. Thanks to Gabi's influence with the local contractor, the remodeling work was in the homestretch with the studio and loft apartment about ninety percent complete. The retail space still had a ways to go, but both Gabi and Harold Benton had assured him that the shop would be ready for the grand opening celebration they had planned for Memorial Day.

He had big plans for his property once his cash flow situation improved. The yard where the kids currently played had been a parking lot for horses and buggies in the church's early days, and a prayer garden in more recent years. When he'd first viewed the footpath that meandered through evergreens and hardwoods across the property last summer, he'd recognized the potential. It provided a good spot to sit and relax and nurture the creative muses. Plus, it gave him space to showcase the outdoor sculptures he'd been planning.

However, that was a topic of thought for another time. Right now, the evergreens along the path offered battlefield concealment for Keenan and his brother and their snowballs, a fact he was reminded of when an icy sphere hit the back of his neck.

"Hoodlums!" he bellowed.

"Kids, two. Uncle Skunk, zero!" Keenan shouted back, then ducked away into the trees.

Cicero wore an evil grin as he bent down to scoop up snow. He cradled six fist-sized snowballs in his arms and had taken one step toward the trees in search of his targets when a blood-curdling scream stopped him in his tracks.

Three

Cicero's blood turned colder than the snow. He took off running before the scream faded or Keenan's frightened voice reached his ears. "Un-cle Hun-ter!"

Twenty seconds later, he spied the boys. Keenan was down on his knees beside his little brother who lay still as death on the snow. Please, Lord, Cicero prayed. Please.

"What happened?" he demanded of the older boy.

"I don't know! He was running then he fell down and he screamed then he just went quiet."

"Did he hit his head?"

"No. I don't know. I don't think so."

Cicero assessed the situation in a single glance. No visible blood. The five-year-old's arm lay at an unnatural angle. Broken arm, probably fainted from the pain. Please, Lord, he silently repeated. Let that be all.

As he reached the boys' side, Galen stirred and

his eyes opened, little blue pools of pain. "Mama. I want my Mama. My arm—"

"It's okay, buddy. Everything is gonna be okay. Let me take a look at you." He crouched down beside Galen. "Did you hit your head?"

Tears began to roll down Galen's cheeks. "My arm. Help me, Uncle Hunk."

"I will, son. I will. Hang in there. You're gonna be fine." Cicero quickly debated the best course of action. He didn't know whether to move the boy or not. He didn't want to leave him lying in the snow, but was it okay to move him? He hadn't brought his phone outside, so he couldn't call 911. Dammit, he had no experience with kids and broken bones! He didn't know the rules.

"Keenan, run inside and tell Ms. Gabi that your brother broke his arm and I need help. Go fast, now."

The older boy turned and darted off. In her previous career, Gabi had been a cop. She'd know what to do.

Cicero patted Galen's leg in an awkward effort at comfort and glanced around the area, trying to deduce what had happened. He couldn't see anything the boy might have tripped over. The kid was accident prone, but how had he managed to fall hard enough to break a bone?

Looking closer, he spotted the jagged edge of a rock peeking out from beneath Galen. He must have come down hard on it. Holy hell. It could have been his head rather than his arm.

Shaky from the thought, Cicero turned with relief at the sound of Gabi's hurried approach. "Oh, no," she said, her voice brimming with compassion. "Baby, what did you do to yourself?"

"Did you call 911?" Cicero asked, spying the phone in her hand.

She shook her head. "Not yet. Let me take a look. I don't see evidence of head trauma or significant bleeding, and the bone isn't poking through skin. It's quicker to transport him ourselves. Cicero, you pick him up and hold him, and I'll drive."

"What about the other kids? We can't leave them alone."

"The clinic is two minutes away. I'll drop you off and come right back. Misty can be in charge for four minutes. How much trouble can they get into in that short a time?"

"Don't ask," he said grimly before he focused his attention on Galen.

The process of lifting the boy, carrying him to Gabi's vehicle, driving the winter-rutted road to the clinic, then toting him into the facility proved harrowing for Cicero. Surprisingly, Galen didn't scream and cry, but he did moan and whimper the entire way. A nurse showed them straight to a treatment room where she cut the coat and shirt-sleeve to reveal Galen's bare arm. The pretty doctor he'd spoken to at the Valentine's Day dance walked in moments later. Cicero had never been so glad to see someone in his life.

"What do we have here?" Dr. Anderson asked, her tone cheerful and upbeat. "Took a tumble, did you young man?"

"My arm is broked."

"Yes, I agree it most likely is. I'm Dr. Rose. What's your name?"

"Galen. That's my Uncle Hunk."

"Hunt," Cicero was quick to say. "Hunter Cicero. This is my nephew, Galen Redmond."

"Nice to meet you, Galen Redmond. Let's take a look at your arm and see if I concur with your diagnosis. Do you know what an X ray is?"

The boy's eyes went round as saucers. "You have X-ray vision like Superman?"

She laughed. "Not me, but my machine does."

"Wow."

Cicero stood back and watched as Dr. R. Anderson, a.k.a. Dr. Rose, or, as he'd mentally designated her, Doctor Delicious, examined and treated his nephew with caring, compassion, and a gentle touch. Despite the disdain with which he held the medical profession these days, he found himself warming to the woman and studying her with an artist's eye.

Rose was an apt name for her, he decided, as the chorus of "My Wild Irish Rose" spun through his mind. Long, slim, and judging from her

41

reaction at the dance last night, thorny. But her face—oh, such an appealing face. Oval and perfectly framed by thick brown hair shot through with red-gold fire and secured in a professional chignon, hers was a face beyond the blush of youth, which made it all the more interesting. She wore no makeup; she didn't need it. A sprinkle of freckles dusted her ivory complexion. Ridicu-lously long lashes framed almond-shaped eyes the smoky green of a forest of fir trees in winter. Her thin, straight nose turned up just enough to beg a playful kiss.

Her full mouth begged a different kind of kiss altogether.

And her hands were as sexy as sin. As her long, slim fingers moved expertly over Galen's body, Cicero's own fingers suddenly itched for charcoal and a sketch-pad. He could see her in glass, shades of green with a thread of fire running through her core. Substantial. Strong. And yet as delicate as spun sugar.

No wedding ring, he noted. No telltale white line where a wedding ring belonged. He perked up. *Well, well, well. How interesting.*

It had been a long time since he'd had any action. Too long. In Texas, he'd been too busy helping Jayne and setting up the studio and working to pay the damned bills to spend any time looking for female companionship. As a result, he was now smack dab in the middle of the biggest dry spell he'd had in years. Probably his entire adulthood.

Dr. Delicious completed her examination and declared the break to be a simple fracture that should heal fine. She sent him off to the clinic's business office to take care of paperwork while she set the bone and applied a cast. As he tracked through the clinic, he considered the possibilities.

His time on Bella Vita Isle had taught him that living in a small town complicated love affairs. Everybody knew everybody's business. Gossip was a primary pastime. Privacy was all but nonexistent. Such realities didn't preclude a liaison, but they meant he should probably do a little recon before jumping into anything.

On the flip side, small-town living made life simpler when dealing with a medical clinic business office, he discovered. He'd been in such a rush that he'd left his wallet behind.

"No problem, Mr. Cicero," a perky, middle-aged brunette told him with a smile when he explained his lack of cash or paperwork. "Bring the insurance card and your medical power of attorney by later. We're open until five. If you can't make it back until tomorrow, that's okay, too. We'll get it all squared away. The important thing is that Dr. Rose is taking care of your nephew."

His mouth lifted in a slow smile.

What a different experience from the blood-

suckers at the various medical centers he'd been dealing with over the past ten months.

"Thanks."

"I hope your nephew feels better soon, but I'm sure he will. I have three grandsons and every one of them has worn a cast at one point or another. Casts make them rock stars at preschool, you know."

"I didn't realize that. I just hope I can get through the rest of his visit without needing a second cast. The kid and his brother are accidents waiting to happen."

"They're boys," she returned with a fatalistic shrug.

It was a statement and sentiment his sister often had expressed, and hearing it caused a pang in his heart. Heading back toward the exam rooms, he picked up his step, attempting to leave the memories behind.

He halted abruptly when he passed the waiting room and spied Keenan. "What are you doing here?"

"Ms. Gabi brought us. Uncle Hunter, is my brother going to die?"

The abject fear in the boy's voice and expression destroyed Cicero. This was what happened when a child's only parent died. He hunkered down beside the seven-year-old, placed a hand on his shoulder, and stared him straight in the eyes.

"No, Keenan. Your brother is not going to die.

He broke his arm and it will be good as new in about six weeks. He's getting a cast."

Keenan's eyes rounded with hope and then narrowed with suspicion. "You swear?"

"I swear," Cicero solemnly replied.

The boy let out a long, heavy sigh of relief. Then his eyes narrowed. "He's getting a cast? That's not fair. I want a cast. Can I get a cast?"

"No."

Cicero rose and looked at Gabi who had entered the building, carrying Daisy. Misty stood beside Gabi. Her posture was tense, her complexion pale, and her eyes dimmed with worry.

"We were concerned," his apprentice explained.

"Understandable." Cicero summarized Galen's injury, and as he spoke, he saw Misty slowly relax. The poor kid. She's always waiting for the next disaster to happen, and after all that's happened, who can blame her? He finished up his story with a reassuring smile. "So it's all good news."

"Lucky duck," Keenan grumbled. "I want a cast."

Misty shot her brother a glare.

"Which arm did he break?" she asked her uncle.

"His left."

"That's good. He's right-handed."

"Like I said," Cicero told her, "it's all good news."

Gabi gave Misty's shoulder a gentle squeeze,

then caught Cicero's gaze. "I brought Galen a blanket for the ride home—and your wallet and phone. I figured you'd need to call the Parnells to let them know what happened."

"Yeah." He dreaded that call. Amy had fussed and fretted enough over leaving the kids with him for the long weekend. She wouldn't take the news well. He might as well get ready to have his butt chewed.

Of course, if she was that worried about it, she shouldn't have left them with him.

Cicero had been peeved that the Parnells hadn't canceled their ski trip. He didn't really care that the couple already had it planned and paid for before Jayne died. It was too soon for them to leave the demons. Too soon to dump them on a babysitter—even if said babysitter was a beloved uncle. These kids needed stability. They needed a routine. They certainly needed to know that their new parents would be there when they were needed.

So far, Cicero had kept his thoughts to himself, but if Amy let him have it once he told her about Galen's accident, he'd damn well let her have it right back.

"Where is my brother, Uncle Skunk?" Keenan asked, intruding on Cicero's troubling thoughts. "I want to see him."

"Let's go find the doctor or a nurse and see if they'll let you in his room." He took hold of

Keenan's hand just as Dr. Anderson appeared in the doorway. Cicero asked her the question.

"If you promise you'll only stay a minute and not excite him so that he tries to move around, you may all peek in on him," Dr. Anderson replied. "Okay?"

"We promise, Doctor," Keenan was quick to say.

"Follow me."

Dr. Delicious led them back to the treatment room where Galen lay talking to a nurse about superheroes. Upon hearing his brother's voice, Keenan darted past the doctor and rushed into the room saying, "We've come to see that you are alive, Galen, and you can't move around and we can only stay a minute. Whoa! You have a red cast! How come it's red?"

"I got to pick the color."

"Does it hurt?"

As Galen's siblings surrounded the exam table where the boy lay, Cicero listened with half an ear to the conversation. He was more interested in what the doctor was saying to Gabi.

"—date for the wedding?"

"August seventeenth. It's the soonest we thought we could pull it off. Flynn made some noise about wanting it to be sooner, but Mom sat him down and told him she's been waiting to plan her only daughter's wedding since the day I was born and not to rush her."

The doctor laughed. "That sounds like Maggie."

"Flynn can't say no to her any more than my brothers can. It was a moot point anyway, since he's planning an extended honeymoon and I won't leave Whimsies until after tourist season winds down."

"Whimsies?" Rose's gaze flicked over to Cicero. "That's the name you've chosen for the glass shop you're opening?"

Gabi nodded. "Yes. Whimsey glass is work that's created for no useful purpose. They were popular as souvenirs in the nineteenth century, so I think it's the perfect name for our retail store."

"I love it," Rose said to them both. "Your shop will be a great addition to Eternity Springs."

The adults' attention was jerked back to the children when Rose spied Keenan removing a pencil from a clipboard lying on the counter.

"Hold on, Kevin, is it? You can't sign his cast yet. It needs time to set."

"Keenan," Cicero informed her, moving forward to smoothly intercept the pencil.

"I'm Misty." The girl waved toward her sister. "That's Daisy."

"It's nice to meet you all, though I wish it had happened in a park rather than the emergency clinic."

Cicero thought the smile she gave the children was the prettiest thing he'd seen all morning. He needed to draw that smile, too. "Your minute is up, you monsters," he said abruptly. "Tell your brother you'll see him later."

"What's for lunch, Uncle Skunk?" Keenan asked. "I'm hungry. Can we have McDonald's?"

"I told you Eternity Springs doesn't have a McDonald's." Cicero reached into his wallet, pulled out a twenty, and handed it to Gabi. "Would you take them somewhere for a burger? I've heard Murphy's has good ones."

"Sarah Murphy runs a bakery. She doesn't serve burgers."

"I'm not talking about your friend's bakery. I mean Murphy's Pub."

"Murphy's Pub," Gabi repeated. "You want me to take these kids to a seedy bar?"

"You haven't been there since you came home from Italy, have you?" Rose Anderson observed. "It's not the same old Murphy's. I eat there almost every day for lunch. A newcomer to Eternity Springs runs the bar now. Her name is Shannon O'Toole. Do yourself a favor and order the shepherd's pie."

"Now I'm hungry," Cicero said. "I love shepherd's pie. Get a couple of servings for me, to go, would you?"

"Will do. You know, I'd heard that Murphy's had reopened, but I didn't realize it had upgraded. Now I'm anxious to check it out."

Gabi and the kids said their good-byes and left—after Cicero threatened to feed Keenan peas for supper if he wasn't good for Gabi until Cicero and Galen got home. When the good doctor also turned to leave, he said, "Wait a minute."

She paused and gave him a polite, professional smile. He propped a hip on the exam table.

"Are you seeing anyone?"

Her smile froze and she blinked. "Excuse me?"

"I'd like to take you to dinner."

"Why?"

Why? A corner of Cicero's mouth lifted in a crooked smile. That wasn't the usual response he received when he invited a woman on a date, and that fact only made her more intriguing. "I actually have quite a number of reasons for asking. Start with the fact that I find you fascinating."

Her brow furrowed and she stared at him like a bug. A particularly unpleasant bug.

"Your nephew is on my exam table."

Yes. I'd like to find my way there, myself.

"I don't date patients."

"In that case, it's a good thing I'm not your patient, isn't it?"

Now her lips thinned.

"Listen, Mr. Cicero, I—"

"Hunt. Call me Hunt, please." Hardly anybody used his first name, especially now that Jayne was gone. Damned if he didn't want to hear his name on Rose Anderson's lips.

"Mr. Cicero," she repeated. "Thank you for the invitation, but I'm not interested."

Whoa. Zing. He let his smile go wide. He'd always loved a challenge. Besides, she might claim to be disinterested, but her eyes said something else. He hadn't missed that flicker of attraction, and she'd dodged his question about seeing someone else. Judging by past experience, he could infer that she probably wasn't dating anyone at the moment.

But before he could say more, an electronic bell sounded from above, ringing three times. She turned on her heel and left the room without another word, crossing directly to a phone on the wall in the hallway. "Yes?"

Cicero glanced at sleeping Galen, then shifted his position to allow himself a line of sight into the hall.

The doctor was listening intently. "We'll be ready," she said. She hung up the phone and spoke to the nurse now waiting beside her. "We have penetrating abdominal trauma two minutes out. I need all hands on deck. And call my sister in."

"Sage left for Denver this morning," said the nurse who had tended to Galen.

Rose muttered a soft curse. In a clipped, professional voice, she fired off her orders. "Call Pete. We want the air ambulance ready to go. Chances are we will be transferring this one ASAP."

"Yes, Doctor."

51

In an instant, the sleepy clinic went into action. Soon Cicero heard the crash of doors and the rattle of wheels on a stretcher as the trauma patient arrived. Over the next twenty minutes, he listened with interest as Rose Anderson and her small medical team fought to save a young man's life. The action took place in a room some thirty feet away from where he waited with Galen, and the atmosphere in the hallway swirled with tension. From what he could gather, the patient was a teenaged boy who'd been thrown from a snowmobile and had the horrible luck to land on the sharp point of a dead tree branch lying on the ground.

"Grade five liver laceration" never sounded good.

The nurse rushed past his doorway carrying bags of blood. Her gaze flickered toward him, and the look in her eyes told him she'd forgotten about their pint-sized patient who now appeared to be awakening from his nap. Cicero turned his attention away from the drama down the hall and onto Galen.

"How you feeling, Robin?" he asked. It was a familiar tease, one sure to distract the boy from his obvious discomfort.

"I'm Batman."

"That's not what Keenan says."

"He's the Joker. My arm hurts, Uncle Skunk."

"I know, Buddy." Cicero gently brushed the

boy's hair out of his eyes. "Good thing Batman is such a badass."

"Aunt Amy says we can't say that word. You say a lot of bad words."

Cicero winced. "Yeah, I know. I'm trying to stop."

"That's okay. I won't tell. Mom said a lot of bad words, too. Sometimes she drank too much, too. Can we go home now?"

"Not yet, buddy. We have to wait for the doctor to come check your cast."

His voice got small. "I don't like waiting on doctors. It's never good."

Pretty profound statement coming from a little mouth, Cicero observed. Over the past year, they'd done a lot of waiting where doctors were concerned. Waiting for appointments. Waiting for test results. Waiting for treatment. Waiting for news.

Once the waiting was over, they would have given anything for more time to wait.

The potent cocktail of anger, frustration, and grief stirred inside him again. He really hated doctors' offices—and he despised hospitals. Frankly, he didn't feel all that kindly toward doctors as a rule, either. Cold fish, most of them. Delivered hard news with either a flat, detached manner or a false compassion you could see right through. He understood that doctors weren't miracle workers, but when their "cures" were more dangerous than the disease, shouldn't somebody be held accountable for that?

Cancer hadn't killed Jayne. No, she'd been whipping cancer's ass. Infection had killed her. From a bug she'd most likely picked up in a freaking hospital, one that her weakened immune system had been unable to fend off.

His gaze shifted to Galen. The cast was dry. Maybe they should beat feet and come back to have it checked later when things weren't so busy. One of the pluses of living in a small town, right?

He checked his watch and decided to wait five more minutes. Some might label his concern as paranoia. He didn't care. Recent experience had proved just how dangerous medical care could be. Jayne had been fine on Monday, dead on Thursday. That fact haunted him. What if Galen . . .

He was just about to slip his arms beneath the boy to lift him from the exam table when he realized something had changed. Sound had ceased. The clinic had gone quiet as the grave. He closed his eyes.

Well, splendid. Modern medicine loses another one.

His stomach did a slow, sick flip, and he shoved his fingers through his hair. A teenaged boy. He thought about a set of parents somewhere about to get the phone call every parent prayed they'd never receive. He thought about siblings and grandparents and cousins. What heartbreak they had facing them.

He absolutely wanted to get out of here now. Thank God that Galen was too young to realize what had happened down the hall. Had it been Keenan wearing a brand new cast, the questions would be coming at him like bullets.

Just as he opened his mouth to tell Galen they were going, he heard the approaching *squeak squeak squeak* of rubber soles against tile. Rose Anderson swept into the room wearing a fresh physician's coat over blue scrubs and a smile identical to the one she'd worn when she'd greeted them on their arrival.

"Sorry for the delay," she said briskly. "Now, let's take a look at that cast."

Cicero watched her tuck and trim, and listened to her chatter with a growing resentment. A boy in her care just died. Couldn't she bother herself to care just a little? His disdainful gaze swept over her, not missing the bloodstains on the tops of her sneakers. He only halfway listened as she explained how to take proper care of the cast because he was busy getting downright pissed. They must teach them this flat-eyed poker face in medical school.

Good thing she'd turned down his dinner invitation. Like one of his foster mothers used to say, pretty is as pretty does. The doctor wasn't nearly as delicious as he'd initially perceived.

The brunette from the business office rapped on the door. "Excuse me, Dr. Rose. The Oldhams just drove up."

A grimace flashed across the physician's face, there and gone so quickly that Cicero would have missed it had he not been looking directly at her. The boy's family, Cicero surmised. Maybe she possessed a smidgen of humanity, after all.

"Thank you. I'll wait for them in my office. Please show them there." She smiled kindly at Galen. "How do you feel, young man?"

"My arm hurts, but it's not too bad. I want to go home and finish the snowball fight."

"Maybe tomorrow. You need to stay quiet today."

"Oh, man!"

To Cicero, she said, "Give him another dose of pain reliever before bed. If you have any questions, feel free to call."

She turned to leave, then hesitated at the doorway. "When you're ready to leave, it would be better if you used the side entrance."

In order to avoid the grieving family. Okay, so maybe she had slightly more than a smidgen of humanity. Slightly.

"Will do."

The sooner, the better. Cicero wrapped the blanket Gabi had given him around Galen's shoulders and led him out of the clinic just as anxious voices became audible.

A bank of clouds had rolled in while they'd been

indoors, and the gray pall they cast over the valley matched his mood. He had a project list a mile long waiting for him and had the rug rats not been around, he would have lost himself in the work. Under the circumstances, he simply didn't have the heart for it. Instead, he called the Parnells, got a thorough ass-chewing, then loaded up the kids and drove to the nearest movie theater. Cicero brooded through the drive and movie, an animated fantasy that kept the little monsters entranced. Memories of those interminable minutes when he stood listening to the teenager die floated through his mind and made him literally sick to his stomach. A bad landing. What craptastic luck that poor kid had.

And it could have been Galen just as easily. He could have come down on a stake instead of his arm. There was a stack of rebar in the alley behind the studio. The kids ran around back there all the time. Any one of them could have slipped and fallen on top of the steel rods.

Cicero didn't know to whom the steel belonged—*but he'd damned well see that it was hauled off first thing tomorrow.*

His thoughts went down the dark rabbit hole of what-ifs. He imagined the reactions of Jayne's children had they suffered another tragedy right on top of the loss of their mom. He wasn't sure they'd survive another blow. Keenan would probably start stealing candy cigarettes from the

Stop & Shop—if they still made candy cigarettes, that is. Galen would revert to wetting the bed every night. Misty would fall into one of her books and never come out. On top of all that, he doubted the Parnells possessed the intestinal fortitude they'd need to support the children through something so tragic.

For about the millionth time, he wondered about the kids' fathers. Three deadbeat dads. *What the hell was wrong with men?* Cicero understood the basic biological drive as well as any guy, but nothing excused carelessness. *Jayne had sure known how to pick 'em.*

Cicero's dark imaginings opened the mental door to additional worry about the children's guardians. He hoped his sister's instincts had been better when it came to choosing guardians than it had when picking bedmates.

Jayne had met Amy Parnell when the two waited tables at the same restaurant in Portland, Oregon. Amy had been the sister Jayne had always wanted. In fact, he always suspected that transforming their friendship into family had contributed to Jayne's decision to accept Amy's brother's marriage proposal. After all, she hadn't married the fathers of her first three children.

He was damn glad she had married Daisy's father. Otherwise, Scott and Amy might not have stepped up to the plate when Jayne asked them to be guardians after her husband was killed. He gave them plenty of credit for that. Heaven knows, he wouldn't have wanted to do it.

Cicero had never wanted kids. He was too selfish. Too involved in his art. Too old at this point to start down that particular road. These short little visits and pockets of responsibility were all he cared to handle, thank you very much.

What would he have done if Galen's accident had resulted in something worse than a broken arm? How would he have managed the others? How was the family of the snowmobiler managing now? He wondered if the dead teen's parents had other children to comfort and cling to tonight.

He hoped Rose Anderson had treated them with compassion rather than a perfunctory "I'm sorry for your loss" like he'd received in that Houston hospital room. He gave her points for ensuring the family's privacy, but he wouldn't forget her perfunctory manner in the wake of the teen's death. Pretty face, but a cold heart. He didn't need that in his life. Wintertime in Eternity Springs was chilly enough. When he went looking for feminine companionship, he wanted warmth. Heat.

So quit imagining how she looks wearing that damned white coat and nothing else.

The movie ended and they made a stop at the beloved McDonald's for dinner before hitting the road for home. Experience told Cicero that the movie popcorn, hot dogs, sodas, and candy wouldn't put a dent in their appetites, and he'd been right. These kids could pack it away.

During the return drive to Eternity Springs, Keenan entertained them with knock-knock jokes. When Galen requested a sing-along, Misty actually stopped reading and joined in. She had a lovely voice, Cicero decided as he hummed along to the theme song from *The Lion King*, glad for the distraction from thoughts of death and frozen-hearted doctors.

Twenty minutes away from town, a telltale shudder indicated that the SUV had a tire issue. He pulled off at a scenic overlook and changed the tire without incident, though the frigid night air soaked into everyone's bones. By the time they arrived home, it was time for baths and bed. Thank goodness.

"Less than twelve hours to go," he muttered once the bedtime ordeal was done and he went to chase the lingering chill away with a hot shower, only to discover that Misty had drained the tank yet again. As he pulled his clothes back on, he recalled the hot mineral springs located beyond the estate's rose garden and tennis court.

Well now, he thought, a smile playing on his lips. The little kids were asleep. Misty was reading. He could slip out for a soak with a glass of scotch and a cigar, and he wouldn't be shirking his duty one little bit. Or breaking the promise he'd made to Amy not to smoke or drink or do drugs in front of the kids. Not that he ever did drugs, and he smoked cigars only on rare occasions—and as a rule, he drank far less than had the little monsters' mother.

But after the day he'd had, he deserved a little indulgence.

He called up to the resort's main house and ordered both his drink and his smoke to be delivered to the hot springs, then changed into the swimsuit and heavy robe the spa provided. He checked on the kids one last time, and headed outdoors.

The cold night air was still; the estate grounds quiet. While he wasn't the only guest at Angel's Rest right now, this was definitely the off-season. He did hear a curious thumping sound he couldn't place, and it got louder as he made his way through the bare winter rose garden.

He didn't hear the voice until the tennis court came into sight. Spying movement, he stopped abruptly and tried to process what he was seeing. Somebody was playing tennis by moonlight in the frigid cold? Yes, alone. Using a ball machine.

"Okay, this is just weird," he murmured.

Then he heard the voice. A familiar voice. One filled with anger and frustration and pain. "Idiot kids!" *Whack.* "Stupid snowmobile!" *Whack.* "Fudge monkey possum sucking tree branch!" *Whack. Whack. Whack.*

Cicero's chin dropped as he realized he was watching the doctor beat the absolute hell out of tennis balls while screeching a curse he didn't think he'd ever heard before. And he knew a lot of sailors.

She held the racket with clenched fingers gone white with the pressure of her grip. Tears streamed down her face. Her voice vibrated with fury—and grief.

He watched her for a few more minutes until the icy winter air chased him to the hot springs, where he discovered his drink and cigar waiting for him. He settled into the water with a sigh of content-ment and reflected upon the scene he'd just witnessed.

Maybe Dr. Delicious wasn't as coldhearted as she'd let on.

Four

"Come on in out of the cold," Shannon O'Toole said when Rose stepped into Murphy's Pub. "It's miserable out there. I'm beginning to think winter will never end."

"That's always how I feel in February." Rose pulled off her hat and gloves, then unzipped her jacket and slipped it off. She hung it on the coat rack beside the door and approached the bar. "I'm tired of the snow, tired of the cold, tired of winter gray."

Tired of death.

She glanced around the empty bar. "Where is everyone?"

"Poker game at the barber shop." Knowing her customer, Shannon set a wineglass on the century-old polished mahogany bar. "Zin or cab tonight?" she asked.

"Neither. It's a vodka martini night. Dirty, with extra olives."

Shannon's brows arched with an unvoiced question.

"Nathan Oldham's funeral was this afternoon," Rose explained.

"Of course." Shannon's caramel-colored eyes softened with sympathy as she began to mix the cocktail. "I heard St. Stephen's was packed to the rafters."

Rose pictured the church pews packed with students wearing letter jackets. "Yes. The Oldhams are well liked in town, and all of Nathan's classmates and their families attended. Lucca Romano coached him in basketball, and he gave a very moving eulogy. Eternity Springs will grieve this loss for some time."

Shannon gave a stainless steel cocktail mixer a shake, then poured Rose's drink into a martini glass. "And what about you? How are you doing?"

"I'm fine," Rose responded automatically. When Shannon pinned her with a doubting look, she admitted, "Okay, I'm a mess."

It was true. All her training and experience had seemed to fail her in the past three days. She burst into tears at the slightest provocation. She had trouble getting to sleep, and once she finally did drift off, she had the most horrible nightmares.

Shannon threaded olives onto a toothpick, dropped the garnish into the martini, then set the glass in front of Rose.

"I'm sorry. Want to talk about it?"

"Not really. Thanks, though." Rose took a sip of her drink, then closed her eyes and savored. "Talk to me about something else. Anything else."

"Okay, then. Want to hear our latest remodel woes?"

"Absolutely."

Shannon had moved to Eternity Springs last year after inheriting Murphy's Pub from a distant relative. She lived in a darling little dollhouse of a Victorian—a real fixer-upper—over on Pinion Street, and she was doing much of the work herself.

Her past was a bit of a mystery. She managed to charmingly thwart the town busybodies every time they pressed her for details. Rose was curious herself, but she didn't pry. She liked Shannon a lot, and the two of them had become friends. Shannon would share her past when she wanted to talk about it—or not. People were entitled to their secrets. Heaven knows, Rose had secrets of her own.

"—dry rot. It's not something I can do, and it's going to take an extra ten thousand for the repair."

"Oh, Shannon. That's terrible. I'm so sorry."

"Thanks. My piggy bank is starting to oink in pain."

"Well, the house is going to be lovely once it's finished. You'll turn a nice profit when you flip it to summer tourists."

"Like they say, from your mouth to God's ears. Of course," she added, her expression going sly, "I'd be remiss not to mention that it would make a lovely home for a physician, too."

"I'm not buying your house, Shannon. I have a cushy deal at Angel's Rest, and I love my garret apartment."

"See, I have an ulterior motive. If you'd buy my house, then the apartment would be empty, and I could rent it. I'd love living there, and I could finish my own novel."

When Celeste first introduced the two women, Shannon had confessed to having a secret desire to write a mystery. Rose had encouraged her, and the shared interest had created a bond between them. "Speaking of writing, will you have new pages for me to critique this week?"

"I will. I murdered two people."

"You go, girl."

"What about you?"

Rose shook her head, then took another sip of

her martini. "Nothing so far. I haven't been able to concentrate."

Her thoughts drifted back to the funeral and her dark mood returned. The alcohol had loosened her tongue just enough to allow her to admit, "This one hurts as much as any I can remember."

The kindness in Shannon's eyes almost undid her. "For a former army doctor during wartime, that says a lot."

"War is different. It's . . ." She searched for the right words to express the emotions inside her. "It's death and maiming and never an easy thing to accept. But I've had it cushy since moving to Eternity Springs. No IED shrapnel or suicide-bomber fallout to deal with, no battle wounds. Even accidental deaths here have been rare. And I've never lost a sixteen-year-old on the operating table just a week after I watched him play high school basketball. I've never had to tell his mother that her son was dead. It sucks, Shannon. Especially since I ask myself if I could have saved him if I'd only had better equipment or more knowledge or more skill. I'll never know. It's impossible to know such things. But the questions haunt me."

"Rose, you can't do that to yourself. You did your best. That's all anyone can ask or expect. Doctors aren't gods."

"Far from it. We're human. Fallible, flawed,

imperfect, human beings. That's why our malpractice insurance is so high."

"Nah," Shannon drawled. "For that, let's blame those who are truly responsible—the bloodsucking lawyers. Not the good ones like Mac Timberlake, mind you. I'm talking the real ticks."

Rose's mouth twisted in a rueful grin as she silently toasted the sentiment. Upon finishing her drink, she signaled for another. She seldom drank hard liquor and rarely more than one, but she wasn't on call tonight. If she needed a crutch to get through the end of this horrible day, then so be it. She wasn't hurting anyone. She'd walked to Murphy's, and she'd walk back home. A little self-destructive behavior upon a rare occasion wasn't the end of the world. She wasn't going out on the prowl, planning to hook up for some indiscriminate, unprotected sex.

More's the pity.

A cold wind blew into the pub when the front door opened and a figure stepped inside. Not just any figure, either, she saw as she glanced over her shoulder, but the fire-breathing dragon himself. *Play your cards right, and maybe sex wouldn't be out of the question.*

Rose snorted at her own foolishness while Shannon greeted the newcomer with a friendly smile. "Hello. You're Gabi Romano's friend, Cicero, aren't you?"

"I am."

"She told me all about the shop you two are opening when she and her fiancé came to dinner last night. It sounds fabulous. I'm Shannon O'Toole. Welcome to Murphy's Pub."

"Thanks. Nice to meet you, Shannon." Approaching the bar, he pinned Rose with an enigmatic gaze. "Good evening, Dr. Anderson."

"Mr. Cicero." She smiled without any warmth. She hadn't missed the disapproval in his eyes in the wake of Nathan's death. He probably thought she failed—which, of course, she had.

She fished an olive out of her martini as tears stung her eyes. She blinked them back, teethed the olive from the toothpick, and tried not to visibly stiffen when Hunt Cicero took a seat on the barstool next to her. Shannon set a coaster down in front of him asking, "What can I get you?"

"What beer do you have on tap?"

He selected a microbrew from the list she rattled off, and she served it just as the door opened again and a half dozen laughing men stepped inside. Members of the team-building retreat at Angel's Rest, Rose realized.

With Shannon suddenly very busy and no other locals in the bar, Cicero turned to her for conversation. "So, 'fudge monkey possum sucking' is one of the most inventive curses I've heard since I worked on a freighter out of Istanbul. Do you have any others?"

"What in the world are you talking about?"

"I happened to walk by when you were, um, playing tennis the other night."

Embarrassment fluttered through Rose, and on its heels, anger. She didn't try to stop herself from going stiff as a scalpel. "You spied on me?"

He met her gaze over the top of his pint. "I rented one of the cottages while the mischief-makers were in town. I was headed for the hot springs."

"Oh." Without a comeback for that, she scowled down into her drink. The Angel's Rest estate was open to guests. He'd had as much right to be there as she. *Wonderful. Just wonderful.* It wasn't enough that this man had been part of the most horrible day of her life in recent years, he'd managed to insert himself into her meltdown, too. Defensiveness blossomed within her and she lashed out in response. "What's your problem, anyway?"

"My problem?"

"I didn't intentionally cause Galen pain, you know. It's impossible to set an arm without it. I acted quickly and efficiently and with gentleness. I challenge you to find a physician who would have done a better job."

"I don't have a problem with your treatment of my nephew."

"Then why the condemning looks?"

She waited for him to deny it, but he surprised her.

"I don't like doctors."

Now it was her turn to lift a brow. "Oh," she replied, her voice dripping with disdain. "You're one of *those*."

A gleam of amusement entered his dark eyes. "Those?"

"People who give more credence to self-diagnosis or something they read on the Internet than to the advice of their doctor who spent years in medical school followed by a residency."

"I don't think anything I've said or done supports that thesis. I took my nephew for treatment, didn't I?"

"Probably were afraid Child Protective Services would be on your butt."

"Speaking of butts, what put the stick up yours?"

She lifted her chin. "I don't like glass artists."

"I'll mention that to Gabi Romano next time I see her."

"Damn," she muttered beneath her breath. He had her on that one. She went for the deflection. "Why don't you like doctors?"

"Because they're fake. They like to project the image of being caring and compassionate, but nine times out of ten, they're hard-hearted and insensitive."

"I guess you blow your glass with a broad pipe, don't you?"

"What?"

"You're not a painter so you don't use a broad brush."

His lips twitched. "Just how many of those martinis have you had?"

She pointed her olive-depleted toothpick at him and scolded. "Generalizations are a poor way to make a diagnosis. Dangerous."

"I think you're dangerous, Doctor."

His words struck like a knife, and while she attempted an offhand manner, the hitch in her voice betrayed her. "That's me, Dr. Dangerous. Show up in my emergency room at your own peril. You saw that firsthand, didn't you? I managed to set an arm, but I couldn't save a life."

"Don't put words in my mouth," he warned. "That's not what I meant at all. You're a beautiful woman with a sharp tongue. That's why you're dangerous."

Cicero shocked her when he reached out and covered her hand with his, giving her a comforting squeeze. "You need to lighten up on yourself. Word around town is that you made a valiant effort, and that nobody could have saved him."

The kindness of his words and action shook Rose, and again tears stung her eyes. She blinked rapidly as Shannon appeared in front of them then and asked, "Another beer, Cicero?"

"Sure. Thanks."

To Rose, she said, "Are you ready for your soup?"

"I'll have another drink, first."

Shannon gave her a long look, then spoke in a chastising tone. "Rose—"

Rose straightened her spine. Her friend was close to crossing a line. "Are you my mother or my bartender?"

"I'm your friend."

Rose closed her eyes. The emotions rolling around inside her were ugly. The sense of failure clawed like a demon. She so wanted to escape the images. Nathan's mother crumpling. The pain on his father's face when he saw his dead child lying on a cold metal table in her ER. Bitterness and regret produced words that sat on her tongue like poison, words she shouldn't speak to a friend.

She fought to find some that weren't so mean. "I was an army doctor, Shannon. I can drink with the best of them."

Shannon's mouth flattened, but worry flickered in her eyes as she set about making another martini. After setting it in front of Rose, she took the opportunity to escape to tend her other customers.

Cicero dragged his gaze away from the basketball game on the television suspended over the bar and stared at Rose. "You were in the army?"

She lifted her empty glass in toast. "Hooah."

"How long?"

"Seems like all my life. I was an army brat, too."

He gave her a close once-over. "How old are you, anyway?"

Rose had to laugh at that. He wasn't shy at all. "You are the rudest man."

Ignoring that, he continued, "I have you pegged for early thirties. Not long out of medical school."

Ah, there it is.

"Because I'm such a craptastic doctor?"

He shot her an irritated scowl. "I understand you being down right now, but don't be stupid."

Intrigued, Rose asked, "So then, how did you come to the conclusion that I'm younger than I am?"

"Other than how you look?" He raised a brow.

She didn't reply, just took a sip of her drink and let her tongue skirt over her bottom lip.

His stare zeroed in on her mouth. Distractedly, he said, "I've been around a lot of doctors over the past year and you're years—decades—younger than any of them."

Pleased with herself, Rose held up her index finger.

"He offers a clue. 'A lot of older doctors.' I suspect that means you've been spending time with specialists. Why is that?"

Even as she asked the question, the answer formed in her alcohol-slowed mind. Celeste had told her that he'd lost his sister to cancer. "Ah, Galen's mother. So that's why you don't like doctors. What type of cancer did she have?"

"Do we really have to be having this conversation?"

"You brought it up. Somebody tells me they don't like me, I want to know why."

He narrowed his eyes. "I didn't say I didn't like you."

"You said you don't like doctors. I'm a doctor. You don't like me." Why was it bothering her? Did she want him to like her? Deep down, maybe she did.

Anderson, you're a fool.

"Maybe I like you too much."

"You don't even know me."

"Precisely."

Rose frowned at the dark-eyed devil. This conversation confused her. Maybe she should switch to club soda. Were they fighting or flirting?

"Do you play darts?" he asked.

"Sure. I spent plenty of evenings in a pub when I was stationed in England. You want to be the target?"

He laughed, the sound a slow, sexy rumble that skittered along her nerves. "On second thought, how about a game of eight ball? Probably be safer for me."

Did she dare? He may as well have a danger sign flashing over his head. Yet Rose found herself reaching deep inside for her poker face.

"I'm not as talented at billiards as I am at darts."

The gleam in his eyes told her she might not have pulled that one off.

"Neither am I." He slid off the barstool. "That should make it fair to wager."

"You want to bet?"

"Sure. Why not?"

"Money?" *Ka-ching, Ka-ching,* she thought.

"Nah, something more interesting. Do you cook?"

"Only if I'm out of poison." After one more sip of her martini, she slid off the stool and onto her feet. She took pride in the fact that she didn't wobble one little bit.

"You are an interesting woman, Doctor. Okay, then. Home-cooked meals are out. Babysitting when the monsters visit this summer."

Hmm. That wasn't such an onerous bet. She liked children. She'd liked those particular children, based on the little she'd seen of them. Besides, on this bitter cold February night, summer seemed like a very long time away.

"That doesn't solve the question of what I'm going to win from you when I whip your butt."

"Dream on, baby."

"I'm not your baby."

"No, you're going to babysit my sister's babies."

"You're not listening. Or else, you're very slow. A wager requires a bet, Mr. Cicero."

"Call me Hunter."

"Why is it that seems to fit you so well?" she mused. "What am I going to win from you, Hunter?"

Now he was grinning openly.

"In the wildly unlikely event that you defeat me in a game of eight ball, I will create a piece of glass especially for you."

Rose attempted to veil her excitement at the thought. Though she wouldn't admit it to another soul, she'd visited his website. His work was fabulous. She moved to the head of the pub's pool table.

"I guess that's a fair enough bet. Want to lag for the break?"

"So, you have played the game. You know the lingo." He positioned himself at her side and chose the solid yellow 1-ball.

Rose chose the solid red 3-ball. "You might just be surprised at how much I know."

At her nod, they both rolled the balls toward the opposite end of the table. As they bounced off the bumper and rolled back toward them, he said, "Actually, buttercup, I don't think I would."

"Rose. My name is Rose. Rosemary, actually."

"Beautiful name." He gestured toward the pool balls, which had rolled to a stop, the yellow ball closest to where they stood. "I break. Rack 'em, sucker."

She shrugged, and did just that. He broke, sank two stripes, and proceeded to run the table, sinking the 8-ball after calling it in the left center pocket. "Don't forget your doctor's bag when you babysit. My nephews and nieces are quite rambunctious."

She wanted to bare her teeth and growl at him. She refrained, saying instead, "I really don't like you."

He moved like a mountain lion and backed her against the table, his arms bracketing her on either side. She smelled the clean, masculine scent of sandalwood soap on him. It was her favorite fragrance in Savannah Turner's local soap shop, Heavenscents.

"I really don't like you, either," Hunt Cicero said, his voice a low, predatory purr. "Want to go back to my place and have sex?"

Yes. Heaven help her, but yes, she honestly did.

Five

Cicero didn't plan the proposition, and when the words slipped out, he knew he could pass it off as teasing. Except, he realized he wasn't teasing. He seriously wanted to take Dr. Delicious to bed.

That he felt that way was no great shock. He often met women he wanted to take to bed; he had a well-earned reputation as a player. But something about this particular thorny Rose appealed to him more than most—despite his prejudice against members of her profession.

And judging by the look in her eyes, she might just take him up on the idea.

So he waited for her response with a surprising amount of anticipation, even though he knew he'd been an ass to ask the question. She'd been drinking and her emotions were a mess from having lost a kid on her ER table less than a week ago. An honorable man wouldn't take advantage of her.

Just call me Cad.

"Rose!" called a feminine voice from near the pub's front door. "Finally! I've been looking all over town for you."

Cicero never took his gaze off the physician, so he saw the flash of emotion in her eyes. Unfortunately, he couldn't put a label on it before she turned away.

"Why?" she asked of the newcomer with long, curly auburn hair and lovely green eyes a shade lighter than Rose's. "Is there a problem?"

"No, not on my end for a change. I'm worried about you."

Rose waved off the concern. "I'm fine."

When the newcomer's gaze shifted from Rose to him, curiosity replaced the concern she'd displayed. Seeing it, Rose said, "Have you two not met?"

"No, but I know who you are." She gave him a brilliant smile and offered her hand. "I've been wanting to come by your studio and talk business. I love your work. I'm Sage Rafferty, Cicero. I own the art gallery in town."

"Allow me to return the compliment. I was familiar with your work, too, even before Gabi showed me the painting you gave her for the retail shop. It's fabulous, and perfect for the store. You have a gift for mood and color."

Sage brightened at the compliment from a fellow artist. "Thank you. I thought a shop named Whimsies should have a fairy or two on its walls."

"You also did that landscape at the medical clinic."

Sage nodded, and Rose explained, "Sage is my sister."

"I see the resemblance in your smiles."

"You've actually seen her smile?" Sage asked, her attention returning to her sibling. "Lately?"

"Sage," Rose said in a warning tone. "I'm fine."

"Honey, you are so not fooling me. I know what it's like to let the work drag you into dark places. Let me help you. Lean on me. Heaven knows it's my turn."

Cicero's expression must have betrayed his curiosity at those remarks because Rose gave him a wry smile and said, "My sister is a physician, too." Then to Sage, she added, "He doesn't like doctors."

"Oh. One of *those.*"

Her disdain so matched her sister's that he had to laugh.

"I know when it's time to make a strategic retreat. I think it's time I wandered home. Sage, it was a pleasure to meet you. Dr. Anderson, I'll let you know when it's time for me to collect our wager. G'night, ladies."

He tipped an imaginary hat, left bills on the bar for the drinks, then departed Murphy's Pub. He walked home on the bitter cold February night feeling pleasantly warm, and he dreamed about stethoscopes and little black dresses.

The following day he had the studio to himself since Gabi was off to Denver with her mother shopping for a wedding gown. Cicero sat in his office with a stack of bills, a few checks, and his adding machine, hoping he'd managed to keep his head above water for another month. His computer sounded an incoming video call. Mitch. Calling from Bella Vita Isle.

Please, don't let this be bad news.

The young man's expression relieved him. "Your mom is okay?" Cicero asked, in lieu of hello.

"So far so good, mon. Praise be. They've scheduled bypass surgery for tomorrow."

"At the hospital in Miami? The place Flynn recommended?"

"Yes."

"Okay, then." Cicero exhaled a slow breath.

Mitch's family was his family, too, and his mother's heart attack in late January had scared them all. Cicero had been so worried that he'd actually overcome his fury with physicians long enough to find the name of a heart specialist for her to consult.

After a little more discussion about his mother, Mitch asked about the Galveston studio, and Cicero caught him up with the progress on that front. "We're still negotiating," he said. "I'm beginning to think that lawyers can give doctors a run for their money when it comes to being asses."

The offer for the building housing his studio in Galveston had been the one bright spot in an otherwise bleak January. The week after his sister's death, a developer had swooped in with a plan to build a resort hotel that required the destruction of the old building Cicero had purchased for a studio the previous year. With Jayne gone, and since the Parnells didn't want him underfoot and offering child-rearing opinions as they worked to form their new family, he'd had no reason to stay in Texas. He'd be close enough in Colorado should the little demons need him, and he stood to turn a tidy profit from the sale. Those funds would go a long way toward paying the medical debts he'd assumed when he'd signed paperwork that ensured that his sister got to see the very best, out-of-her-insurance-network doctors. Those bills hadn't died with his sister.

Talk about the Texas studio evolved into conversation about the Colorado one. Cicero was relieved to learn that Mitch still intended to spend June through September in Eternity Springs, barring any unpleasant surprises concerning his mother. As the conversation wound down, Mitch asked, "So, just how cold is it in your little mountain metropolis today?"

Cicero thought of Doctor Delicious. "Not as cold as I expected, actually. You'll call me after the procedure?"

"I will."

"From the hospital. Use your cell. Don't make me wait until you get home to your computer."

"Yes, boss."

Cicero returned to his figures, and after a few more calculations and projections, he decided he could afford to wait out the developer a little while longer. He honestly believed that if he remained patient, he could milk the man for another fifteen percent. With any luck, by the end of summer, he'd find himself free of the financial rough patch he'd been slogging through for months. It would be so nice to throw this yoke off his shoulders.

After all, since he'd promised Jayne and the Parnells that he'd help with financial support for the kids, he had college to save for.

He came close to banging his head on the table at that thought.

Sighing, he took out his checkbook and began tackling invoices. He was halfway through the stack when he heard the front door open. Happy for the distraction, he looked up to see his friend and Gabi's fiancé, Flynn Brogan, stride into the studio.

Cicero took a good look at his friend's expression and rolled out an old joke. "A horse walks into a bar—"

"And the bartender asks, 'Why the long face?' Yeah, yeah, yeah. You're right. I'm not a happy man."

Not an unhappy one, either, Cicero decided. More disgruntled. He took a guess at why. "You have a fight with Gabriella?"

"You mean Ms. Hard Head? I don't want to talk about it."

Cicero leaned back in his chair, ready to be amused. He knew his friend. "Of course you want to talk about it. You wouldn't have come here and plopped down in a chair otherwise."

"You're wrong. I'm here because I have something to discuss with you that doesn't have anything to do with the fact that my beloved fiancée refuses to move in with me."

"She's cut you off?"

"I didn't say she won't sleep with me, but she won't spend the night. She won't move in. She wants to wait until after we're married, and that's not happening for months yet because it takes months to plan a wedding."

"Oh, the horror."

Flynn flipped him the bird.

Cicero laughed. "Gabi's a girly girl. Of course she wants a wedding."

"There should be some compromise here," Flynn grumbled. "If she's so determined not to live with me until we're married, then why can't we quietly get it done at the courthouse now, then have the wedding like she wants this summer?"

"Makes perfect sense to me."

"Me, too!" Flynn's voice rang with righteousness. "But when I suggested it, you'd have thought I proposed that we rounded up some kittens to dye purple and sprinkle with glitter."

"I don't know what to tell you, man. In my experience, once Legs takes a position, it takes an earthquake to move her off of it."

Flynn nodded his agreement and sighed. "True enough. By the way, don't you think it's time you dropped that nickname you have for my wife-to-be?"

Cicero considered the question. He knew the term needled Flynn. That's why he used it every chance he got. What were friends for if not to give one another grief? He shook his head. "Maybe after the wedding. So, you mentioned another reason for visiting this morning?"

"Oh, yeah." Flynn rubbed the back of his neck. "I'm here to give you a heads-up. Ms. Granite Head is bummed that she's not here to give you this news herself, and don't think I refrained from pointing out that the nuptial extravaganza is the cause. Anyway, the way she tells it, sometime last fall, she decided you should participate in this thing, but she knew you'd say no, so she took it upon herself to throw your hat into the ring."

Warily, Cicero asked, "What ring?"

"Have you ever heard of the Albritton Fellowship?"

Cicero shook his head.

"Doesn't ring a bell."

"I didn't think it would. You're not the type to bother with competitions."

"Competitions?" A seed of anger sprouted within him. "What has Gabi done?"

"She submitted your work for consideration for the Albritton, and they're announcing the three finalists this morning. You're one of them. Gabi had put her cell number on the application, but she was halfway to Denver when they called. She told them you wouldn't be available to speak with them until this afternoon in order to give me time to come by here and clue you in. She's afraid you would blow off the phone call if you didn't know what it's about."

"I will blow them off. I don't do competitions."

"You really should do this one, Cicero," Flynn said with a knowing smirk. "The prizes are substantial. As a finalist, you're already assured of a cash award—if you participate, that is. If you were to win, there's a fellowship that pays an additional stipend for a year. Not to mention the boost you'd surely get from all the publicity. The Albritton is a big hairy deal, and apparently, you're the first glass artist to ever make the finalist cut."

"I don't enter contests."

"Then you'll be throwing away a minimum of fifty grand."

Fifty grand? Cicero sat up straight. "What did you say?"

"Second place is one hundred and first place is a cool quarter mil."

"Mil—what? Million? The winner's prize is two hundred fifty thousand dollars?"

"Plus the stipend of the same amount."

"Holy hell. What do you have to do to win? Kill someone?"

"Actually, I think you'd have to create something in your medium."

"How many somethings?"

"Just one, I think. I don't know all the details. That's the information you'll be given in the phone call. You can get online and read about it, too. Now, back to Gabi. You're a ladies' man. Do you have any ideas for me about how to win her over to my way of thinking?"

Cicero couldn't drag his attention away from the half-million-dollar dangle. Distractedly, he said, "Try sex."

"What do you mean, try sex? That's the whole problem here. I want to have more of it, and that means she needs to be there."

"That's all I have, Brogan. Frankly, it's all I ever need. Not that I've ever wanted a woman to move in with me, mind you. I tend to have the opposite problem. Once I take them to bed, I have a hard time getting them to leave."

"You are such an egotistical ass, Cicero."

"Just telling the truth, my man. Just telling the truth."

They traded insults a bit more in the manner of good male friends, before Flynn took his leave. The moment the door shut behind his friend, Cicero opened his laptop and keyed in a search for Albritton Fellowship.

It was a biennial contest for artists of any medium. And the prizes really were what Brogan had claimed. He scanned the home page, then followed a link to read about the most recent winner and finalists. Two painters and a potter. They'd been given a theme and asked to produce a representative work by a deadline. The board of directors of the Albritton Foundation chose the winner.

Cicero read the artists' bios and studied the photos of the work they'd produced for the contest. Impressive. And he was a finalist? Not that he wasn't confident of his own talent, because he knew he was good. But still.

His mind spun. Worst-case scenario, he made fifty big ones and could pay off a chunk of the medical bills. *Best-case scenario, I make sick bank. Sick.* He continued reading from the website. There were shows in New York, Los Angeles, and Dallas, attended by everybody who's anybody in the art world.

Now that he'd thought about it, Cicero realized he had heard about this competition, but he'd never considered entering. Why had Gabi? How had she done it without his knowledge? What had she submitted? He clicked around some more and discovered further details about the entry requirements. Then he remembered the photographs she'd asked him to email last fall.

"She put together a catalog," he murmured to himself.

He would have chewed her out if he'd known. He didn't go in for this sort of stuff. But now— he owed her. Big. He'd have to do something nice for her. Make a grand gesture. She wouldn't expect that from him. Cicero didn't make grand gestures to his apprentices—but then he didn't enter contests, either.

"Live and learn," he said, tossing his checkbook back into his desk drawer. Financial matters could wait. He needed to think, and he did his best thinking with a punty in his hands. Besides, working would help him pass the time until he received the phone call. *If I receive the phone call.* He knew that Gabi and Flynn wouldn't B.S. him about something this big, but until he actually spoke to the Albritton people himself, he'd worry that a mistake had been made. His luck had been running just that way.

He'd taken two steps out of his office when the phone rang. He glanced at the wall clock. Only ten after eleven. Caller ID showed an unfamiliar number. Ordinarily, he would have ignored the call, but now, he picked up. "Hello?"

"Am I speaking with Mr. Hunter Cicero?"

His heart thudded. "You are."

"Excellent. I'm glad to have reached you. It just occurred to me that you're in the mountain time zone and I'm calling a little early. My name is Elliott Goodson. I am the Executive Director of the Albritton Foundation. I am pleased to inform you that you are a finalist for this year's fellowship competition."

Damned if Cicero didn't go a little bit weak in the knees. He propped a hip on the corner of his desk for support and said, "I'm honored, Mr. Goodson. Thank you so much."

By the time he hung up the phone fifteen minutes later, all thought of working had disappeared. His thoughts spun like a waterspout off Bella Vita Isle. He had a deadline—August 31. He had a theme—a quote from a poem by Emily Dickinson:

Hope is the thing with feathers.
That perches in the soul
And sings the tune without the words
And never stops at all.

Now all he needed was an idea.

A grand idea. The idea of all ideas. A half-million-dollar idea.

He needed inspiration.

His best ideas always came to him when his mind was empty of everything else following strenuous exercise. When he ran a marathon or swam the channel between Bella Vita Isle and neighboring Sunrise Cay, ideas flowed like rum in the islands. Of course, his most creatively spectacular ideas had happened in the aftermath of a vigorous session between the sheets.

He couldn't go swimming in Eternity Springs. He could go running. Skiing. Mountain climbing. But he needed a spectacular idea.

"Guess I'll go see if Dr. Delicious has plans for lunch."

He grabbed his coat and exited his studio wearing a self-amused grin. Such sacrifices a man made for his art.

Six

This year the annual Eternity Springs Ice Fishing Derby at Hummingbird Lake boasted a record number of entries. Held on the last weekend in February, the festival went on in sunshine, rain, snow; and once even in a blizzard. Luckily, this year the weather cooperated, and as Rose parked her car in the lakeside campground lot on Sunday afternoon, bright sunshine beaming in a cloudless sky teamed with a nonexistent breeze to make the temperature hovering in the twenties seem almost balmy.

The mouth-watering aromas of grilling brats and roasting nuts drifted from the concession stands erected around the campgrounds, and she stopped and bought a paper cone full of nuts before making her way out onto the ice in search of Shannon. Her friend wasn't difficult to find since she'd planted a Murphy's Pub pole banner beside her fishing hole.

Rose couldn't help but smile. Raised a city girl, Shannon had jumped into the outdoors life with both feet. Rose enjoyed most of what life in a mountain town had to offer, except she honestly didn't see the appeal of ice fishing. Fly fishing bubbling rivers and frothing streams in summertime, yes. That was an art and a joy. Sinking a line through a hole in the ice? She didn't get it.

And yet, now that she'd visited the Derby—a first for her—she had to admit that she found the atmosphere appealing. It was like a party on ice. She popped a warm cashew into her mouth and greeted Shannon.

"You look like you're having fun."

"I am. It's a gorgeous day and I've caught two fish."

"You go, girl," Rose said with a smile.

"Whoa! Not two. Three. Got another one!" Shannon pulled a rainbow trout from the water and chortled with glee.

Rose wrinkled her nose when her friend grasped the wiggling rainbow and began to extract the hook from its mouth. "Yuck. That is why I don't fish unless I'm with someone who will do that nasty task for me."

Shannon glanced up at her in surprise. "You don't like to remove fish hooks?"

"Or touch fish. Fish skin and scales creep me out."

"What? That's crazy. You're a doctor. You touch things that are a million times worse than fish skin. I imagine since you moved to Eternity Springs, you've removed a fish hook from a human being a time or two."

"More times than I can count. But I'm always gloved and there are no scales involved."

"That's just weird." Shannon efficiently freed

the hook, then dropped the trout into the cooler at her side. "So I guess it's safe to assume you're not ready to chop a hole in the ice and join me?"

"The fish are safe from me." She pulled a thermos from a tote bag and handed it to Shannon. "I brought us hot chocolate."

"God bless you. I have a camp stool in that green bag at your feet. Get it and sit down and let's dish. I have information about your boyfriend."

Rose couldn't help but be intrigued. "He's not my boyfriend."

Shannon released a puff of air that fogged on the chilly air. "Ha," she said in disbelief. "Then why do the two of you have dinner together at Murphy's every night?"

"It's not every night."

"Almost. Word is getting around town that the two of you are an item."

"We live in a small town. Word gets around when somebody buys extra toilet paper at the Trading Post." Rose shrugged and pulled the camp stool from the bag Shannon had indicated. "I've been having dinner at your place regularly since I discovered the ambrosia that is your potato soup. As far as Cicero showing up, too, well, Murphy's is a public place. I can't stop him from choosing to eat his supper there."

"Don't give me that. You both wait for the other to arrive before you place your meal orders.

Seriously, Rose, the two of you are like teen-agers." Shannon laughed and added, "It's been going on for almost two weeks. And given it's my restaurant, I've had a front row seat!"

"We are just being polite. They're not dates. We're not dating. The term boyfriend implies dating."

"He asks you on a date every night."

"Eavesdropping?"

"I'm not deaf."

"Then you've heard me refuse every night, too." Rose waved that away as she set up the stool and took a seat. "It's a joke. It's become a joke between us."

"Maybe so, but he is a man on the prowl and he has you in his sights. I've worked in enough bars over the years that I recognize the signs. Okay, girlfriend, spill. He's hot. He is obviously fishing. Why don't you let him reel you in?"

Rose filled a Styrofoam cup with hot chocolate from her thermos as her friend lowered her line into the icy water. Handing over the steaming drink, she said, "It's complicated."

Shannon studied her through narrowed eyes. "It's your ex, isn't it?"

"I'm not sitting out here in the cold to talk about *him*. You promised dish on Hunt Cicero. Whatcha got?"

"Well, I hate to spread gossip"—Shannon ignored Rose's snort and continued—"but word is that your local fire man has been spending a lot of time at the library. Reading poetry."

"Poetry? Seriously?" Rose was intrigued.

"But that's only part of it. The librarian told the nail tech at the salon that he gathers up a stack of books and carries them to one of the private study carrels. He reads for a little while, then he leaves the library and goes for a run. He comes back, reads some more, then runs some more. The nail tech says she's seen him out jogging, and that he looks really good in running pants."

"The woman does have a keen eye." Rose sipped her hot chocolate and considered the tidbit of news. She wouldn't try to deny that Hunt Cicero was interesting, well traveled, and well read. His interest in poetry shouldn't surprise her, but it did. "He has a PEZ collection."

"A what?"

"PEZ. You know, those little candy holders? He has a collection of them. Like over 300 of them."

"A collector. Hmm." Shannon twisted her head to look behind her. "See, that fits him. I'll bet he's collected plenty of women over the years."

Rose followed the path of Shannon's gaze and spied Cicero standing with his arm draped familiarly around a woman's shoulder. A lovely young woman whom she didn't recognize. Something ugly stirred inside Rose. "Who is that?"

"The blonde? She's pretty, isn't she?"

"She's young."

"Twenty-one. I know. I carded her last night." Shannon gave Rose a knowing look as she added, "Pull in your thorns, Rosie. She and her fiancé had a beer at the pub last night. Her father is one of Flynn Brogan's closest friends so it makes sense that Cicero knows them. The whole family is here for the engagement party."

"Oh." Rose winced. "Was I that obvious?"

"Yep."

She sighed. After Brandon ditched her then married someone ten years younger than she, young women and older men were a sore spot for her. "That's embarrassing."

"Actually, I think a little jealousy is telling. You can deny it all you want, but you're interested. The man is obviously hot for you, too. And didn't I overhear him invite you to be his date tonight? You didn't tell him no."

"But I didn't tell him yes, either. I said I'd see him there. I received my own invitation and since the party is at Angel's Rest, I just have to walk downstairs."

"So it's a semi-date?"

"No. I don't know. Maybe." In an effort to deflect her friend's attention, she asked, "What about you? Are you going?"

"I am." Shannon dusted her knuckles over her shoulder. "I received invitations from two handsome men, I'll have you know."

"Excellent. Although, considering all the times

you're hit on at the pub each night, I'm not surprised. Let me guess." Rose mentally reviewed the pub's customers. The owner of the Trading Post, Eternity Springs's grocery store, had been coming around Murphy's Pub quite a bit. "I bet Logan McClure is one of them."

Shannon lifted her line from the water, checked the bait, then sank the hook once again. "Correct."

"He does make it pleasant to buy groceries. And the second guy? This shouldn't be difficult since we don't have that many single men in town. Of course, mystery man could be a visitor. Since you said handsome, the name Romano pops to mind first."

Shannon made a patting gesture over her heart.

"Oooh, you scored a date with one of the super-studs? Max or Tony?"

"Max invited me first, so I'm going with him."

Rose studied her friend, picking up a vibe that surprised her. *He's not the guy you'd like to be going with, is he? But neither is Logan.* Rose wanted to ask, but Shannon's manner broadcast that the topic was closed.

"You'll have fun with Max." She glanced down at the fishing line and observed, "I think you have another fish."

"Oh!"

While Shannon dealt with the trout, Rose thought about her own plans for the engagement party. Her attention wandered back to the group that included Hunt Cicero. It wasn't surprising that she found him intriguing. Any woman with a heartbeat would. Darkly handsome, he seemed always to be . . . simmering. Yesterday on her way to the clinic, Celeste had asked her to drop off a bridal magazine at the studio for Gabi. She'd watched him work. He'd been hot and sweaty, his movements graceful. When he'd wrapped his mouth around the blowpipe and lifted his gaze to hers, the intensity in those gorgeous dark eyes had melted her. In that moment, the expression playing with fire had taken on an entirely new meaning.

Hunt Cicero. Passion, poetry, and PEZ collections.

He was nothing like her ex.

Brandon had looked like a Nordic god, light and bright and beautiful. A brilliant and talented surgeon, he'd had a charismatic personality and he'd walked the hospital corridors like a king whose confidence knew no bounds even before he'd earned renown in his field. Her father had admired and respected him. In her most vulnerable moments, Rose wondered if even from the beginning, Brandon had pursued her for professional reasons rather than personal ones. Her father's mentorship had been a valuable boon to his career.

Looking back, she understood why she'd fallen for Brandon. Less clear to Rose were the reasons why she'd stayed with him for seven years. After canceling plans to marry three separate times due to deployment—twice for him, once for her—they'd put the idea on hold. In hindsight, she could see that having her around made it easier for him to concentrate on what really mattered—his career. She'd been little more than convenience for him. Someone to pick up his dry cleaning. Someone to cook for him. Someone for sex. Of course, once he was established and she had needed *him* for a change, he'd dumped her for a younger, healthier model.

Stupidly, she hadn't seen that one coming.

Maybe that was part of the appeal where Cicero was concerned. With a man like him, there would be no ambiguity. A woman would know from the first that she was just another notch in the bedpost. *Maybe it's time you start notching your bedpost, too.*

What would it hurt? It's not like she could get pregnant.

Shannon interrupted her reverie. "Speaking of brooding, where did your thoughts run off to?"

"Cold fish. Hot tamales."

"Excuse me?"

"Men. Maybe I should take a lesson from them. Except for one stumble, I've been a good girl all of my life. Maybe it's time I practiced being bad."

"Ooh." Shannon's eyes rounded with intrigue. "Tell me about this stumble."

"Not now. I'll play *True Confessions* with you

another time." Maybe. Maybe not. Probably not. That particular story wasn't one she ever planned to publish.

Just then an air-horn sounded, signaling the end of the day's competition and dragging Rose's thoughts away from her barren love life. While Shannon removed her line from the water, Rose stood and helped her friend pack up. "Are you going to the weigh in?"

"Of course. I won't even make the top fifty, but I want an official basis point so I can point to my progress next year."

"I like your style, O'Toole."

Shannon nodded regally, then said, "I'm all-in on life in Eternity Springs. So, in addition to bringing me hot chocolate, didn't you say you wanted to listen to the school choir concert? Isn't that next on the day's agenda?"

"I did, and it is. I have a large number of patients in the K-to-5th-grade demographic. My inbox overflowed with invitations."

Rose helped her friend tote her supplies to her car, then while Shannon stood in line with her catch for the weigh-in, Rose grabbed a front row concert seat. The kids began taking their places on the risers. She smiled at the sight of rosy cheeks and the girls' excited grins and boys' feigned boredom. Gabi's niece, Holly Montgomery, spied her doctor and gave Rose a little surreptitious wave.

"What a doll she is," a deep voice rumbled. Cicero slid into the seat to Rose's left. "Gonna be a heartbreaker one day."

"No," Rose countered. "She's destined to be a heart mender. Have you heard her story?"

"About being kidnapped?" When Rose nodded, he said, "Gabi told me. So great that there was a happy ending to that one."

"Absolutely," she agreed. "The world needs more happy endings. So, did you enjoy the fishing today? Have any luck?"

"Fishing was okay. I caught a few, but just between you and me, I don't see the allure in ice fishing. That said, this little festival has been nice. Love the way the whole town participates."

"Wait until tomorrow when the hot air balloons go up. It's truly a beautiful sight. They're predicting perfect weather for it."

"So I hear. Gabi's been fretting about the weather all week, hoping that the balloons get to fly. We have friends in town for the party tonight, and she's planning on bringing them back out here tomorrow to watch. I admit I've been pleasantly surprised by the number of tourists the event has brought to town. Gabi made a couple dozen glass balloons to sell as souvenirs and she told me she only has a few left."

"She's opened the retail shop?"

"Not yet. Her sister-in-law has set aside space for a display in her soap store during the festival."

"That's nice of Savannah."

"She and Gabi are good friends."

The school choir began their concert, and Rose settled back to listen. Events like this were always bittersweet for her. As a rule, she managed to keep her regrets at bay, but invariably when she sat in a crowd as a spectator rather than a parent, the *what-ifs* sneaked in like thieves in the night. Nevertheless, she enjoyed the concert, and afterward, she congratulated her pint-size patients on a job well done. All the while, she remained cognizant of the fact that Cicero stood at the edge of the crowd watching her. Waiting for her?

She couldn't deny that it gave her a little thrill.

He fell in beside her as she began her walk to her car. "I had a nice talk with your sister earlier."

"Was Sage here? I didn't see her."

"No, she came by the studio this morning to pester me about getting her pieces for Vistas Art Gallery. She gave me some dirt on you."

Rose checked her step and almost slipped on the ice.

"She said you're a writer. That you have an agent and everything."

Oh. That.

"There's no 'everything.' We haven't sold the book."

"Sage said you've written more than one. Mysteries and medical thrillers. In all of our dinners together, you've never mentioned that to me. Why not?"

"There haven't been that many dinners, and it's never come up."

"You have a creative streak, Dr. Anderson. I find that fascinating. I thought doctors were all left-brained people."

"I think we've already established that your perceptions about physicians aren't accurate."

"I want to read one of your manuscripts."

The idea both thrilled her and frightened her to death. He made his living off of his creativity.

"I'm just a dabbler. I find writing relaxing. It's fun to use my medical knowledge to plot scenarios."

"Sage said you live in a regular writer's garret. I want to see that, too. Why don't we plan to slip away from the engagement party tonight and you can show me?"

Seriously, he was amazing. She rolled her eyes at that. "Why am I not surprised that you would invite yourself up to my bedroom?"

The look he gave her was a knee-weakening combination of innocence and devilish desire.

The memory of that look stayed with her the rest of the day. As she got ready for the party, she tried to tell herself that she'd intended to clean her room today all along. That she'd intended to file the stacks of paperwork on her desk this afternoon.

And that she'd planned to wear matching red lace underwear beneath her dress anyway.

Rose looked at her reflection in her bathroom mirror, a mascara wand in hand, and muttered, "You are pathetic."

She was not going to invite Hunt Cicero up to her room tonight to show him her manuscript or her etchings or her underwear.

No way.

Well, probably not.

Could she do it?

She closed her eyes, shook her head, and silently chastised herself. Was she seriously thinking about going to bed with a man with whom she'd never even had a date?

You have dinner with him almost every night. He picks up the tab.

Only half the time. She paid the other half. Those didn't count as dates.

Says who? The only reason he hasn't taken you out somewhere is because you shoot him down every time he asks. He walks you home after dinner, doesn't he? That's a date.

No. Dates include a good-night kiss. She hadn't kissed the man yet.

Idiot.

Not that she hadn't thought about it. Bet he was great at it. He had that intensity thing going, after all. She picked up a rust-colored lipstick and painted her mouth.

Wonder if he taps into his creative streak in bed?

A hookup. That's what they called it these days. Easy, breezy, no strings sex. Could it really, truly be that way for a woman? No emotional entanglements? Just physical fun?

It had been so long she she'd had sex. Years.

Talk about pathetic.

It would be fun with Hunt Cicero. Of that, Rose had no doubt. But she also had no experience with such things. After her disastrous first time as a teenager, she'd waited until she was in a committed relationship to venture into sex again.

Look how that turned out.

At this point the memory of Brandon's betrayal was more an annoying paper cut than a vicious stab to the heart, but the experience had changed her. Never again would she trust her heart to a man.

She exited the bathroom and crossed to her dresser where a half dozen bottles of perfume sat on a mirrored tray. She reached for one, then froze. These were all scents Brandon had favored. "Why in the world have I kept them?"

She glanced at the clock. Twenty minutes before the party was due to start. She had time.

She pulled on a pair of jeans and a sweater, grabbed her wallet, and headed downstairs to the Angel's Rest gift shop. Celeste had commissioned Savannah Turner to create a unique line of scents for Angel's Rest, and they'd recently added perfumes to the collection. Five minutes later, she was back in her room dabbing a spicy, exotic scent named Angelfire between her breasts.

As she walked to her closet and removed the emerald-green cocktail dress she planned to wear, she told herself that maybe the time had come for her to broaden her horizons, to leap into the unknown, to do the unexpected.

She knew better than most that life was short.

And she wasn't living hers to the fullest. In the past twenty years, she'd never done anything crazy or wild. She'd never done a kegstand or flashed her boobs at a Mardi Gras parade. She'd done what was expected of her—college, medical school, being the devoted daughter.

She'd never had an affair.

She'd never played with fire.

In this day and age where casual sex seemed to be accepted as the norm, she was an oddity. She could count on two fingers the number of partners she'd had. The consequences from her first foray into sex had been enough to keep her celibate until Brandon.

In the end, that hadn't worked out so well for her either, had it?

She'd been the good girl, the supportive partner, putting her lover's career above hers while ignoring her self-doubts. And when she had entertained those concerns, she'd turned to the rock in her life for advice—her oh-so-traditional army colonel father. Brandon had been the son he'd never had, and to the Colonel, men's needs, wishes, and desires always came before females'. That's the way she was raised. That's the way she'd acted.

Well, maybe it was time to change the status quo.

Dr. Rose Anderson—Bad Girl. She liked the sound of that. She liked the idea of it. Why not go for it? What would it hurt? Who would it hurt? Her father was gone. Sage was forever telling her to kick up her heels.

She stepped into her dress and did a twist-and-turn pretzel dance to get it zipped. She stepped into a pair of Christian Louboutins—shoes were her indulgence—and dug out her evening bag from the back of her closet. She touched up her lipstick, dropped it into her bag, and snapped the bag shut. As she stared at her reflection in the mirror, her stomach took a nervous roll. She looked all right for a woman her age, but she'd left dewy and fresh behind long ago. Did she actually have the guts to go through with—a hookup?

"It is the day of the Ice Fishing Derby," she muttered, making fish lips at her reflection.

Suddenly out of nowhere, tears flooded her eyes. An engagement party hookup. How pitiful was that? She attempted to blink the moisture away before her mascara smeared, but when a pair of teardrops overflowed, she grabbed for a tissue and headed for the bathroom.

Great. Just great. A pre-party pity party. Pre-engagement party. Another engagement party. How many did this make since she'd moved to Eternity Springs? And she wasn't even going to count the baby showers. She'd end up a sobbing mess.

"Stop it," she scolded, dabbing away the wetness and glaring at her reflection. "Just stop it. This is stupid. This is your choice. You have a good life. You are a happy person. You have a man who has twice the sex appeal of Daniel Craig wanting to jump your bones. What do you have to cry about?"

Nothing. She was nervous, that's all. Frightened half to death at the thought of getting naked in front of Cicero. Nearly a decade had passed since she'd stripped off her clothes in front of someone new. Her stomach wasn't quite as flat. Her butt wasn't as high. Her boobs weren't as perky.

She drew in a deep, bracing breath, then exhaled a sigh. Okay, so maybe she wasn't ready for sex with a man who was little more than a stranger.

A little voice whispered in her head: *You could start with a little necking.*

Her lips twitched. "Rosemary Anderson, you are a mess."

She scowled at the dark smudges beneath her eyes, and set about making the repairs. By the time she exited her suite and headed downstairs, she felt calm again and once more in control.

She was on the second floor landing when her sister glanced up, spied her and gave a little wave. Rose waved back.

The figure standing near the reception desk looked up. Dressed in a dark suit and silver tie, Hunt Cicero gave her a slow once-over, his gaze lingering on her breasts, her hips, her legs.

His tongue languidly licked his lips.

When he finally raised his gaze to meet hers, the heat in those chocolate eyes raised chill bumps on her skin. His intimate smile made her shiver. His roguish wink sucked the breath right out of her.

Maybe I'm ready, after all.

Seven

Cicero was feeling edgy.

As he dressed for the party at Angel's Rest, he found himself prowling his loft apartment. He'd spent another fruitless afternoon with his sketchpad. Were he not already running late, he'd spend some time on the weight bench he'd installed in the storage room downstairs. Not that exercise would help his situation. He'd spent hour upon hour in physical exertion, thinking about the Albritton and about Emily Dickinson's feathered hope since receiving that life-changing phone call; and still, inspiration eluded him. He'd never struggled like this before.

He'd come up with a few ideas—small ideas. Small ideas wouldn't cut it for a chance like this. He needed something colossal, something spectacular, and so far he'd managed little more than humdrum. It was driving him crazy.

He needed to clear his head. He needed to blow out the cobwebs.

He needed to get laid.

He could drive up to Crested Butte and pick up a ski bunny, but that idea didn't have much appeal. Not when Doctor Delicious starred in his night-time dreams and daytime fantasies.

His fascination with Rose Anderson bemused him. The last time he'd focused this intently upon one woman, he'd been fifteen years old and crushing on a girl in math class. Why now? Why this woman? Who knew? It didn't really matter, did it? Like Jayne used to say after her diagnosis, *it is what it is*.

And what it *was* was he had a bad case of the hots for Rosemary Anderson, MD.

He grabbed his keys and headed out, his mind filled with images of Doctor Delicious. Laughing with Shannon O'Toole this morning. Staring into the hole cut through the ice of Hummingbird Lake. Wrinkling her nose at the wiggling fish the barkeep yanked from the water. Her tender smile and encouraging wink to the little Montgomery girl. He was drawn to her like Keenan to trouble.

Cicero didn't know exactly why she appealed to him so much. Over the years, he'd had a bevy of beauties revolve through his bed—actresses, models—he'd even scored a *SI* swimsuit edition centerfold one time. Rose Anderson was pretty in a girl-next-door sort of way, built long and lean with curves where they were meant to be, but she wasn't drop-jaw breathtaking. She was smart, witty, and delightfully stubborn. Passionate about her beliefs, her work, her family and friends. He found the whole writing thing intriguing. He sensed that she harbored secrets, and he wanted to learn what they were.

If she'd let him.

She was a mixed bag of signals. Slow. Caution. Detour. Yield. Warning, curve ahead. Stop.

His libido waited less patiently each day to see a green light.

The drive to Angel's Rest took only a few minutes. He parked and walked inside, meeting the Callahans and Timberlakes on the walk. Inside, the official hosts of the evening, Zach Turner and the Romano brothers greeted their guests. Cicero congratulated the honorees. Dressed in turquoise blue, Gabi sparkled like sunshine on the water off Bella Vita Isle, while Flynn's eyes had that heavy-lidded sexually satisfied look that made Cicero green with envy.

He wandered into the parlor, on the hunt for Rose.

He didn't find her anywhere, so when Celeste walked by, he asked if she'd seen her. "Not yet. I suspect she'll be down shortly. Why don't you grab a plate and eat before all of Ali's crab cakes are gone? They always go fast."

"I'll do that. Thanks for the tip."

He filled a plate with meat and cheeses and crab cakes, then loitered in the hallway, his attention never far from the staircase. Anticipation rolled through him like a dream. He could be Rhett Butler waiting for Scarlett.

Wouldn't he just love to see Rose in that famous red dress with feathers and cleavage?

The fanciful idea made him roll his eyes. Yes, he had moved into the realm of the ridiculous. He'd polished off his snack, and had just set his empty plate on the tray of a passing waiter, when movement at the top of the staircase caught his attention. He looked up and sucked in a breath. Not red and feathered. She wore a strapless, clinging, emerald-green dress that ended just above her knee and made him think of mermaids.

Green means go.

Watching her descend the Angel's Rest staircase, her hips swaying with each step downward, he mentally stripped away the top half of the dress. The kind of probing he wanted to do had nothing to do with learning her secrets.

He met her at the bottom of the stairs. "Good evening, *Sirena Bellissima.*"

"*Sirena*?" She arched a patrician brow. "Should I confess that I understand Italian?"

Delighted, he asked, "Are you offended that I called you 'beautiful mermaid'?"

"I think I shouldn't have chosen stockings that shimmer."

"Stockings? Not pantyhose?"

She arched her brow again, this time flirtatiously. "Are you really asking me about my underwear, Mr. Cicero?"

He gave her a slow once-over. "Just trying to fill in the blanks for my fantasies, Dr. Anderson."

"I think you think about legs too much. I understand that's your nickname for Gabi. What does Flynn think about that?"

He shrugged and slipped his arm through hers. "She's tall. I'm not going to call her *Stumpy.* Besides, I only use the single word. No adjective to go with it. Certainly not *beautiful.* I could just as easily call her Bird Legs or Spaghetti Legs or Green Giant. Any of those suits her."

"Liar. She's tall and athletic and has great legs from playing basketball."

He touched her hair, wrapped a silken curl around his index finger. "Why are we talking about her, anyway? You are tall and delicious and have spectacular legs. It's so easy to imagine them wrapped around me—in shimmering stockings or bare-legged skin. So, what can I get you to drink?"

She stammered a moment before saying. "Wine. Red, please."

"Sure you don't want something green tonight? A margarita, perhaps?"

"I don't think they're serving margaritas tonight."

"Pity. Green is my new favorite color." He slid his finger down her cheek, then along the neckline of her dress. "Green means *go,* you know. It means *yes.*"

She visibly shivered. Satisfied that he'd piqued her interest, Cicero sauntered off into the parlor toward the bar station standing in one corner. When he returned holding two glasses of cabernet, Rose stood safely beside her sister in a group of five. Cicero joined them and handed her a glass.

Nic Callahan was talking about a stray dog that Sheriff Zach Turner had picked up at a campground outside of town and left at her animal clinic, which doubled as Eternity Springs's shelter. "He's just a doll, a lab mix who is just as friendly as can be. He's obviously been on his own for a while, but I'm sure he was someone's pet at some point in his life."

"You should adopt him, Cicero," Gabi suggested. "You need a dog."

"To quote my late sister's standard reply to that suggestion, I need a dog like I need a hole in the head."

"The kids would love it," Gabi said. "Misty especially. Keenan wants an iguana. That's all he talked about during their last visit."

"Not true. The kid talked about everything under the sun when they were in town. He never shut up."

"He's seven," Rose said. "That's what seven-year-olds are supposed to do."

"He wears me out. He only wants an iguana because his mother had a picture of the two of us with an iguana in a California bar."

"So get him a dog," Gabi said. "If he had a dog to play with, he wouldn't bother you so much."

"I can vouch for that," Nic said. "Pets make great distraction devices."

"Thanks, but no thanks." Cicero turned to Lucca Romano and lobbed a distraction of his own onto the court. "How did the basketball team do today?"

Lucca's lips twitched, but he made the save. "Man, it was an ugly game, but we squeaked it out."

When Nic's husband added his opinion of the game, Cicero breathed an inward sigh. He'd successfully changed the subject. The last thing he needed was somebody around here dumping a dog on him.

Despite his best intentions, a flash of memory distracted him.

"He's a wheaten terrier," his new foster father had said. *"He's just the best dog. If you*

don't mind, we thought we'd let him sleep in your room."

A burst of laughter dragged him back to the present as more guests arrived and filled Angel's Rest's walls to near bursting. It was a happy crowd gathered for a happy occasion. Cicero pushed off thoughts about pets and pests, and concentrated on the here, now, and—

His lips twitched with self-amusement as his gaze lingered on Rose's cleavage. Here, now, and green.

"Scarlett O'Hara has nothing on you, *Bellissima.*"

"I'm sorry, I didn't hear you."

"You look beautiful tonight."

"Oh." Delightful color stained her cheeks. "Thank you."

At eight o'clock, Gabi's brother Zach called for attention and thanked their guests for coming to the party. He then offered the first toast to the happy couple, and soon had everyone laughing with tales of Gabi's escapades when she worked as his deputy sheriff.

It was a nice event, an enjoyable evening. Cicero liked his new friends and neighbors.

But he still felt edgy.

Throughout the evening, he circled Rose like a shark, at times keeping his distance, occasionally brushing up against her just to remind her that he was still around. She flicked her tail at him more than once, and Cicero was ready to follow her right into the deep. The party was beginning to wind down when he spied Celeste carting a tray filled with dirty glasses toward the kitchen. It looked heavy. Smoothly, he swooped in and lifted the tray from her hands. "I've got that."

Celeste smiled up at him. "Thank you, dear. Your assistance is timely. I'm afraid my eyes were bigger than my muscles, and I overloaded my tray."

"I'm glad I can help." He followed her into a room that was a cheerful cross between a commercial kitchen and a kitchen in a private home. The angel wing motif made him smile. Even though the symbol appeared everywhere he looked, the effect wasn't overdone. "I like your kitchen, Celeste."

"Thank you." Her blue eyes twinkled. "It makes me happy."

"You make everyone around you happy."

"Why, what a lovely thing to say. Thank you, Hunter." Celeste gestured for him to set the tray on a counter beside a large sink. After doing so, he unconsciously rolled his shoulders.

Eagle-eyed Celeste noticed. "Are your shoulders stiff? You should scoot over to the hot springs and soak for a little while before you go home. You'll find swimsuits in the pool house."

"Thanks, but I—"

"Get Rose to go out there with you. Soaking in

the mineral springs is one of her favorite things to do after a busy workday. It'd be good for her."

"I'd like that," he finished, changing his mind. "That's a great idea. Thanks."

A self-satisfied smile lit her up like a sunbeam.

"Playing matchmaker, Celeste?"

"Actually, I am. And I'm very good at it."

"Then I'll consider myself warned," he replied.

"If you land Rose Anderson, Hunter, you should consider yourself lucky."

"I can't argue with that." Of course, he wasn't sure that his definition of "landing" was the same as Celeste's.

Cicero rejoined the party and looked around for Rose. He found her in the parlor listening politely to Maggie Romano babble on about wedding plans. Cicero liked Maggie, but he'd already heard her and her daughter debate floral bouquet choices at length when Maggie visited the studio. Something told him that by his apprentice's wedding day, he'd be an expert on all things bridal.

Maggie interrupted her talk of daisies and dahlias to give him a warm smile. "You have the look of a man on a mission."

"I am that. I had a long session in the studio today, and my back is stiff. Celeste is sending me to the hot springs, and she told me to drag Rose along with me." He challenged Rose with a look and added, "You'll come?"

Indecision glimmered in her eyes.

"Your feet must hurt after standing in those stilts all evening," he added. "I'll rub them for you, *Bellissima*."

"Italian endearments," Maggie observed, patting her hand rapidly over her heart. "You are a dangerous man, Cicero."

"Training," he replied, adding a bit of the devil to his smile. "I lived in Venice for two years. So, you'll join me?" He waited a bit and added, "*Per piacere?*"

She slowly nodded.

"Excellent." He offered her his arm. "Shall we track down our hosts and say our good-nights?"

"I think they're all out on the front porch," Maggie said helpfully.

As they moved toward the front door, Rose murmured, "My feet don't hurt. These are great shoes. I don't need a foot rub."

"Yes, they most definitely are great shoes." He reached down and pulled an errant curl behind her ear and ran his finger down the skin of her neck. "I'd like to see you wearing them and nothing else."

She visibly shuddered and briefly closed her eyes, then asked rhetorically, "What are you doing?"

"Trying to take the edge off, *Sirena Bellissima*. Trying to take the edge off."

Rose almost chickened out. The doubts that

had assailed her before joining the party downstairs returned with full force once she went upstairs to change into her swimsuit. She wasn't stupid. The man was looking to get laid. There was only one way this evening would end if she went with him to the dark, private hot springs. Yet, here she was wriggling into a swimsuit. Was she weak? Wanton? Both?

Both. She wanted this—wanted him. It had been so damned long for her.

It was only when she slipped the swimsuit strap over her shoulder that she remembered that this wasn't a usual winter's night in Eternity Springs. This was the evening between Ice Fishing Derby and the balloon race. Town was packed with people. The mineral springs would be packed, too.

Her stomach sank in disappointment.

Wait a minute. Crowded hot springs aren't a deal breaker. You could always invite him up to your apartment to . . . see your manuscript.

Before she could change her mind, she pulled on the boots and full-length down coat she used for her walks to the springs, grabbed a towel, and headed back downstairs where Cicero waited. With his earlier mention of Scarlett O'Hara planted in her brain, she had a sudden mental flash of the scene from *Gone with the Wind* where Rhett Butler stood at the base of the staircase looking up.

Except Hunt Cicero was better-looking than Clark Gable.

And frankly, my dear, you've never had a fourteen-inch waist in your life.

Who cares? He told me I look beautiful.

The engagement party crowd had departed, and they were able to slip out the back door without any delay. A three-quarter moon shone in a clear, dark, star-studded sky. "I love the night sky here," Cicero said, his breath fogging on the bitter air. "It's something I missed during my time in Texas."

"Too much city light?"

"Way too much. Bella Vita spoiled me."

"I'd love to visit the island someday," she said wistfully. "Gabi makes it sound like paradise."

"It is. It was a great place to live for a little while."

"But not forever?"

"No. I don't do forever. I've been a wanderer all my life."

A timely reminder, Rose thought, trying to ignore the little sting, then deciding the comment was exactly what she needed to hear in order to manage her expectations. They reached the fork in the path that led to the hot springs and Cicero turned the wrong direction. "No," she said. "This way."

"Actually, we're going to a different spot. While you were upstairs changing, Celeste tracked me down. She said that with all the tourists in town, the hot springs pools will be packed. There's a private cottage this way that had a late cancellation. She gave me a key."

A private cottage this way? Rose well knew that there was only one cottage in the direction they were taking. Beneath the light of a lamppost, she stopped short, pulling his hand from hers. "Celeste gave you a key to the honeymoon cottage?"

Now a step ahead of her, Cicero looked around. Golden lamplight illuminated the slow smile that spread across his face.

"It's the honeymoon cottage?"

How typical, Rose thought. Celeste enjoyed playing Cupid more than anyone on the planet. If she and Hunt started an affair, she'd need to remember to have a talk with her friend and explain that her lover was a wanderer—and Rose was fine with that.

Her lover. Whoa.

"She didn't mention the honeymoon thing when she offered it," he continued. "She asked if we'd rather have a soak in a private fresh water hot tub or a crowded mineral pool. I'll take privacy over crowds any time, won't you?"

"Umm . . ."

"Yes?"

"You know that old saying about out of the frying pan into the fire?"

It took him a moment to make the connection. That smile turned devilish. "You're saying I make you hot."

She lifted her chin.

"I'm saying you're trying to seduce me."

"I've been doing that since the day we met. You haven't been cooperating. Until tonight." He stepped close to her and took her in his arms. Lowering his voice to a sensual rumble, he said, "Don't worry, *Bellissima.* I promise I won't do anything you don't want."

He kissed her, softly, sweetly, and so tenderly that she wanted to sigh. As first kisses went, it was perfect.

"That's the problem," she grumbled in a moment of honesty when he lifted his mouth from hers. "I'm more afraid of myself than I am of you."

He laughed and stepped back. Grabbing her hand once again, he pulled her toward the honeymoon cottage.

Rose hadn't seen the inside of the cottage since it was completed, but she'd definitely heard about it. Celeste had built it the previous year and she was very picky about to whom she rented it. She wanted the honeymoon cottage to be a luxurious retreat for special couples.

So why the heck had she given Eternity Springs's newest fox the henhouse key?

Warm, yellow lamplight glowed in the window of the charming Victorian cottage painted baby blue with white gingerbread trim. As they approached, she wondered about the late cancellation. Had a groom somewhere walked out on his bride at the altar?

Been there, done that—sort of.

She and Brandon had already booked their honeymoon eight months out when her world fell apart. On the night that would have been her wedding night, she'd wondered who was sleeping in the ocean view bridal suite.

Don't go there, she warned herself. Hunter Cicero wasn't Brandon. He'd used her for her connection with her father. Cicero just wanted to connect.

As Rose stepped onto its front porch, she attempted to combat the nervousness rolling through her stomach by talking. "I've been meaning to take a look through this cottage for weeks. I walked through it when it was being built, but I haven't seen the finished product. You'd think that since I live at Angel's Rest, I'd keep up better with all the improvements Celeste is making around here. I know the cottage is becoming very popular. I recall her mentioning that a magazine writer visited earlier this month and is going to write an article about it. I'm surprised anyone would consider Eternity Springs as a honeymoon destination, but I guess if they're looking for an out-of-the-way spot that's still within driving distance of an air-port, this valley is a good choice. I think—I'm babbling."

"You're nervous. Don't be nervous with me, *Bellissima*."

Cicero unlocked the door and opened it, then put his hand on her waist and ushered her inside. The front room was a sitting area furnished with a plush, oversized love seat and rocker big enough for two positioned in front of a stone fireplace. A kitchenette had granite countertops, gleaming cabinets, stainless steel appliances, and fresh red roses on the small drop-leaf table.

"It's beautiful."

Romantic.

Dangerous . . .

"Celeste said there are switches for the outdoor lights and heaters along the back wall," Cicero said, striding into the bedroom. Rose followed him to the threshold of the French doors where she hovered, unable to make herself follow the man toward that huge bed.

Until he flipped a switch and light flooded a walled-off courtyard outside.

"Oh, wow."

Fingers of steam rose from the surface of a large, infinity-edged hot tub. Small waterfalls spilled from the hot tub into a plunge pool below. "Looks inviting," Cicero observed. "I'll go change."

Rose nodded, then took advantage of his absence to open the door and step outside with the thought of slipping into the concealment of the bubbling water before he returned. She had never been the type to prance around strutting her stuff in her swimsuit, even as a teen. It had taken her the longest time to get comfortable being naked around Brandon.

She couldn't believe she was contemplating getting naked in front of this gorgeous man.

The hot water felt divine and the clean smell of the water a welcome change from the stinky smell of the mineral waters at the hot springs pools. She settled back against one of the jets so that the water pounded the muscles between her shoulder blades and started to relax.

Then the lights dimmed, soft jazz began to drift from unseen speakers, and the door to the cottage opened. Her tension flooded back. Cicero stepped outside wearing a spa robe and flip-flops and carrying a tray that held two flutes, a bottle of champagne and a plate of fruit and cheeses. He set the tray down beside the steaming water, and when his hands went to the belt on his robe, Rose's mouth went dry. She felt a little light-headed.

Had he put on a bathing suit?

The robe pooled to his feet. Yes, he'd put on a bathing suit. She didn't know whether she was glad or disappointed.

Not that there wasn't plenty of skin to see. The man was built with broad shoulders, a muscular chest that declared him to be an outdoorsman rather than gym rat, and a flat stomach that hinted at a six-pack. All that exercising he'd been doing in the library, she thought. He had just enough chest hair to give him that masculine appeal without being hairy.

Rose sank a little lower in the water as he stepped into the pool.

"This feels great," he said, taking a seat at an angle to her, his knee accidentally brushing hers. At least, it could have been accidental. Knowing him, though, he'd planned it.

"Champagne?"

She loved champagne. Absolutely adored it. But it went to her head faster than anything, and add that to possible dehydration from soaking in steaming hot water—not to mention the intoxicating effect of sharing said water with this fallen angel of a man—if she had any sense at all, she'd tell him no. "Yes, thank you."

A moment later, the familiar pop echoed through the night. Cicero filled a glass and handed it to her, then poured one for himself. Holding it up in a toast, he said, "Cheers."

"Cheers." She sipped her drink, consciously going slowly when what she really wanted to do was chug it. Tension rippled through her. Doubts assailed her. What in the world was she doing here? She reached for a distraction. "How did you break your nose?"

He stretched out his long legs and smiled.

"I've been assured that the break isn't obvious. You've been studying me closely."

"I'm a physician. I notice lots of things."

"I'll just bet you do." He took a leisurely sip from his glass, then said, "I usually tell anyone who asks that a jealous husband did it. It makes for a more interesting story than the truth."

"What is the truth?"

"Someone was bothering my sister and I tried to stop it."

Curious about the incident, she wanted to ask more but his voice held a note of finality so she held her tongue. He changed the subject by saying, "So, tell me about your writing."

Her writing? Now that surprised her. It was also the easiest question he could have asked her. "What do you want to know?"

"Everything. What I'm most curious about is where you get your ideas."

She laughed. "You're kidding, right?"

"Because it's the question an artist always gets asked? The creative process is different for everyone. I'm interested in yours."

The sentiment was one of the sexiest things he could have said to her because it showed interest in her beyond the surface. "My canned answer is that inspiration comes from everyday experiences."

"What's the truth?"

Rose took another sip of her champagne and

absently shifted so that a water jet pounded against her spine between her shoulder blades. "I can tell you because you won't think it's crazy, right?"

His lips twisted in a self-deprecating smirk. "Honey, believe me, I'll understand."

She drew in a deep breath, then confessed, "I hear voices."

"Oh, yeah?" He sat up a little straighter. "Your characters speak to you?"

"Yes."

"Now that's cool."

"Yeah, well, not so much. Usually—unfortunately—the villain begins the conversation."

"Oh." He took a contemplative sip of his champagne. "That adds a measure of creepiness to the process, I imagine."

"You can't begin to guess."

"Once you write their story, do they leave you alone?"

"That depends. I've written one sequel."

"Ah. Have these characters spoken to you all of your life?"

Rose hesitated, inwardly debating just how open she wanted to be. But the shadows and the privacy and yes, the company, added an intimacy to the night. She confessed something she'd never told another soul, not even Brandon. She'd only admitted it to herself in the last couple of years.

"It started after I was deployed to Afghanistan.

I think it's my mind's way of dealing with some of the things I've seen. That's what happened with my sister. She was with Doctors Without Borders and survived a horrible situation in Africa."

She told him about Sage's experience, and how it had driven her away from medicine. She told him about the dark paintings Sage had produced that were so different from those whimsical works for which she was known. Rose talked for some time about her sister's situation, answering his questions and sharing some of what she'd learned about the political realities of the war-torn region.

"In my twenties, I spent a few years back-packing—primarily in Europe, but I traveled through parts of Africa, too," Cicero said. "It's both a beautiful and a horrible continent. Now, tell me about Afghanistan."

Rose delayed answering by sipping her champagne. This was not the focused, intense seduction she'd anticipated. "I don't talk about it."

"Afraid you'll lose your character's voices?"

"No, that's not it. Writing is my hobby, not my passion. I'm different from Sage in that respect. Her therapy became her passion. Mine has remained a therapy."

He reached for the cheese plate, then silently offered it to her. As she selected a plump straw-berry, he suggested, "Maybe if you talked about it rather than write about it, that would help."

Rose hesitated. Something about him compelled her to share the story, but caution held her tongue. "You know what they say: Doctors make the worst patients. I don't think I can talk about it."

"Okay, then. Tell me about one of your villains."

That she could do. "His name is Brian Stebbins. He's a surgeon whose stint in Iraq drove him crazy. He's a serial killer who re-creates IED attacks then attempts to save his victims by doing field surgery. He always fails. Well, until the last two chapters."

Cicero popped a grape into his mouth and slowly shook his head. "Whoa. That's pretty scary, Dr. Anderson. So who defeated him? Who is your protagonist? A sexy, beautiful female physician?"

"Not hardly. My hero is a portly, balding gentleman who looks a little like Alfred Hitchcock."

"Now you've totally ruined the fantasy."

"He's actually very charming, which is part of the reason he has three failed marriages." She stretched out a leg and flexed her foot. "He is a complicated man, an orthopedist with a brilliant mind and a mild alcohol problem. His oldest illegitimate son is a detective on the case, which is what pulls him into the story."

"I want to read it. Seriously. That sounds like the type of book that's right up my alley. So, tell me how it works. You sit down at the computer and your characters dictate to you?"

"I wish it were that easy. Usually I sit down at the computer and I write two paragraphs, then delete one, then write three paragraphs, then delete two. So, how does the creative process work for you?"

There was a long pause then he said, "Lately, not very well."

She heard a note in his voice that she'd never heard before, one of uncertainty with an amazing dash of insecurity. Hunt Cicero insecure? She found the idea both surprising and intriguing. He'd always seemed to be the most confident of men, the kind never to back down from a challenge. "Is there something similar to writer's block for glass artists?"

"Apparently. I admit it's a new experience for me. Not one I particularly enjoy." He refilled his glass, then stared at the rising bubbles for a broody few seconds before asking, "Do you read poetry?"

That one came out of left field. "I'm afraid I've never developed an interest," she confessed. "I blame it on my ninth grade English teacher. She made us memorize poems and stand up in front of the class and recite them. Pure horror for a beanpole of a ninth grader, let me tell you. From then on out, my only exposure to any type of poetry has been the limericks my unit used to compose during our stint in Kandahar."

"Limericks," he repeated, his brow knitting thoughtfully.

"And bacon haikus."

His grin flashed. "Bacon haikus?"

"State fair pig races.
Poor showing blue ribbon run.
Bacon for breakfast."

"Your contribution?"

"No, my anesthesiologist's—a former farm boy. Most competitive man I've ever met. He was very bitter about some of his stock show competitions."

Cicero's laughter rose on crisp night air, and the sound sent a sensual shiver running up Rose's spine. To distract herself, she reached for a piece of cheddar cheese.

"Maybe that's my mistake. I've been thinking about feathers instead of farm animals," Cicero said.

"Feathers?"

This time when he hesitated, the silence stretched longer. Rose was about ready to conclude that he wouldn't respond when he recited:

"Hope is the thing with feathers.
That perches in the soul
And sings the tune without the words
And never stops at all."

"That's lovely," Rose said.

"It's from an Emily Dickinson poem, and it's a pain in the ass."

He told her about how he'd come to be entered in a significant arts competition, and the challenge of the final round. "So far, a concept has eluded me."

"What an exciting opportunity for you. I'm surprised I haven't heard anything about it. I'd expect something like this to be the talk of the town."

"I asked Gabi and Flynn to keep the news to themselves. People are curious enough as it is about what's happening in the studio, and right now the last thing I need is for random people to stop by and grill me on a competition piece that doesn't exist. If creativity is a lush rain forest, then these days my brain is a barren desert."

He said it so glumly that she couldn't help but smile. "Surely it's not that bad."

"Honestly, it's never been worse. I've had a creative rough spot or two in the past, but I've never known anything like this."

"That's why you've been spending so much time in the library. Looking for inspiration?"

"You know about that?"

"Our library is gossip central in the winter. And since we're on the subject, why the reading-and-running?"

"Endorphins. My most creative moments come in the midst of vigorous exercise."

He reached for her hand and brought it up to his mouth for a kiss, followed up by a gentle nibble, then a suggestive lick of his tongue. His gaze steamier than the vapor rising from the water and with a panther-on-the-prowl tone, he purred, "Want to help inspire me?"

Instinctively, she snatched back her hand. Then embarrassed by her reaction, she scoffed. "Oh, for heaven's sake. Do you use that line often, Cicero?"

Now he flashed a tiger's grin.

"Is it really considered a line if it's the truth? Don't you find great sex to be inspirational, Doctor Anderson?"

The sound of the *S*-word on his tongue made her ache. Yearning washed through her. She couldn't recall the last time she'd had great sex, so she couldn't really say, but she wasn't about to admit to that. Especially not to him. Dodging the question, she said, "*Great,* hmm? That's a bold adjective you threw down there."

"Grammar smack. I love it." He laughed. "But then, I am sharing a spa with a writer, aren't I? I have to tell you, I find adjectives incredibly sexy. Maybe not as sexy as adverbs, but then I've always been different."

"You're looking for inspiration. I suspect you'd find gerunds sexy."

"Probably. If I remembered what a gerund was."

Playfully, he pulled her to him and settled her on his lap. His thighs were rock hard, his thick arousal unmistakable. His dark, magnetic gaze focused hotly on her mouth. He reached up and brushed a thumb across her lower lip. "Define it for me, *Sirena Bellissima*."

Rose's body went deliciously liquid. She wanted to wiggle her bottom, to shift her position that inch to the right where she needed to be. She wanted to tease him and watch the heat burning in his eyes flame hotter.

She knew she was playing with fire—with a man who played with fire for a living. Already, she burned. Was she ready for this? For him? An affair? Maybe even simply a one-night stand?

Live a little, Rose. While you still can.

You spend way too much time dying.

"Do it," he repeated, sliding his thumb across the line of her jaw then trailing it down the length of her throat.

Beneath his touch, her pulse pounded. She drew a deep breath, then moistened her lips with a slow circle of her tongue. "A gerund is a verb that functions as a noun and ends in I-N-G."

He nipped softly at her lower lip. "Like kiss*ing?*"

"Like kissing." She leaped from the frying pan. "And touching. And, lovemaking."

His eyes flashed with victory and perhaps a bit of relief. His fingers tightened on her skin. Then his mouth swooped down upon hers.

And Rose Anderson fell into Hunt Cicero's fire.

Eight

They called it the art of seduction for a reason.

Cicero knew that proper seduction required patience, consideration, attention to detail, and the investment of time. Some had called him a master of the art; he considered himself a well-practiced student. No one would argue that he qualified as experienced.

So why in the world he totally lost control with Rose Anderson he couldn't begin to guess.

Sure, he'd felt that little zing of arousal during the meals they'd shared at Murphy's. Yes, she'd occupied his dreams more than a time or two on long, cold February nights and starred in his daytime fantasies more times than that. But Cicero wasn't a green boy sharing his first hot tub with a beauty. He knew his way around the jets.

He enjoyed the challenge of the chase. He liked to indulge in long, slow, wet kisses. He pleasured his partners with new sensations, aroused them with the leisurely explorations of his eyes, his hands, his mouth. He'd never been a skip-straight-to-the-good-stuff type of guy.

Until tonight.

Rose's kiss set him ablaze, and all thought of leisurely seduction and practiced finesse went up in smoke. With the first touch of his mouth against hers, he went primal. Instinct directed his actions. Conscious thought disappeared.

As did their swimwear.

He wanted to believe that he held on to his sanity enough to heed any sign of resistance on her part, but thank God, it wasn't an issue. The woman gave as good as she got, matching every stroke of his hand, flick of his tongue, and nip of his teeth with one of her own. When she dropped her head back and arched her back, offering herself to him with total abandon, colors flashed in his mind's eye.

Then he realized she'd activated the spa's specialty lighting system, and he laughed aloud.

Her eyes fluttered open. She looked dazed.

"What? You make me see stars."

"It's a special talent of mine."

He took a reverent moment to feast on the sight of her full, coral-tipped breasts as they bobbed above the bubbling water. "Are we going to finish this, *Sirena Bellissima*?"

"Oh, I do hope so."

"In that case—" Bracing himself against the winter's chill, Cicero swiftly stood. He kept Rose cradled tightly against his chest.

She let out a little shriek. "What are you doing?"

"Hot tubs are nice, but I do my best work in a bed."

Thankfully, he reached the toasty warm indoors in only a few long strides. He kissed her as he set her on her feet in front of the fireplace, reached out to throw the switch on the gas logs, and snagged the towels that good planning on his part had left within reach.

He took his time and considerable care while drying her off, the cold night air having banked the fire inside him. However, once Rose took a towel and began to return the favor, she soon had him teetering right back on the edge of his control. When she leaned in and gently kissed the old cigarette burn scars on his chest that he'd carried since his months in the foster home from hell, a huge well of emotion rose within him.

She wasn't the first woman to make that gesture. It had proven to be something that many felt compelled to do. But Rose's tender ministrations felt different. They reached into a hidden place inside him to which he seldom allowed access—even to himself.

Cicero reacted to the swell of emotion the way of most men. He ran from it.

He ran from it by leaping headlong into sex.

He swept her up and carried her to the bedroom where he deposited her in the middle of the big bed, climbed over her, then unleashed the sexual demon inside him.

Soon his hands and mouth had her shuddering and whimpering. Judging her ready, he sheathed himself inside her tight, wet heat and relentlessly demanded more until she rewarded him with moans, groans, and gasps. Only after he made her scream out her climax did he allow himself to follow her, pounding into her until he erupted, intense physical pleasure scorching along his nerve endings.

When he heard her cry out a second time, he allowed himself a moment of personal satisfaction. Guess he shouldn't feel badly about skimping on slow seduction this time. Sometimes, like that old saying goes, art was in the eyes of the beholder.

He lay down beside her, tucked her next to him, and murmured, "Sleep for a little while?"

She replied in a soft, sated tone. "Perfect."

"Yes, it was. You are."

Then Cicero drifted off, his body sated and relaxed, his mind a clean slate ready to receive the flash of feather-and-hope creativity he needed.

Dozing with a deliciously warm body cuddled against him was a pleasure he'd missed during his nights in the mountains, so Cicero slept more soundly than he'd anticipated. He awoke some time later, not to an Albritton-worthy image floating in his mind's eye, but to whimpers of pain coming from the woman in bed beside him.

Oh, hell. Was this a case of morning-after regrets? He'd dealt with those a time or two—and it was never pleasant. It could seriously complicate life in a small town, too. Still, the dismay curling in his stomach caught him off guard.

He swallowed a sigh, then rolled up on his elbow. Firelight and the muted glow of lamplight from the front room illuminated her face, and Cicero saw that she was still asleep. Crying in her sleep.

Not regrets, then. Dreams? She'd mentioned Afghanistan earlier. Had that stirred up haunting memories?

Another little mewl escaped her lips and broke his heart.

So he leaned down and brushed a featherlight kiss against her lips.

"*Bellissima*, wake up."

She didn't stir, so he kissed her again, a little harder this time. Her eyelashes fluttered. She gazed up at him without really seeing him, he could tell, her eyes twin forest-green pools of pain. "Bad dreams?"

She blinked. Her eyes widened with awareness of her surroundings. Fresh tears filled her eyes and she nodded.

"Afghanistan?" he guessed.

She remained silent and he could see the inner battle reflected upon her face. It was obvious that she didn't want to tell him, and he'd almost given up when she murmured a name.

"Elizabeth."

He waited a beat, then asked, "Who is Elizabeth?"

She closed her eyes, and teardrops spilled, trailing across her temples.

"My daughter."

Oh. Cicero took a moment to absorb that. She'd never mentioned a daughter to him. He'd never heard any gossip about a daughter, either. He did know about an ex-fiancé, but he didn't remember kids. There was obviously a story here. A sad one. He was curious, but should he push it? He wanted to know because it was her story, but he didn't want to hurt her.

"I'm sorry," she said softly before he made up his mind. "This isn't like me at all. I guess your mention of backpacking in Europe jogged the memories. That, or the mind-blowing sex."

He wiped away the tears with the pad of his thumb. "Mind-blowing, hmm? You have a way with your words, Dr. Anderson."

"You have a way with your mouth."

The wry note in her voice had the corners of his mouth lifting. He gave her another soft kiss, then asked, "Want to tell me about her? About Elizabeth?"

A long moment of silence followed. Finally, she said, "I never talk about what happened. Dad was stationed in Germany at the time, and the subject was verboten. I don't even talk about her with Sage."

"So, is that an answer to my question?"

"No, actually, I think I *would* like to talk about her. Don't look at me, though. It'll just make me nervous."

He rolled his eyes, but did as she asked, going down onto his back with one arm propped behind his head. He wrapped the other around her and pulled her close so that she rested her head on his chest. "So, you still lived at home?"

"I was sixteen. Have you ever been in Germany for the Christmas market season?"

"I have. I sold sketches in a booth one year."

"Your own sketches?" He nodded, and she continued, "He sold his photographs and bought me my first German mulled wine. And my second. And my third."

He sensed where this was going. Poor Rose. "*Glühwein* is potent."

She sighed heavily. "So was he. He was nineteen and had long blond hair and blue eyes and an Australian accent. He was passing through Germany on a backpacking tour around Europe. His name was Will and I said yes and six weeks later, he was long gone and I realized I was pregnant. Being pregnant was scary, being the colonel's pregnant daughter was terrifying."

"I'm so sorry."

"Me, too. I'd never seen my father so angry. I looked up to him. He was my hero. He was never a warm man, but after I told him what had happened, he went arctic on me. Totally froze me out. He told me if I chose adoption or abortion he'd support me. If I decided to keep the baby, I was on my own."

"Cold," Cicero muttered.

"Tough love. He did what he believed was best for me. As a widower with two young daughters, he learned firsthand the challenges of single parenthood. Honestly, he was right. I chose adoption, he sent me home to the States to have her, and a private agency placed Elizabeth with an infertile couple desperate for a child to love who could give her all the advantages I couldn't. I met them one time. They really were good people. I liked them."

"There are a lot of good people out there who should be parents, but can't be. Your choice was a real gift."

"I know."

"So, no regrets?"

The length of her pause answered his question.

When she finely spoke, pain rippled in her voice. "That's a complicated question. I have lots of regrets. I regret overindulging in *glühwein*. I regret going to bed with a young man without using condoms—or learning his last name. I regret spending the next fifteen years trying to make it up to my father by living the life he thought I should live, and then doing it with the person he thought I should live with. I let guilt and regret make choices for me, and I'd like a do-over on some of them. I wish I hadn't missed a few particular life experiences. But do I regret choosing adoption? No."

Cicero was intuitive enough to deduce that one of the missed life experiences to which she referred was having other children.

"Do you have any contact with Elizabeth?"

A full half-minute passed before she responded, and she did so with a catch in her voice. "I got to hold her after she was born. Beyond that, no. My father told me a clean break would be best, so that's the way we set it up from the beginning."

What a prince, he thought as he idly stroked his thumb up and down her arm.

"After he died, I added my information to a registry that will match us up if she ever goes looking for me. That's what I dream about. She's lost and looking for me, and it's dark and I can't find her. I hear her calling me, but I can't see her. In my dream, I know that I'll never find her, never see her, and"—she gave a little despairing laugh, and Cicero felt the warm splash of a tear against his bare chest—"and I don't have a clue why I'm yammering on about this to you. Seriously, I don't do this sort of thing. Tell me to shut up."

"I'm not gonna tell you anything, but I think I

can coax your thoughts into a new direction." He slid his large hand lower across her hip and between her legs.

The art of seduction.

He was the master. She, the canvas. He took his time and concentrated on detail, and devoted himself to making the moment a masterpiece.

So why, he wondered, when she lay sated and asleep in his arms, did he feel as if he were the student, and she the artist?

The following morning, Rose awoke to the mouth-watering aroma of frying bacon, and her thoughts immediately turned to bad haikus. She grinned into her pillow until she realized that the pillow wasn't hers. The bed wasn't hers. And she lay as naked as the day she was born.

She went still.

Oh, yeah. Hunter.

The memories of the night came roaring back. She'd done it. She'd had sex with a near stranger, a man she'd known all of two weeks. A handsome man. An obvious player. Only that hadn't been shocking enough. She'd also managed to spill at least some of her guts about Afghanistan and the whole miserable story of her teenage pregnancy.

Her eyes fluttered open. She waited for shame to wash over her or embarrassment to warm her cheeks. Neither happened. Instead, she felt almost *free.*

Go figure.

Sunshine sliced through a gap in crisp, white window curtains and cast a wedge of light on the earth-toned rug in front of the bedroom fireplace where yellow flames flickered from gas logs. She heard the nudge of the refrigerator door shutting and moments later, the crack of egg-shells against a bowl. If she wanted to shower before breakfast, she'd better get a move on.

She rolled from the bed and scooted into the bathroom. Eight minutes later, wearing a white terry spa robe with the Angel's Rest logo on the lapel, she joined Cicero in the kitchen. He'd forgone a spa robe and wore only a pair of plaid boxers. His dark eyes warmed and he said, "Good morning, *Dolcezza.* I hope you like waffles."

Beautiful flower, she translated. "Good morning, *Cuoco.* I love waffles."

"*Cuoco*? Not *Innamorato*?"

She'd called him a cook, not a sweetheart. She didn't know if he realized that he never used her given name. She thought it might be a defensive tactic utilized by a man who'd undoubtedly had legions of women in his life. If he didn't use a woman's name, then he didn't get it wrong. She shrugged.

"What can I do to help?"

Amusement flashed across his face.

"I've got it. Coffee?"

"Please."

He filled a mug and set it on the bar in front of her. Rose propped a hip on a barstool, sipped her coffee, and watched as he poured batter into a waffle iron. "It's nice of you to make breakfast. Thank you."

"Completely self-serving. I woke up starving and thinking about words that rhymed with bacon. I was so relieved to recall that the refrigerator was stocked."

As the waffle cooked, he studied her over the top of his own coffee cup. "And how are you this morning, in addition to being beautiful, of course?"

The man had a way of making lines sound sincere.

Suddenly ill at ease, she misjudged the distance as she set down her mug, leaving it halfway off the edge of the bar. It teetered and started to fall. She grabbed for it, and coffee sloshed onto the bar and hardwood floor. "Oh, for crying out loud."

Cicero reached for the paper towels.

"Did you burn yourself?"

"No. Only embarrassed myself." She took the handful of towels and bent to wipe up the floor spill. When she straightened, she saw his big hand wiping the counter and she had a sudden flash of memory of it stroking down her hip. Heat stung her cheeks. "Honestly, I'm nervous. I have very little experience with things like this."

"Waffles for breakfast?"

"A man cooking me waffles for breakfast. In fact, I have little experience with the whole morning-after thing entirely."

"Ah." Judging the first waffle done, he transferred it to a plate then added two pieces of bacon beside it. He set it in front of her and gestured for her to dig in. "If it makes you feel any better, this is new territory for me, too."

"Excuse me? You don't have experience with one-night stands? How gullible do you think I am?"

Frowning, he removed warm butter and syrup from the microwave. His voice held a grumpy note as he said, "I don't think you're gullible at all, and if I had considered last night a one-night stand, I'd have gone home afterward rather than spend the night."

"Oh." As she dribbled syrup onto her waffle, she decided she might as well be direct. "So what exactly was last night?"

"That's a fair question. I guess it's up to us both to decide. From my perspective, I'd like to think of it as a beginning."

"Beginning *of?*"

"You tell me."

She didn't know. An affair? A friendship with benefits? Neither one sounded right to her. "Maybe we don't need the preposition, after all."

He pointed his fork at her and warned, "Don't start with the grammar smack again. We'll end up back in bed, and then I won't get any work done this morning."

She laughed in response. It proved to be the first of many times he made her laugh during the first month of their "beginning."

March blew in with a blizzard and frigid air that hung around two weeks, but Rose's new love life kept her toasty warm. While she and Cicero continued to meet regularly for dinner at Murphy's Pub, they also began to broaden the scope of their activities. They enjoyed official date nights when he took her to the Yellow Kitchen for dinner or drove over to Gunnison for Mexican food. They went skiing at Crested Butte and snowmobiling on the property Flynn Brogan owned in Thunder Valley. She caught some speculative looks and fielded a few questions about the budding relationship from friends, but it wasn't until after they attended a Mardi Gras party as a couple at the end of the month that she faced the expected third degree from her sister.

Bright and early the morning following the party, Sage sailed into Rose's office at the clinic, toting a brown bag and wearing yoga pants and an intense expression. Rose braced herself for interrogation. Sage set the brown bag on her desk and demanded, "So, what's the deal with Cicero? Are you sleeping with him?"

"It's nice to see you, too, Sage," Rose said dryly.

Sage waved a dismissive hand. "Don't try to

change the subject. Tell me everything, Sister-mine. Dish!"

Past experience had taught Rose the futility of trying to dodge Sage's questions, but folding easily would be a bad precedent to set. "Do I ask you about your sex life with Colt?"

"So there is a sex life. Good for you. Rosemary, I love Colt with all my heart and I couldn't be happier in my marriage, but I have to say that Cicero is one fine looking man. He's a grand addition to Eternity Springs's merry little band of hot and sexy men."

The phrase startled a laugh from Rose.

"Did you say merry little band?"

"Of hot and sexy men, yes. It's a term Sarah Murphy coined. You have to admit we have more than our fair share of gorgeous guys, the vast majority of whom are blissfully married, thus merry. I'm so excited for you! Is it serious or just a fling? Not that there's anything wrong with flings—well, unless you're married, of course. But you're not married and you've been alone for too long and—tell me—is he as good as he looks? I bet he is. Those hands of his are huge." Sage gave a dramatic shudder and added, "I'll bet he's just a whole lot of fun in bed."

"Sage, I'm not going to talk about this."

"It's a waste of time to try and put me off. You know I'll pester you until I wear you down. That's what little sisters do."

"Maybe so, but I have to try."

"I know. That's what big sisters do." Sage nodded toward the brown bag and added, "I figured you probably skipped lunch again. You need something light before yoga class. I brought you yogurt and nuts from the Blue Spruce."

"Seriously? The Blue Spruce isn't ordinarily open this time of year." She reached for the bag.

"They're opening for spring break this year. Celeste convinced them that they'd have enough business to make being open worthwhile. I'm thrilled because I've been craving their pimento cheese. Nobody makes homemade pimento cheese like the Blue Spruce."

In the process of pulling a yogurt cup from the bag, Rose stilled. A fierce combination of joy and envy struck her like a fist. The last time her sister had craved pimento cheese, she'd been carrying her son.

Sage is pregnant again.

She pinned her sister with a look. "Pimento cheese? Really?"

Sage went still, then winced. "Well, shoot. I just lost a hundred dollars. Colt said I wouldn't be able to keep the secret until Easter. He is going to win the bet. It's just not fair that you know me so well. Unless you keep my secret?"

"You mean you don't want me to tell anyone that you're pregnant?"

A madonna's smile spread across Sage's face. "Yes."

Tamping down the envy and giving joy free reign, Rose hurried around her desk and pulled Sage onto her feet. She wrapped her arms around her sister saying, "Congratulations, honey. I'm so happy for you. For all three of you. Wait. Make that four. How are feeling?"

"Thanks. Fine." Sage hugged her back, then said, "I'm a little scared. I had hoped I got past all my phobias when Racer was born, but the minute I missed my period, the nightmares returned."

Rose gave her sister another hug for good measure. Sage had been delivering a baby when thugs directed by an African warlord attacked the medical clinic and ordered unspeakable horrors done to physicians and patients alike. As a result in her sister's damaged psyche, babies and terror had been intertwined. "You've told Colt about the nightmares."

Sage nodded. "He immediately went online and booked a long weekend for us in sunny Southern California. We're leaving on Friday morning. We can take Racer with us, of course, but I wondered if—"

"Of course I'll babysit," Rose interrupted. "You know how much I love to do it. Racer and I are pals."

"I know. But since you have a new man in your life, maybe it's not good timing?"

"The timing is just fine. Although"—her words trailed off as a thought occurred—"now that I think about it, I'd like you to give me a chit to hold in reserve."

Warily, Sage asked, "A chit? What kind of chit?"

"Babysitting."

Sage gave her a confused look. "I'm sorry, but I'm not following."

"Hunt and I have this thing about wagering. We do it a lot. One of the bets I lost requires I babysit his nephews and nieces when they visit Eternity Springs this summer. So, how about if I keep Racer for you and Colt this weekend, then when Hunt calls due our wager, you have to pitch in to help."

"All right—whoa. Wait a minute. These are the kids Gabi talks about? One of them ran through the Valentine's dance? Another broke his arm?"

"Taking care of multiples will be good practice for you."

"There are two girls, right? That makes four of them. I'm not having triplets, Rose."

"How do you know?"

"Bite your tongue."

"How far along are you, anyway?"

"I'm due the first part of August."

Rose flashed a grin. "Have to do something on these long winter nights, right?"

"Absolutely. Now, tell me about your winter nights."

"What time are you planning to leave Friday?" Rose countered.

"Rosemary," Sage groaned. She gave her long, wavy red hair a toss. "Give me something, here. Just because I'm married to the sexiest man alive doesn't mean that I can't appreciate the attributes of a man as potent as Hunter Cicero."

Potent. Yes, that was a word that suited him.

"How serious is this?"

I don't know.

"It's barely been a month, Sage."

"So? Sometimes love happens fast. Believe me, I know."

Rose didn't recall Sage's romance with Colt being fast—just the opposite, in fact. "Whoa, there. I haven't had very good luck with serious. I think I'm much better off keeping things casual."

"Don't take this as a criticism, because it's not. But you're not one who usually indulges in casual sex."

"I never said I was sleeping with him."

"Phfttt. Pull the other one, Sister. You're glowing."

"It's from the radiation," Rose shot back, flippantly.

Sage's complexion drained of color and her expression grew stricken.

"Rose? Are you keeping something from me? Are you in some sort of treatment I don't know about?"

"No. I'm sorry. I shouldn't have said that. I shouldn't joke. Everything's fine."

"When is your next checkup?"

"June."

Then, because she really wanted to deflect the conversation from that particular conversational path, she said, "Okay, I'll admit I'm sleeping with him. He's a fabulous lover. Yes, those hands of his are magic—and he speaks to me in Italian when we're making love."

Her ruse worked. Sage immediately brightened, and she patted her hand over her heart. "Oh, Rose. That's so *romantic*. Do you remember enough of the language to know what he's saying?"

"Let's just say that it's not difficult to infer the meaning of the words I don't recognize." She opened her yogurt and said, "Tell me about your trip. Where in California are you going?"

"Palm Springs."

The sisters talked about babysitting arrangements while Rose ate her yogurt and nuts, then Sage glanced at the clock and said, "You'd better change or we'll be late. I don't want to miss the opening stretches. They're my favorite part."

The Monday night yoga class was a relatively new item on the Eternity Springs activity calendar. Upon discovering that Shannon O'Toole had been an instructor prior to moving to town, Ali Timberlake had convinced her to begin a class for local residents on a night when the bar was closed. The class had become so successful that Shannon had added a couple of early morning sessions, too.

Rose enjoyed the classes. Shannon was a patient instructor who made all her students feel comfortable, no matter their age or ability—a character-istic that Rose was counting on tonight. "Speaking of Hunter and wagers," she said, as she and her sister approached Murphy's, "I think there's a chance he might join our class."

Sage abruptly halted midstep. "Yoga class? He's coming to yoga class? Like Lenny Winston?"

"No, not like Lenny Winston. Lenny needed the exercise, but that's not why he came to class. He was being a creeper. Hunt isn't a creeper."

"He doesn't need the exercise, either. The man runs every morning, skis at least twice a week, and does push-ups in the library. That doesn't count the more personal exercise he gets with you. He's a hard body in a town full of hard bodies. So what's the deal?"

"It's my idea. The man is focused and intense and overstressed. I'm not exactly sure what's going on, but I walked into his studio the other day and he was punching the keys on a calculator as if they were a speed bag. Before I could say hello, his phone rang and someone laid some sort of problem at his feet. When he hung up the phone he had enough torque in his jaw to run a motor."

"Yoga is great for stress relief."

"Yes. But I think the main problem is that he's struggling creatively. He's only mentioned it once weeks ago, but I sense that he's not happy with the work he's producing."

"That I totally understand. Nothing makes me more cranky than to see an image in my head and be unable to get it onto my canvas. Artists have earned the term *temperamental* honestly."

Rose understood it, too. It made her downright grumpy to sit down to write and not know where to go with her story. "I think Hunt needs a little balance in his life, and yoga just might help."

"Feed the creative Zen. I get that. So, you call him Hunt? I've never heard anyone use his first name before."

Rose didn't want to get into the whole name-use silent battle she had going on with her lover. A month into their relationship, he still hadn't called her by her given name. As a result, she'd taken to using generic endearments with him, too, her favorite being Fireman. She doubted he'd even made the connection, but it had become a matter of principle with her.

"I like being different. Anyway, once I had the idea to drag him to yoga, I lured him into a bet on a game of darts."

Aware of the many hours of playing time Rose had put in all over the world, Sage murmured, "Sucker."

"Yeah, well, he accused me of being a ringer, so

I'm not sure he'll show up. He's skeptical and I think maybe just a little bit intimidated."

"Because it'll be a class full of women?"

"No, he'll like that part." Rose popped almonds into her mouth. "He is probably the most competitive person I've ever met. He knows he's not going to win the pose wars."

"Pose wars? Since when are there pose wars in yoga?"

"Don't try to tell me that you don't sneak looks at Nic Callahan's poses wanting to do yours better."

"We started class the same night. I want to be sure I'm keeping up. Besides, what I'm really checking out is the way she looks in yoga pants. I'm so totally jealous of those long legs of hers." Sage tapped her finger against her lips in thought for a moment, then added, "Speaking of yoga pants, what do you think the man who plays with fire will wear to class tonight?"

"I gave him some yoga pants, but I don't know if he'll wear them. The look on his face when I gave them to him was priceless. I told him if he chooses something else he needs to go either tight or loose. And no going commando."

Sage waggled her eyebrows. "Does he ordinarily go commando?"

Rose made a zipping motion across her lips.

Her sister laughed and added, "I thought about skipping tonight's class, but now I'm sooooo glad I decided to be healthy. Enough of this lolly-gagging around. Hurry up, Rose. Let's get there in plenty of time to get a good spot in the back row. I want to be sure I have an unrestricted view of a certain downward facing dog."

Nine

Cicero stood outside of Murphy's Pub and muttered, "Nothing like getting an early start on being an April Fools' joke."

He tried to remember the last time he'd felt this awkward. What the hell was he doing here anyway? Carrying the rolled up piece of puffy plastic Rose had dropped off at the studio for him along with the pants he had on. Yoga pants made for guys. Who knew they even made such things?

He wasn't going to wear them. He'd put them on, taken them off, pulled on sweats, thought about how cute Rose had been when she'd given him the damned things, then put them back on.

At least they were damned comfortable— though he wondered if they didn't hug his package just a little too much. Is this how women felt when they asked if pants made their butts look big? Ordinarily, he didn't give what he wore a second thought, so the fact that he thought about it now only increased his sense of discomfort.

He couldn't believe he'd let Rose manipulate

him into giving yoga a try. When she'd suggested the dart game, he'd known by the look in her eye that she had something sneaky up her sleeve. The fact that he went along with her was a sign of just how desperate he really was.

He'd been working on the Albritton project for over a month and had nothing worthwhile to show for it. The ideas he'd entertained—and pieces he'd produced—had been about as pedestrian as anything he'd ever done. Hell, he'd done more inventive work when he'd been making souvenirs for the tourists in Venice.

So far, the ideas that flowed following physical exertion hadn't been worth a damn. Nothing had sparked his artistic fire. Doing push-ups hadn't helped. Running hadn't helped.

Not even sex had helped.

Lots of sex. Lots of really great sex.

The situation unnerved him. His creativity had been one thing he'd always been able to count on. Sure he had a lot riding on this project, but he'd always been one to thrive on pressure. He should be cruising along with a clear vision of his design and half a dozen test pieces sitting on his studio's shelves.

Instead, he had empty shelves and a yoga mat tucked beneath his arm.

Wuss. You're pathetic, Cicero. Totally pathetic.

At least his mat was black and not hot pink or aqua. He knew that yoga wasn't the exclusive domain of women. He could name male members of every professional sport who'd added yoga to their physical routines. Some guys swore by it.

Cicero was just swearing, period. He truly didn't want to do this.

Once he'd gone down in ignominious defeat in their dart game, Rose had promised him he'd shift from stressed to blissed in ninety minutes worth of yoga. He'd been quick to point out that a round in the sheets only took a fraction of that time, but of course, she hadn't considered that an argument in his favor.

Muttering a curse, he opened the door and stepped inside to see the pub's interior transformed. Tables and chairs had been pushed against the walls and a dozen or more women sat on a rainbow of yoga mats lined up in rows. An elevated platform had been positioned at one end of the room, and Shannon O'Toole sat atop it, donning socks that had no toes.

Cicero hesitated, wondering where he should put his mat. He looked closer at the other participants. He recognized about half of them: Celeste Blessing, Sarah Murphy, Nic Callahan, Gabi's two sisters-in-law and her mother. His apprentice wasn't here, which relieved him. Knowing Gabi, she'd give him grief about doing this.

The women he didn't recognize were older, closer to Celeste's age, though admittedly he could be totally off base where the owner of Angel's Rest was concerned. Sometimes he'd peg her as being in her sixties. Other times, she seemed older, almost ageless.

It doesn't matter how old Celeste is. Quit delaying. Pick out a spot for your mat.

If he put it in the back row, he'd look like a perv. If he spread it out in the front row, he'd look like he was trying to avoid looking like a perv. Safest place would be the men's room, except he wouldn't sit down in there with three layers of yoga mats between him and the floor.

"You made it!"

He turned toward Rose's voice like a lifeline, then was distracted by the sight of her. She wore a patterned sports bra in shades of red and black and matching pants that hugged her ass and hips. Maybe this wouldn't be such a waste of time, after all.

"Yes I made it. I don't welch on bets."

A grin teased her lips. "We'll start in a few minutes. Want to spread out your mat?"

Not particularly.

"Where?"

"I'm over here." She gestured toward a blue mat at the end of one row. "I saved room for you beside me."

"Great. Thanks." He stepped around the mats, nodding hello to familiar faces, trying not to let his eyes linger on cleavage or Lycra-clad hips. At

Rose's direction, he rolled out his mat, then knelt on one knee. That's when he noticed the woman in front of him. Cat Davenport stood bent over touching her toes. She wore a long, oversized yellow shirt over formfitting Spandex—and her ass was directly in his line of vision.

That gave Cicero pause. He'd met Cat's husband, Jack. The man struck him as one scary dude. He shifted his gaze to Rose.

"Tell you what, I'll set up behind you. That way I can copy your movements."

And watch your *ass, not Mrs. Davenport's.*

What followed was ninety minutes of near humiliation set to music that made him want to sleep—or slit his wrists. He was bigger, taller, and stronger than every other student in the room. He was athletic. Coordinated. Competitive. But tonight in Murphy's Bar, he was the proverbial bull in the china closet, awkward and cumbersome and clumsy.

When it came to yoga poses with names like Warrior and Tiger and Tree, these women made him look like—Loser. They twisted themselves into pretzels, and did it with grace and ease. He tried to stand on one leg and damned near fell over. He shot a silent glare toward Rose.

Where the hell is the bliss in this?

Two thirds of the way through the class, when his head was on the floor and his butt was in the air and sweat dribbled down his forehead and onto his mat, a sensation of light-headedness had him swaying. He fired a hiss just loud enough for her to hear.

"If I pass out, Dr. Anderson, you have to promise to give me mouth-to-mouth."

She looked back at him through her spread legs, blew him a kiss, and wiggled her butt. He groaned and surrendered and lay prone on the floor.

Damned but yoga was hard work.

"It's okay to take a break, Cicero," Shannon said from the dais.

Gee, thanks, for calling attention to my general wussiness.

As a dozen pairs of eyes turned his way, he gave a beauty queen wave and a smile, though mentally he was shooting the finger at both Shannon and Rose. *Evil women.*

He propped himself up on his elbows and fastened his gaze on his lover. Look at her, he thought as the class continued. Long and lean and curved in all the right places. He needn't have worried about ogling Cat Davenport, or any of the other women here tonight. He couldn't take his eyes off Rose—until a cry of pain grabbed his attention and that of everyone else in the room.

An older woman standing near the front of the room at the end of a row grabbed her knee. Voices rose in alarm and Shannon cried, "Christine!"

Rose and Sage moved toward the woman before anyone else reacted. "Oh shoot oh shoot oh shoot," the woman said. "I've tweaked it again."

Even before the woman finished her sentence, Rose moved a chair into position so that all Christine needed to do was to lower herself into it.

"What happened, Christine?"

"It's my bad knee. I slipped on the ice last week and pulled something. I know to be careful, but I wasn't paying attention. I stepped the wrong way."

"Shall I get some ice?" Shannon asked.

"That would be great," Rose replied.

"I'm all right. Please, dears. I don't need a doctor."

"She means she doesn't need a doctor's bill," another woman piped up.

"Now, Sandra," scoffed a third woman. "That's not very nice."

"It's the truth. You know her husband is a skinflint. He has been that way ever since high school. I should know. I dated the man."

"Why, Sandra Thompson!" exclaimed the third woman, her voice bristling with offense.

Christine shook her head, wincing from pain. "She's right. Larry is tight with the dollar. Oh, dear. This really does hurt."

Rose knelt to examine the knee as Shannon emerged from the pub's kitchen with a plastic bag filled with ice. "We've had more injuries from slips and falls this winter than I can remember since I arrived in Eternity Springs."

Cicero watched the caring, compassionate physician at work and wished she'd been a member of Jayne's team. He recalled the first time he'd seen her at the Valentine's Day dance. Her white coat had waved at him like a bullfighter's red cape, but his attitude hadn't fazed her. Every day she exhibited caring, compassion, and strength.

He'd appreciated that strength these past weeks. Meeting her so soon after Jayne's death had been good for him. She'd given him something positive to think about. She'd soothed his grief.

Celeste spoke from just behind him. "She's a special person."

"Yes, she is."

"Both of the Anderson girls are blessings for our town, but Rose's decision to settle here made it practical to build the new clinic which in turn allowed us to attract Dr. Coulson to Eternity Springs. A town can't thrive without readily available medical care. Yes, she is definitely a positive force in all of our lives. I pray that we don't lose her."

He whipped his head around to stare at Celeste. "Lose her?"

"Oh, dear." She gave her lashes an innocent flutter. "Did I speak out of turn?"

"She's never said anything to me about moving." When another thought occurred, he demanded, "Oh, hell. She's not sick, is she?"

"Not that I know of." She patted his arm

reassuringly. "Life is like Angel Creek, dear boy, flowing toward the unending ocean of that which is after. Sometimes it's bubbly and frothy and active. Other times, it's a slow and quiet eddy. Sometimes it's frozen. The only constant is that it will constantly change."

Cicero waited, but it appeared that she'd said all she intended to say. Now if he could only figure out just what it was she'd said.

He tried again. "Is Rose thinking about leaving Eternity Springs?"

"I'm sure she doesn't want to, but sometimes life presents us with choices that take us in directions we don't expect. One must always be ready for a detour. Time will tell. It always does."

At that point, Shannon stepped back up onto the platform and said, "Christine has called Larry to come help her get home. Let's begin to wrap things, shall we? Clear your minds—"

Distracted by Celeste's comments, Cicero didn't attempt to follow Shannon's instructions. He sat staring at Rose, recalling how Gabi had mentioned to him that Celeste had a sixth sense like nobody she'd ever met.

He hoped her senses were as mixed up as the spiel she'd just given him.

He wondered why the thought of Rose leaving town bothered him so much. He refused to think that she might be sick.

He liked her, yes. He liked her very much. He

liked her heart and her wit and her passion. He liked her sexy way of walking and the little mewling sound she made when she came apart in his arms. She filled an empty place inside him, one he'd not recognized existed prior to meeting her.

Like Celeste Blessing, he didn't want to lose her.

In all the years he'd been playing around with women, he couldn't recall a particular time or a particular woman who'd affected him just this way.

In front of him, Rose rolled onto her side, dislodging bobby pins from her long auburn hair. It spilled onto her shoulders, the color of fine red wine. Wine and Rose, he thought, triggering the memory of lines from a poem that he'd run across while doing his Emily Dickinson library research.

"They are not long, the days of wine and roses. Out of a misty dream, our path emerges for a while, then closes, within a dream."

Something flittered through his thoughts, an idea just beyond his reach.

Days of wine and roses.

Wasn't that the title of an old movie? Or maybe a book?

Days of wine and Rose.

His pulse sped up. His fingers suddenly itched

to sketch, to hold a punty as images—shape, color—flashed in his mind. He levered himself up to a seated position and focused on the coral colored polish on Rose's toenails without really seeing it. Color, shape—a dreamy mist. Something—he dragged his gaze away from Rose and looked for paper—a pen—a pencil.

Hell, a crayon and a blank spot on a wall would do.

He rolled up onto his feet, all thought of yoga class forgotten, his thoughts divided between the image taking shape in his brain and his need to find a drawing implement. He headed toward the section of the bar where he'd seen Shannon stash her order pad just as the injured Christine's Larry walked inside wearing a pocket protector that held two pens. "May I borrow that?" he asked, smoothly removing the pen from the man's pocket.

"Uh—"

Cicero ignored him, his focus on the Kelly-green stack of Murphy's Pub paper menus. He grabbed one, flipped it over and reached for the idea. It was still there—hovering—but he just couldn't pull it in.

He shut out his surroundings. He wanted music, loud pounding music. He willed the vision to take form and inspiration to feed his creative fire, but when he set the pen point to paper, nothing happened. Not a damned thing.

Waves of frustration rolled through him accompanied by an undertow of panic. Why couldn't he push through the haze?

Maybe if he went back to the studio, he'd be able to block out all of the distractions and concentrate. He set down the pen, then glanced around for Rose and saw that she was busy talking to Christine and her husband. He grabbed his stupid yoga mat and ducked out of the pub.

Back at the studio, he sat in front of his drawing board and tried to recapture the moment. *The days of wine and roses.* What was the connection between wine and roses, and hope and feathers?

He was thinking about it hard, when his phone rang. He wanted to ignore the call, but Amy Parnell was on the line. This could be another broken bone—or a broken neck.

After a twenty-minute conversation with Amy about the new stack of medical bills in the mail that day, he abandoned the hope of recapturing the creative wind. He'd missed his chance—but he decided that yoga had possibilities.

For the next week, he showed up at Murphy's, mat in hand, for each yoga class Shannon held. He claimed the spot behind Rose for his mat, and tried to think about wine and roses.

After each class, he produced a halfway decent sketch that would make for gallery quality work, but fell far short of Albritton worthy.

Then, right before his second Monday night

session, he received a phone call that offered new possibilities. Forget wine and roses and yoga. Sun, sea, and sand might be just the change he needed.

Better yet, sun, sea, sand—and Rose.

"I can't just drop everything and go on vacation," Rose told him. "I have responsibilities. I have patient appointments."

"Ask your sister to cover for you. I'll bet she'd be happy to do it. When was the last time you took a vacation?"

Rose's teeth tugged at her bottom lip. It had been a long time ago.

"You don't want to miss a chance to meet Avó. Her mind is still sharp as a palm frond. She loves to tell stories and listening to her is like living history. You'll love it."

Cicero had explained that Avó was the great-grandmother of his apprentice, Mitch, and a beloved figure on Bella Vita Isle. She'd just celebrated her 100th birthday, and now that she'd actually made it to the milestone, she'd allowed her friends and family to schedule a birthday party. Cicero planned to go early and stay on afterward in order to put in some studio time with Mitch.

He slipped his arm around her waist and tugged her close. "It's twenty degrees and snowing outside. Come with me, *Sirena Bellissima.* I want to see you in a bikini, and swim with you in the warm Caribbean waters. I dream of rolling with you in the sand."

He nipped at the sensitive skin on her neck, and she shuddered in response.

"I don't own a bikini and I'm not a spur-of-the-moment kind of girl. Things like that always get me into trouble."

"A little trouble is good for you," he replied.

"Spoken like a man."

"Which I am." He licked and nibbled at her earlobe. "I'll buy you a bikini."

"I'm too old to wear a bikini."

"Fine. We're staying on a private beach. We'll go naked."

"You're hopeless."

"No, I'm full of hope. Come with me. Call your sister. I want you with me at Avó's party. They are like family to me."

He'd said the magic word—family. Then he captured her mouth in a thorough kiss. When he finally lifted his head and gazed at her with magnetic, hot chocolate eyes that willed her to agree, she sighed. "Okay."

He gave her two hours to be ready to leave Eternity Springs. They had a long drive to Amarillo, Texas, where first thing the next morning, they'd catch a flight to Houston and from there, on to the Caribbean. On the way back, he explained, he'd scheduled a visit with the urchins. It took Rose an hour and a half to line things up at the clinic with Dr. Coulson and Sage, so when she went to pack, she did so in a flurry. The fact that she didn't need to pack winter clothes made the task easier, as did her memory of the beautiful island skirts and dresses that Gabi had brought home after her visit to Bella Vita Isle.

She did pack her one-piece swimsuit. The man could hope, but skinny-dipping in the ocean qualified more as a fantasy. Private beach or not.

The seven-hour drive to Amarillo took eight because they hit rain in the Texas Panhandle. Tired from the drive, they checked into their hotel room and fell into bed—and into sleep—almost immediately. Their wake-up call felt like it arrived mere moments later.

Cicero proved to be an entertaining travel companion. They talked about the places they'd visited, discovering a shared interest in both art museums and jungle treks. Though Rose tried hard not to compare her current lover to her former fiancé, she couldn't help but recall Brandon's resistance to adventure. Shoot, the vast majority of vacations they'd taken during the years they'd been together had revolved around medical association meetings. She'd told herself that having grown up an army brat, she hadn't missed traveling. In hindsight, she could see that hadn't been true.

"I'm excited about visiting Bella Vita," she told

him. "Gabi talked a lot about how beautiful the island is."

He laced his fingers through hers and brought her hand up to his mouth for a kiss. "It's a lush tropical island with lots of flowers and vegetation and water as pretty as I've seen anywhere in the world. But what makes it beautiful for me are the people."

"I'm surprised you left it."

He didn't reply for a long time.

"I wasn't ready to leave when I did," he said, finally.

"Did you consider moving back there instead of going to Eternity Springs after you lost your sister?"

This pause lasted even longer than before.

"I need to be able to see the kids. I promised Jayne. Flying four of them round trip from Houston to the Caribbean just wasn't feasible."

She gave his hand a squeeze. "I hope those children know how lucky they are to have you as their uncle."

"It's temporary. Once they've had enough time to bond with the Parnells, then they'll have a family and they won't need me. Well, except for my money. Guess they'll always want that. I'm going to help support them financially no matter what. Scott's salary as a bookkeeper for a small business doesn't stretch far enough to raise four kids. If Amy went to work, they'd have to sink her whole paycheck in day care. I promised my sister I would contribute cash for their support. However, beyond that I figure I'll be off the hook."

"You'll always be their Uncle Hunk."

"No, not necessarily. A lot of that depends on the Parnells. They may decide the kids are better off without me and give me the boot."

"Why in the world would they think that? You're their uncle. They're your family."

"According to Scott, I'm a friend of the family. He doesn't recognize the bond because Jayne and I weren't related by blood."

Rose sat up straight. "I thought she was your sister."

"She was—because we declared it so. We were definitely not the traditional family. We weren't related to each other. We were two kids, each with a troubled parent, who both ended up in the same foster home. We declared ourselves family."

"You were in foster care? For how long?"

"On and off my whole childhood."

Her thoughts went to the burn scars on his chest. She'd never been able to work up the courage to ask him about them. He had completely ignored her hints. Now that he'd brought up the subject of his childhood, she wanted to know more.

"You said a troubled *parent*. Father? Mother?"

He shook his head. "I'll tell you that story

another time. Let's enjoy the last leg of our trip to BVI."

She gave him a look that questioned his veracity.

He pointed out the window.

"You can see the islands below."

As deflections went, the Bahamas were an excellent choice.

Rose had visited Nassau eight years ago for the destination wedding of a colleague. While waiting to deplane, she mentioned to Cicero that the trip had been a fast in-and-out so she hadn't done much sightseeing.

"Since we have three hours to kill before we're due to meet Mitch at the marina, how about we grab a late lunch at a Salvadoran restaurant I know of, and then we can rent scooters and play tourist until it's time for Mitch to show up. We can have our suitcases delivered to the marina."

"Sounds great."

And it was. The food was wonderful, the scenery lovely, the city alive with people and colors, scents, and sounds. Cicero drove like a maniac, as did everyone else on the road, so she swallowed her nervousness and did her best to keep up.

Cicero was a great tour guide, and as the time for their rendezvous with his apprentice approached, their route took them past a land-mark Rose recognized from her previous visit, the place where her co-worker's beachfront wedding had taken place. She remembered rows of white chairs at the water's edge, and walking down the flower-lined aisle on Brandon's arm shortly before sunset.

Imagine if she'd made that walk with Hunt instead. Imagine if she were making that walk toward Hunt. Wearing white, carrying a bridal bouquet. He'd wear a white shirt open at the neck and—

"Whoa!" She startled, and jerked the handlebars. Her scooter weaved left into the oncoming lane of traffic. She yelped and overcorrected, shooting right, and hitting a pothole hard. She wobbled and teetered—and fell on her butt.

Cicero was there before she tried to stand. "Are you hurt, *Bellissima*?"

"No. I'm mortified, but okay."

"Let's get you out of the street." He helped her to her feet, asking, "What happened?"

"I got distracted and I overreacted. I hope I haven't hurt the scooter."

"Don't worry about the scooter. Worry about you. You scared ten years off of me."

"I scared myself, too. I've been a doctor far too long, seen too many vehicular accident victims to be so careless."

"I should have warned you about the— distractions. That wasn't an official nude beach, but there is always a lot of skin on display on there. You don't see many people walking around in the nude in Eternity Springs."

They'd just passed a nude beach? She totally hadn't noticed.

"Not this time of year. You'd be surprised at the number of, let's say *nature lovers,* we see in our little slice of Colorado. Every summer I treat sunburns where sunburns shouldn't happen."

"Are you okay to go on? If not, we can ride double. We're about ten minutes from the marina."

She brushed off the bottom of her jeans, glad she hadn't changed into a dress. "I'm okay as long as the scooter is."

He cupped her chin, then pressed a light kiss against her mouth. "Take care of yourself, *Bellissima.* I'd be devastated if you deprived me of my rolling-in-the-sand fantasy."

She closed her eyes.

Yes, absolutely.

She needed to keep her thoughts on his sort of fantasies, not the crazy idea she'd entertained.

When they arrived at the marina, a young man with café au lait skin and Rastafarian braids, who'd been sitting on the bow of a center console boat, stood, smiling widely, and waved.

He loped up the wooden pier and called, "Mon. It's about time you came home."

Home. Rose focused her gaze on Cicero as the two men shook hands, then clapped each other on the back. *Did he still consider the little island his home?*

He introduced her to Mitch Frazier, who, rather than shaking her hand, bowed over it and gave her a courtly kiss. "Another beautiful lady from Eternity Springs? Maybe I make a mistake by not visiting already, no?"

"Keep your lips off this one," Cicero shot back. "She's mine."

Mitch blinked in surprise, then his smile grew even wider.

"Sure thing, boss."

Cicero handed the scooter keys over to Mitch and asked him to deal with the rental return. "Our luggage should be in the marina office. You should change into a swimsuit, *Bellissima.* We may want to stop and swim on the way home."

Fifteen minutes later, Cicero cast off the line and Mitch guided the twenty-four-foot boat away from the courtesy slip and slowly out into the harbor. Upon reaching open sea, he said, "Hold on, beautiful Rose."

She braced herself, and Mitch opened up the engine.

It was a glorious sensation—wind in her face and warm sunshine toasting her winter-weary skin. She'd never ridden on a boat like this one before, and she found she loved the experience. When Mitch offered her the opportunity to take the wheel, she jumped at the chance.

At a spot Cicero said was the halfway point, they stopped and everyone jumped in for a short swim. It was one of the nicest days Rose could recall spending in years.

Then, they arrived at Bella Vita Isle. The island's lush beauty took her breath away.

"I don't know about you, but I'm looking forward to kicking back and being lazy for a little while," Cicero told her after making plans with Mitch to meet at the glass studio the following day.

"I am tired," she agreed. "The sun feels wonderful, but I'm ready to get out of it. How long will it take us to get to where we're staying?"

"About twenty minutes." He stowed their bags in the back of a rented Jeep. "It's not far, but the road is winding. Bella Vita is shaped like a boomerang. The place Flynn owned was at the long end of the island. We'll be at the shorter tip, in a hillside house. Heliconia. There's a pathway down to that little cove that I mentioned."

"And we're staying in a private residence? At a guest house?"

"The main house. The owner is a patron of the arts."

A ghost of a smile hovered on his lips.

"He walked into my studio one day when I was working on a project that I'd intended to send to a gallery. He took one look and wanted it. Bad. We did a deal for it and a few other pieces that included an open invitation to use his place when I wanted. It's a pretty great place; the most imaginative house I've ever been in. I don't believe this guy is quite as wealthy as Flynn, but he's not too far off the mark. A dot-com guy."

"Was the piece he wanted a sculpture?"

"Yes, but we added lighting and hung it from the ceiling so you might call it a chandelier now. You'll see it at Heliconia. He hung it in the entry hall." He shook his head and added, "He named his house after it."

"Really?" She shifted in her seat to better see his face. "How cool is that?"

"The owner does have a unique sense of style."

"I have to admit my ignorance, however. What exactly is *heliconia?*"

"It's a tropical flower. The blossoms look like lobster claws, so sometimes you'll hear them referred to that way. Also 'parrot beaks.' The name comes from Greek mythology. Mount Helicon was the home of the muses of the arts and sciences."

"So this work you created—did you begin with the flower or the mountain in mind?"

"Actually, it was both. I was climbing a cliff face on an island not far from here and I could see flowers above me. The idea for the piece grew from that."

He turned off of the main road onto the lane

leading to their destination. Bella Vita was a volcanic island, and the road up to Heliconia was narrow and winding, not unlike some of the roads around Eternity Springs. Of course, the trees and vegetation were lush and tropical, rather than alpine, and the colors were a feast for the eyes. They climbed high, and when a curve in the road revealed an unfettered view of turquoise ocean, she gasped aloud.

"Oh, wow."

"Told you that you'd love it."

The house sat hidden behind a wall and an electric iron gate. Cicero pulled up to a box and punched in a code. After the gate swung slowly open, he moved the Jeep forward. When the house came into view, Rose did a double take. Part of the structure looked like the decks of the Starship *Enterprise* with rounded walls of windows; but the castle turrets blew that comparison, as did the realization that part of the house appeared to be built in trees.

"It's like a *Swiss Family Robinson*/*Star Trek*/*Cinderella* mash-up—that works."

Cicero grinned.

"That's a good description. The architect who designed it told me the owner was his most challenging client ever. He let his children collaborate. Two boys and a girl."

He punched a code into the keypad beside the front door. Locks snicked open. Cicero's gaze remained on her as he opened the door and ushered her inside.

The first thing she saw was the teardrop of glass hanging by an invisible thread in the center of the entry hall. It drew her gaze upward and she stopped and caught her breath. It was as if a canopy of tropical flowers stretched across the ceiling. Bright reds and oranges and yellows flowed from shades of green.

"Oh, wow, Hunter. That's fabulous. It's like it's raining flowers."

He lifted his gaze toward the ceiling.

"It was a tricky piece, but I must say, it fits this crazy house. It's especially nice about half an hour before sunset when the sunlight hits it."

"You have an incredible talent," she said.

A shadow crossed his face.

"I'm afraid it needs a jumpstart. I'm hoping the change of scenery will be the fuel it's been missing."

He carried their bags upstairs to the guest suite where she saw more of his work. They showered together, and then he opened a bottle of champagne to celebrate their first night in the Caribbean. They watched the sunset, both inside the house and on the western horizon. Personally, Rose found the light show created by sunshine and his sculpture on the ceiling to be more compelling than Mother Nature.

The next day they slept in, then hiked down to

the private beach and went for a morning swim. Afterward, they shared cooking duties and prepared a big breakfast. As they sat down to eat, he said, "I need to head to the studio. Do you want to come into town with me and explore a bit, or would you rather stay here and laze around today?"

"I think I'll stay here. I'm feeling a little inspired, so I might get my laptop out and write for a while." She'd fallen behind with her word count goals lately. This would be a good chance to do some catching up.

"Do you plan to murder anyone today?"

"Actually, I'm seriously considering it."

"Thata girl. How are you going to do it? A gun? A knife?"

"I'm leaning toward a pie."

"Crust as heavy as an anvil?"

"Rhubarb. It can be poison, you know."

"You are one scary woman, Dr. Anderson."

"Thank you. I do try."

He left a short time later, after telling her he'd be back by three and to call if she needed anything. She settled down with her computer and went to work on murder.

By noon, she'd killed one person and had moved on to a second. By two, she'd added more words to her manuscript than she'd managed in a month. She was downright gleeful when she threw a red herring into the mix at ten after three. She went upstairs and showered and dressed for the party, expecting to find him downstairs when she was ready.

By four, she'd grown concerned by his continued absence. At four-thirty, she called. His phone rang and rang and rang. She imagined that winding road and a blown tire and a flipped Jeep. She tried again at four forty. Again at four forty-five. At four-fifty, she went online in search of a phone number for the studio, or a way to contact Mitch. She had no luck whatsoever.

At five o'clock, she went in search of another mode of transportation. The garage was locked. She tried the key codes that had given them access to the house, but had no luck.

She envisioned the Jeep at the bottom of a ravine, Cicero bleeding out for want of a doctor's skill. Tears of concern and anxiety stung her eyes. She would try his cell number one more time, then call 911. Surely Bella Vita had a 911 system. She'd never asked.

She pulled her phone from her pocket and hit redial. It rang and rang and rang. It was still ringing when the Jeep came into view, Cicero behind the wheel. Seeing her, he gave a jaunty wave.

First Rose's knees went weak with relief. Then her spine snapped straight with her fury. He pulled the Jeep to a stop in the drive a short distance from her, unfolded his long legs from inside, and shot her a carefree grin. "Hello, *Sirena Bellissima.* Did you commit any murders today?"

She took a deep breath. Brandon had been a workaholic. As she focused on Cicero, she thought of all the times her ex had left her waiting without a phone call, of all the times he'd been late or simply hadn't shown up. As a physician herself, she'd understood how work interfered with social plans. It was the lack of simple courtesy that she'd resented. One she darned well wouldn't put up with again.

"Two." She advanced on him. "I committed two murders today. And the day's not over yet."

Ten

Cicero arrived at Heliconia flying high, his mood better than it had been in weeks. He'd felt at home in the studio today. He'd felt confident and relaxed and inspired. He'd actually found his creative zone for a change.

He hadn't started with a sketch but instead went straight to the furnace with a clear mind and the intention of turning out some tourist kitsch in order to ease back into the island state of mind. He'd done exactly that for a time, producing a handful of dreamweavers for Mitch to sell at his booth.

The feather image had seeped into his mind

like a zephyr. Just when he'd caught fire with the idea, he couldn't say. All he knew was that for the first time in a very long time, he'd found his fire.

The piece that had gone into the annealer was the best work he'd done in months, the only piece he'd produced that came close to being a possibility for the Albritton entry. It would require three days of gradual cooling before he'd see the final result, of course, but he knew it would be good.

He'd felt as if he'd flung a thousand-pound gorilla off his shoulders. He couldn't wait to get back to Heliconia and share the news with Rose.

Then he drove up and saw her standing by the garage wearing a flowing yellow dress. She looked so fine. He wondered if they had time to—

He parked the Jeep, switched off the motor, then greeted her.

Her reaction was less than promising. She didn't smile. She didn't act too happy to see him. In fact, she looked annoyed. "Something wrong?"

"You said you'd be back at three. I was beginning to worry."

"Oh. Sorry. I should have called. When I'm working and the work is going well, I lose track of time. You know what it's like, don't you? You're deep into your fictional world and the real world fades away?"

"It's happened upon occasion," she admitted. "That's why I use the alarm on my phone when I need to be somewhere."

"You're right. I'm wrong. Please forgive me."

That took the wind out of her sails. Nevertheless, he meant it. As he meant it when he took hold of both her hands, held them out to her sides, gave her a thorough once-over and observed, "You look fantastic. I don't think I've seen you wearing yellow before. It's a great color on you. You're like a breath of spring. Is that what you're wearing to the party?"

The hesitation in her eyes reflected her inner debate. Was she going to let the subject drop or continue to beat him up for being late?

"Yes, this is what I planned to wear. Is it appropriate?"

"It's perfect. You're perfect." He leaned down and kissed her. "I can't wait to introduce you to Mama T and Avó and the rest of Mitch's family. They're going to love you."

Forty-five minutes later, they walked onto the white sand beach where a bonfire burned, drinks flowed, and food roasted, simmered, and steamed. As the sights and sounds and smells swirled around him, Cicero took a moment to shut his eyes and experience—home.

"I love it here," he murmured.

"I can see why," Rose replied. "It's a fabulous spot."

"Cicero!" called a feminine voice. "Are you planning to ignore me all night?"

He turned around to see Mitch's mother looking hale and hearty. Cicero let go of the last fear he'd been holding on to since he'd heard the news about Tabitha Frazier's heart attack. He stepped forward, his arms opening wide, a big smile on his face. "Mama T. Just look at you. You look spectacular."

He wrapped her in a hard hug that she returned just as fiercely. "Of course I do. I look half my age. I could be my Mitch's sister rather than his mother. It is about time you came home where you belong. Now, introduce me to the lovely lady. My son tells me she is a healer."

"She is." Cicero grabbed Rose's hand and pulled her forward. "Mama T, meet Doctor Delicious, Rose Anderson. Isn't she lovely?"

Rose released a little sigh of exasperation and extended her hand. "I'm pleased to meet you, Mrs. Frazier."

"Welcome. Welcome. Welcome." Mama T took Rose's hand in both of hers. "You are a friend of our Gabriella's, too, are you not? From the snowy little town?"

"Eternity Springs. Yes."

Mama T tucked Rose's hand around her arm, saying, "Come with me. Let me introduce you around. Cicero, go get me and your lady something to drink."

"Yes, ma'am. What would you like?"

"Punch."

"Of course." He met Rose's gaze. "Rum punch? I should warn you. It's potent."

"I don't think—"

"Of course she'll have punch," Mama T said. "It's our own special island recipe. You must at least taste it."

Not giving Rose the chance to naysay, Mama T waved Cicero off. The line in front of the punch bowl was long, and by the time he'd managed to fill two cups and returned to Rose, he found her sitting on the sand at Avó's feet, listening with rapt attention to the birthday honoree. He handed Rose and Mitch's mother their drinks, greeted Avó with a kiss to her cheek and birthday well wishes, then went to find a beer for himself.

When dinner was served, they sat at a table with Mitch, who kept Rose laughing with stories from his early days of working with Cicero. After dinner, they joined in the dancing until Rose begged off, claiming a desire to rest her feet. He suspected that mostly, she wanted to sit and listen to more of Avó's stories.

"Want some ice cream?" he asked her as she rejoined Avó's circle.

The smile she offered him sparkled. "No thanks."

"I do. I'll be right back."

She nodded, her focus already on a story about

gold doubloons, Irish whiskey, and the false bottom of a breadbox. Cicero wandered away, scored a chocolate sundae with which to indulge his sweet tooth, then stood watching the sunset as he licked whipped cream from a plastic spoon.

"Firefall," he murmured, recalling a particularly nice piece he'd done in yellow, orange, and scarlet a few years back after watching a Bella Vita sunset. This was one of his favorite spots on the island, and he'd watched the sun sink into the ocean from this spot more times than he could count. He found something about sunsets and the sound of the sea especially inspirational. He'd done some of his finest work after spending an evening on the beach.

"Firefall," he softly repeated. Then, just as the Emily Dickinson poem floated through his mind, the crowd around Avó erupted in laughter. Rose's voice called to him like a siren song, and he turned away from the sunset. His gaze fastened on her.

Disjointed visions and thoughts and sounds spun through his head. Fiery hair and a yellow dress. Hope is the thing with feathers. Firefall. The echo of Celeste Blessing's voice. *She has an angel's heart.* Laughter. Rose Anderson's laughter.

An image formed in Cicero's mind. His heart began to pound.

Rose could sit and listen to Avó for days on end. Such an interesting life she'd had, a real insider's view of Caribbean history. Rose had just begun to wonder if anyone had ever recorded Avó telling her tales when Avó mentioned that she'd written them all down in a memoir that everyone could and should buy from an Internet bookseller. "It's available as a printed book, but I recommend the e-book. I love my e-reader. Everyone should have one. You can adjust the size of the letters."

Rose laughed aloud, and clapped her hands in delight. What a gem this woman was. She glanced around, looking for Cicero, wanting to share her amusement. She didn't spy him in the circle around the guest of honor, and she realized she hadn't seen him since he went for ice cream. That had to have been half an hour ago at least.

Hmm. She wasn't being a very attentive date. Standing, she made her way out of the gathering and wandered toward the food tables. Twilight had descended into near full darkness now, and away from the bonfire and lights, the other party-goers were little more than shadows. Nevertheless, Cicero shouldn't be too difficult to spot. He was taller than most men she'd seen on Bella Vita Isle.

She didn't find him on her first pass through the crowd. Nor on the second. Frowning, she decided she'd better go about her search more systematically. She began at water's edge and walked the length of the beach. Turning around, she walked the opposite direction, searching in a grid until she was confident that she'd covered the entire beach.

He wasn't there. Her date had disappeared on her.

Her temper simmered. She'd bet her favorite pair of flip-flops that the man had hied himself off to his glass studio to work. Leaving her behind. Probably forgetting he'd even brought her along to the party. Shoot, he might not remember that he brought her along to the island, either.

That sorry glassblowing son of an iguana.

Rose stifled the childish urge to kick the sand. She had a choice to make. She could pack her suitcase and go home—literally—or she could confront the inconsiderate conch and tell him off before she packed her suitcase and went home.

She was an army brat. She'd never been one to shy away from a fight.

She turned toward the bonfire where she'd spied Mitch on her last trip up the beach. As she approached, she saw him toss his drink cup into a trash can and begin walking away.

"Mitch! Wait a minute," Rose called.

He stopped and turned. "Yes, beautiful lady?"

"How far are we from the glass studio right now? Is it within walking distance?"

"Yes. Of course. It's only two blocks off the north end of the beach. About a ten-minute walk from here."

Rose nodded. That's what she had thought. They

had driven past it on the way to the party tonight. "Will you give me directions, please?"

The young man looked confused. "Cicero will take you—"

"No," Rose interrupted. "He won't. I'm afraid he's forgotten that I'm here tonight."

"Oh." Mitch winced. "He had an idea?"

"So I assume. Either that or space aliens abducted him."

"Judging by the look on your face, I suspect he'd be better off in a spaceship than in the glass studio."

Rose offered up a wan smile.

"You really shouldn't take it personal, Rose," Mitch said, making a valiant attempt to explain away his boss's boorishness. "He's a creative being and when the wind is upon him, he's consumed. He does this sort of thing all the time, although it's usually at the end of a date rather than in the middle of one. However, I know that one time he left a woman in bed during—"

He broke off abruptly when she drilled him with a glare, then he added, "You're right. He's a cad."

"How do I get to the studio from here?"

Mitch rubbed the back of his neck. "Maybe I should take you."

"Thinking he needs protection?"

"Take a look in a mirror, beautiful lady. What's the saying? *If looks could kill?*"

"I won't hurt him. I'm a doctor. I save lives."

She paused for a beat before adding, "That said, I do know some inventive ways to take lives, too."

"I think I'll pretend I didn't hear that last part." Mitch gave her directions, then hesitated a moment before saying, "Go easy on him, Doc. He's a good guy despite his tendency to get distracted when he's working. You're the first woman he's brought to meet my mother, so I know you're special to him."

Rose started off. As a rule she was slow to anger, but once her fuse was lit, she did a fair job of what her father used to call "getting her Irish up." Her Irish was in its full glory right now. Mitch might have been wise to tag along to protect his reptile of a boss, after all.

The ten-minute walk took her seven, and she arrived to find the studio lights shining brightly. She pushed open the door and marched inside. Cicero sat at his drawing board, a pencil in hand.

She waited for him to look up. He didn't.

"You jerk," she declared, her voice dripping with scorn. "I gave you a pass earlier today. You only get one. I understand there are times in life when work comes first. Sometimes, lives depend on it. But I don't see anyone bleeding out here tonight. Being ignored for work twice in one day crosses my line. I've been here, done this with my ex."

At that, his head shot up. "What? Did you just compare me—"

"Yes, I did," she interrupted. "I'm not going to do it again, Hunter. I won't accept rudeness. I won't be a doormat."

"Doormat? Don't be crazy. I didn't dump you for a younger woman. I'm working, Rose."

Her chin dropped. Her temper blew.

"Now? *Now,* you use my name? For the first time? And it's not in normal conversation. Not while we're making love. No. You use it now when I'm furious with you."

"I've never used your name?"

"Not when speaking directly to me, no."

"Huh."

He studied her, his gaze sweeping over her from head to toe. Then damned if he didn't put his pencil back to paper and continue to sketch.

He might as well have plunged it into her heart.

Tears stung her eyes and she whirled away. She would not let him make her cry. She refused to do it. She fled the studio, walking fast, and when she heard the door open behind her and his annoyed voice call out "Rose, stop it!" she started to run.

To where, she didn't have a clue.

She had no ride back to Heliconia. She didn't know how to get there on her own. She hadn't brought her purse because she hadn't wanted to keep up with it during a beach party, so she had no money. How stupid was that? She knew better. She always took money or at the very least a credit card with her on dates in case this exact sort of thing happened. Shoot, even when she lived with Brandon she always took cab fare with her. *Why had she picked tonight to be so stupid!*

You've been stupid since Valentine's Day. Getting involved with the likes of Hunt Cicero. You deserve to be stranded.

At least she was on a tropical island rather than somewhere cold and snowy. She could spend the night on the beach if she had to. There was a public restroom. A fire burning. Bet she could scrounge up something to use as a pillow.

A hand caught her shoulder, tugging her to a stop.

"Rose, what the hell?"

She whirled on Cicero.

"I want to go home."

"Okay. Okay. Fine," he said, scowling. "I don't like airing laundry in public either. The car is this way." He hooked a thumb over his shoulder.

"To Colorado. I want to go home to Eternity Springs."

He muttered an epithet, then said, "Just calm down, Rose."

At that, she blew. She punctuated her words with a hard poke of her index finger on his chest. "Don't. You. Call. Me. Rose! And don't you tell me to calm down, either. I'm perfectly calm. I'm perfectly, calmly pissed. The only calling I want to hear is you calling whoever needs to be called in order to get me off this island. And while you're at it, call a cab to take me back to the house tonight, too!"

He let a long moment pass before he reached into his pants pocket and pulled out his phone. He thumbed a number, then said, "My companion needs a ride to Heliconia. Pick her up in front of the studio. Make it fast."

He ended the call and spoke in a frigid tone. "I may not save lives like you do, Dr. Anderson, but I have four young children depending on my financial assistance. My work isn't without value."

Cicero turned and walked away, reentering the studio and leaving her alone on the street. Rose breathed short, shallow breaths as she attempted to calm her pounding heart and hold back the tears that once again threatened to overflow.

It seemed like days before Mitch arrived driving an old Ford Crown Victoria. He pulled to a stop beside her and rolled down the passenger side window.

"Climb in, Dr. Anderson."

He didn't say anything to her during the first few minutes of the drive. She paid him little attention, her thoughts a whirlwind as the reality of the evening's events sank in.

She'd let her temper get away from her and voted herself off the freaking island. Okay. Well. Was she having second thoughts about the demand?

My work isn't without value.

That's not what she thought. He'd jumped to a huge conclusion, fired it like a bullet, then walked away before she could set him straight. The jerk. He didn't even pay her the courtesy of fighting fair.

Had he displayed that tendency before tonight? She hadn't noticed. Of course, they hadn't really fought about anything in the weeks they'd been together, had they? They'd argued music and politics and sports teams, but they'd never had a real disagreement. Before now.

They'd certainly started off big.

No. They hadn't started anything. They'd already had their beginning. What they'd done tonight was end.

In the wake of her breakup with Brandon, one thing she demanded in every relationship—romantic or otherwise—was basic common courtesy.

"You are a friend of my friend Gabriella, are you not?" Mitch asked, drawing her from her reverie.

"I am."

He nodded and drove another block.

"What has she told you about Cicero?"

Rose went still. "What do you mean?"

"About Cicero and women. Has she—"

"*Warned* me?" Rose guessed, her stomach sinking.

Mitch shrugged. "I don't want to speak out of

turn, but you seem like a very nice lady. Like a lady. You're different from all the others."

All the others?

"He told me the day he took me as his apprentice that glass isn't art. It is life. He meant it. He is serious. Anyone who is part of his life must compete with his art for his attention. Up until recently, I thought art would win every time. Up until recently, I saw it win every time."

"What happened recently?"

"His sister, Jayne. The children. He put his family before his work. I'd never seen him put anything before the work, lovely Rose. It was the first difference in him I witnessed, but not the last. When Flynn was injured, Cicero went out of his way to be a friend. Family. Friends. Women. You are not the beach bunny/bored trophy wife type who he ordinarily hangs with on Bella Vita. With you—with the way he looks at you—I see something more, something bigger. Maybe something special. He's changed. He's not the same man he used to be."

A lump formed in Rose's throat and she swallowed hard as Mitch concluded, "The point I want to make to you is that if he matters to you, then you shouldn't give up on him too easily."

The young man's words stayed with her after he dropped her off at Heliconia and as she packed her suitcase and moved her things to a bedroom on the opposite side and different level of the house.

He's changed. I see something bigger. Maybe something special.

She'd thought she had been special once before, but she'd been wrong. She'd been a connection to her father, a boon for a career. At least Cicero had wanted her for herself.

You shouldn't give up on him too easily.

She hadn't done that, had she? That wasn't her way. She didn't give up easy. She'd tried to make her relationship with Brandon work. Oh, how she'd tried. She'd dedicated seven years to trying. She'd given up her chance to have the family she longed for. How could she possibly take a risk on a man again?

She certainly hadn't intended to risk anything when she'd begun this affair. She'd thought her heart had been sufficiently hardened after the beating Brandon had given it. Cicero was supposed to be a fling, but apparently, she wasn't cut out for flings. The man had managed to worm his way into her heart when she wasn't looking. Otherwise, his neglect today wouldn't hurt so bad, would it? She wanted—she needed—to matter to Hunt Cicero.

If he matters to you, then you shouldn't give up on him too easily.

"Easy for you to say, Mitch," Rose murmured, standing at the bedroom window, gazing out to where silvered moonlight reflected from the surface of an indigo sea. "You didn't have your heart sliced from your chest and shredded the last time you didn't give up."

If he matters to you.

Rose released a long sigh. Heaven help her. He mattered.

Eleven

"She doesn't matter," Cicero muttered as he ripped the sheet from his sketchbook and started over with a fresh page, a clean slate. Women never mattered. Ideas were what mattered.

And damned if the idea that had lured him to the studio tonight hadn't disappeared in a cloud of Shalimar perfume.

Disgusted, he threw down his pencil and shoved away from the drawing board. He wanted a drink, and he didn't keep alcohol in his studios. Impaired senses didn't mix well with furnaces hotter than two thousand degrees. His gaze lingered for a short moment on the sketch he'd been drawing when Rose burst into the studio. It was good. The work he'd done today was good, the best he'd done since getting the Albritton call.

Maybe he'd truly needed the inspiration of Bella Vita in order to break through his creative malaise.

Returning to the island had breathed fresh air into him. He felt energized. Recharged. Relaxed.

Here on Bella Vita life was simple. He worked. He played. He could go barefoot and outside without pulling on three layers of clothing to stay warm.

He didn't worry about medical bills, or music lessons, or the ridiculous cost of braces.

He dragged his hand down his face and muttered a curse. He picked up his pencil once again and resumed his seat and—nothing. Nada. The creative wind had gone silent.

Grimly, he turned away from his drawing board and moved toward the furnace. Maybe he'd done enough drawing for the day. Maybe what he needed was to work with glass. He was still on Bella Vita, wasn't he? He could smell the sea in the air, hear the surf. He'd go straight to the pipe and let the island work its magic.

He took a long iron blowpipe from the pail of water, extended it into the crucible, and gathered glass. For the next twenty minutes he worked by rote.

He produced a piece so flawed that he wouldn't even sell it as a second.

He broke it into the scrap bin and surrendered. Bella Vita might have contributed to the quality of his work today, but in his heart of hearts, he suspected that his true inspiration was Rose.

She *mattered.*

She wasn't just another woman in a long line of women. She wasn't just candy for his arm or a scratch for his itch. Hell, she wasn't simply *Bellissima* or baby or sweetheart or honey. She was Rosemary Anderson, M.D. His Rose. She mattered to him.

And his actions today had hurt her.

She didn't truly understand his world—his fault because he'd only shared a little bit of it. She didn't know about his money issues. Didn't understand that the Albritton meant so much more than a career boon.

"You really are an ass," he said to himself.

Then he grabbed his keys, switched off the studio lights, and headed for his Jeep.

On the way back to Heliconia, he plotted his apology. He was sailing uncharted waters here. He couldn't recall the last time he'd gone begging to a woman. Hell, he didn't think he'd *ever* gone begging to a woman. Women usually begged him.

But not Rose.

He downshifted to make the climb up the mountain. Like they say, there's a first time for everything.

The house was dark when he arrived. The door locked. He punched in the door code, then went straight to the bedroom they'd shared. He wasn't surprised to discover it empty and her things gone. He called Mitch.

"Did you take her somewhere?"

"To Heliconia, just like you asked me."

"She didn't ask to go somewhere else?"

"Where would she go, mon? How would she get there?"

Cicero hesitated.

"Did she—?"

"You need to fix this, mon. That's all I'm gonna say."

The dial tone sounded in his ear. His apprentice had a point, Cicero conceded as he pocketed his phone. Bella Vita had a taxi. A single taxi. But you had to know to call Jorge to avail yourself of the service. Rose wouldn't know that. It worked in his favor.

This house had seven bedrooms. It made a lot more sense for her to have moved to another room for tonight than to have decamped entirely.

The first three bedrooms he checked showed no signs of having been disturbed. The fourth door was shut. Bingo.

He rapped on the door with his knuckles. She didn't respond.

"Rose, please open the door."

Still hearing no sound from inside, he wondered if she'd fallen asleep. He tried the knob. It turned. He opened the door and breathed a sigh of relief upon seeing the silhouette of her suitcase on the bench at the foot of the bed.

He glanced toward the connecting bathroom. No lights there. However, a filmy white window curtain billowed as the night breeze floated in through the door leading to the verandah. *She's outside.*

His deck shoes squeaked against the wood floor as he crossed the room. His nerves jangling, he pushed back the screen and stepped outside. It was bright outside. The full moon cast a silvered glow across the land. Cicero searched the beach below for Rose. Then a creak behind him caused him to turn around. *There.*

She sat in the wooden porch swing, one leg folded beneath her, the other extended to push against the floor and keep the swing swaying.

Cicero shoved his hands into the pockets of his jeans. Now that the moment had arrived, the words he'd planned to say stuck on his tongue. They didn't feel right, but he didn't know how else to start. He wasn't sure what to say. Should he go with a simple "I'm sorry"? Should he attempt to explain? Should he go all out and grovel?

He opened his mouth, still unsure about what to say. The words that emerged shocked the hell out of him because he never, ever, talked about this.

"I never knew my father, and I was four years old the first time my mother went to jail. She was an addict, in and out of jail, in and out of rehab, for the next nine years. As a result, I was in and out of the foster system. She OD'd when I was thirteen."

Hidden by the shadows, Rose stopped swinging.

"By then, I was too old and too much of a troublemaker to be an attractive prospect for adoption. Jayne had a similar background, only her surviving parent was her father. We had the same caseworker and he placed us with the same family, when I was nine and she was six. We bonded. We both bounced back to our parents more than once, but our guy placed us in the same foster house as often as he could manage. When I aged out of the system, I took off. But I always stayed in touch."

He fell silent then, remembering. Rose resumed swinging, and the chain made a rhythmic squeak.

"She was my sister. I was her brother." He cleared his throat, ridding himself of the lump of emotion that had formed there. "I'll bet you are wondering what the hell this has to do with my being an ass to you today."

She let out an audible sigh.

"Well—"

He laughed without humor.

"I'm selfish, Rose. I learned to be selfish to survive. Before you, I've never had a romantic relationship last longer than—I don't know—a week? Two at the most? I've walked away from women all of my life, but I stuck with Jayne. She was the one constant, the only lasting female relationship that I've ever had. When she was diagnosed with cancer, it shook me to my core. I promised her and I promised myself, that I would stick by those kids."

"That's admirable."

"It's scaring the stuffing out of me. I've never wanted kids of my own. Most of the foster homes

I was placed in had lots of kids. Growing up the way I did made me prize my solitude. Jayne's reaction was the polar opposite of mine. I'm honestly surprised she only had four of the little curtain climbers.

"They're depending on me. The Parnells are depending on me. I gave my word to my dying sister that I'd bankroll the kids. I won't let them down. I need to win this blasted competition, and the pressure is making me a little crazy, but that's not what I want to tell you. I want to tell you that I'm sorry I ran out on you tonight and this afternoon, and I could promise not to ever do it again, but I probably couldn't keep that promise. Not all the time, anyway. You know what they say about old dogs and new tricks.

"The main thing I want to tell you is that you matter to me. You matter to me more than any other woman I've been with. I don't know what that means or where if anywhere it could lead. I'm in uncharted waters here. What I do know is that I want to keep sailing. I'm probably not a good bet, but I'm asking you to give us—give me—another chance. You matter to me, Rose."

At his use of her name, she turned her head. He felt the weight of her stare.

"I think I've figured out the name thing," she said. "Most people use nicknames as terms of endearments. You use them to hold people at arm's length, don't you?"

"I can't say that I've ever given the question any thought. I'm not that deep a thinker."

"Actually, I suspect you're one of the deepest thinkers who has ever crossed my path." She scooted from the center of the swing to one side.

"Sit down, Hunter."

He relaxed just a little and took a seat beside her.

"After I moved my stuff into this bedroom, I went down to the beach and walked along the edge of the water for a little while. The sound of the surf calmed me. I was able to think again, and not just react. I'd like to explain why I got so angry tonight."

"You had every right to be angry."

"Yes, I did. You were a total jerk, but you are also an artist. I understand artists. Medicine is an art. My ex was a brilliant surgeon, but I very seldom came first for him. I understood it. I even encouraged it. Frankly, my career was important to me, too, and it took priority for me more often than not. In hindsight, I regret that. I regret that more than I can possibly put into words."

"Because your relationship failed?"

"No." She leaned back in the swing and paused in reflection. "You know that old saying that youth is wasted on the young? Well, I'm the poster child for that. Five years ago—no, it's closer to six, now—my world crumbled. I lost an opportunity that was much more important to me than I realized."

"Marrying your ex?"

"No, but the 'what' isn't the point. What's important is that after my relationship with Brandon ended, I reassessed every aspect of my life. I decided that if I want my life to count for something, I need to count for something in the lives of people who are part of that life. What happened today, when you disappeared on me—twice—well, it pushed that button."

He winced and because he was a man, went for the deflection.

"Did he cheat on you?"

"Brandon?" Surprise tinged her voice. "No. I could be wrong, but I don't believe he ever did that. Brandon was a jerk, but he wasn't a liar. He was very upfront about his reasons when he decided to leave me."

"Want to tell me about it?"

"Not particularly, no. But I guess I probably should."

Cicero sensed more than saw the tension that seeped into her. They sat with probably a foot of space between them. He wanted to reach out and take her hand in his, but her manner didn't invite it.

"We were together for seven years, engaged for four. Actually had a wedding date picked three times, but the Army had other plans for us. The relationship ended in a way that left a seriously bad taste in my mouth. I vowed I'd never care for another man as long as I lived. Up until now, I haven't."

"Up until now," he repeated.

"You matter to me, too, Hunt," she said, her voice little more than a whisper. "Go figure. It's not what I'd planned. I thought I could keep things casual. That's what I wanted."

He gave the swing a push with his foot. "Isn't that a bit at odds with the whole count-for-something philosophy?"

"Yeah, well. This is where we get into the whole fling versus relationship thing. I looked at you and me as a fling that would one day be a memory and a smile. I wasn't looking for a relationship. I didn't want a relationship. Not after everything that happened."

" 'Everything' being what, Rose?"

"I like the way you say my name."

"Don't try to distract me. Talk to me."

The swing's chains gave three rhythmic creaks before she finally dropped her head back and sighed. "I despise talking about this. Completely and totally despise it. Invariably, it changes how someone looks at me. Don't give me those stares, Hunt. I can't bear the thought."

"Dammit, Rose. You're starting to worry me. What bit of news are you dancing around?"

Her hand inched closer to his.

"When you were simply a fling, you didn't need to know. I didn't feel one bit bad for keeping it to myself. Now that you matter to me and I to you, you absolutely deserve to know. But I'm afraid to tell you. What if you have more in common with Brandon than the affinity to lose yourself in your work? You'll dump me, too. Considering your recent history, I can't blame you. But I have to tell you, Hunt, it totally sucks being dumped by your boyfriend because you had cancer."

Cicero's blood turned to ice.

Cancer? She has cancer?

Dear Lord, not again. Please, not again.

Instinctively, he reached for her hand, and crushed it in his grip. His voice emerged in a raspy croak. "You said *had* as in past tense, right? Isn't that what I heard?"

"Yes. Past tense. I've passed my five year anniversary." With deliberate casualness, she asked, "So are you going to give me the old heave-ho?"

He exhaled shakily.

"No, but if you don't spit out the whole story right now I might throw you off this balcony."

She laughed, then told him how she'd been diagnosed with endometrial cancer, about her chemotherapy and radiation—and about the hysterectomy that ended her chance to have children of her own.

"My first reaction was that I was being punished for giving away my baby. I'd had my chance at motherhood and now there would be no more chances. I'd wanted to start a family for a couple of years, but Brandon kept putting me off."

"I'm so sorry, *Bellissima*."

"Me, too." She shook her head sadly, adding, "He waited six whole weeks after my surgery to tell me that he'd decided he wanted a shot at fatherhood, after all."

Cicero took a moment to absorb that information. Anger on Rose's behalf whipped through him. He knew more than he wished he knew about cancer protocols. The radiation she'd mentioned would have happened after her surgery. That meant the bastard lobbed that grenade while she was going through treatment.

"Whoa. What a gold-plated ass. That makes me look like a prince of a guy."

"I think I'll refrain from comment on that," she replied, her tone wry with amusement. "But it isn't really about Brandon and his behavior. Like I said, I spent a lot of time in self-examination in the wake of my diagnosis and breakup. I realized I needed to make some changes. Life is short. It shouldn't be squandered. I want to live my life with joy and purpose. I want it to mean something."

He stroked his thumb across her knuckles.

"Your life means more than most. I've watched you. You are of great value to your sister and her family, and to your friends. You are vital to the health and safety of the people of Eternity Springs.

And I might have a strange way of showing it, but you are important to me."

"I believe that." She paused a moment before adding, "You groveled."

He stretched out his long legs, crossing them at the ankles.

"That's pretty harsh. I don't know that I'd agree that the word grovel is appropriate."

"Sure it is. You groveled nicely, too. I was quite impressed."

"You have a smart mouth, *Bella Rosa*." He brought her hand up to his mouth and kissed it. "So, are we okay?"

"I'm okay. Are you okay?"

"I'm good. A little shaky, I'll admit. You threw me a curve ball. Supporting my sister through her cancer battle was the hardest thing I've ever done."

"I can understand that. Especially given your history. My father wasn't perfect and heaven knows he made mistakes, but I can't imagine what you went through with your mother."

"My mother was young when I was born. She'd been mixed up with a bad crowd—you know the drill. In the end, I mattered less than the high. It consumed her."

"Drug abuse isn't an excuse."

"No, it's not. But drug addiction is a monster. I try not to think about those years. It just makes me numb. Enough about me. I want to know—five years is one of those magic milestones, isn't it?"

"Yes."

"Don't get me wrong. I wouldn't bail on you because you got sick. I don't do that."

"Yes, you've proven that."

"It's just—it's hell to go through. I'm so sorry you had to do it, Rose."

"You're a good man, Hunt Cicero. Except when you're being a temperamental jerk of an artist."

"Yeah, well. Where do we go from here?"

"Where do you want to go?"

"Skinny-dipping."

She rose from the swing and pulled him to his feet.

"First one in the water gets to be on top."

That evening marked a change for the two of them. The fling had officially grown into a relationship. For the rest of their visit to Bella Vita, life fell into a rhythm. They awoke early and spent a couple hours together, usually swimming or hiking or running, then they both went into town. While Cicero worked in the studio, Rose played tourist or worked on her book or both. He did have one instance where he lost himself in his art and was late meeting her, but Rose let him off the hook. She understood him better, she told him, and she wasn't nearly so insecure herself. Besides, the fact that he'd been so honestly contrite made all the difference in the world.

Cicero left Bella Vita with Rose at the end of their two weeks recharged and ready to return to Colorado and perfect the design he'd created for the contest. They endured a long day of travel with weather delays for their flights both into and out of Miami, and when they finally arrived in Houston, he looked forward to seeing the ankle biters.

That changed the moment Amy Parnell answered his knock on her front door.

Twelve

As a physician, Rose dedicated herself to healing, so the power of her urge to take one of the steak knives from the block on the kitchen counter to Amy Parnell caught her by surprise.

The woman had just informed Cicero that she and her husband were bailing on their promise to be guardians of his sister's children.

"I know what I promised," the woman said to Cicero. She opened her dishwasher and began unloading the silverware. "I tried. We tried. But we can't do it. My marriage can't handle the stress. Scott has said I have to choose. It's either him or the kids."

"You can't do this," Cicero said with fire in his eyes and fury in his jaw. "You made a commitment!"

"Well, they'll be committing me if I'm responsible for them much longer." She tossed the final spoon into the drawer and shoved it shut with a snap. "You won't believe how much work they are."

"I damn well do know how much work they are. I helped Jayne with them a lot when she was sick. I offered to help you after she passed. You're the one who didn't want me around. You told me to move away."

"That was a mistake."

"So you're going to throw them away like so much garbage?"

"No, absolutely not." She stacked red Fiesta plates into her cabinet. "Child Protective Services said they'd be placed in good foster homes."

"What? Foster care?" Visibly shaken, Cicero leaned back against the counter. "Foster homes? Plural? You're splitting them up!"

The pulse at his temple visibly throbbed. The man was so angry that Rose worried he'd stroke out.

Amy tucked her classic blond bob behind her ear and used a white dish towel to wipe water spots from glassware. "Of course they'll try to find a home to take them all, but realistically, it's a lot to ask for."

"Sort of like you keeping your word, huh?"

Cicero paced the kitchen like a panther.

"I tried! We both tried. I feel terrible about this

but really, we're not to blame for Jayne's irrespon-sibility. We will keep Daisy—she's blood kin—but the other three—it's just too much. I'm pregnant again, Cicero. I've already suffered one miscarriage. I'm not going to do anything to put this baby in jeopardy. I have to put my own family first."

"Blood kin? Did you really just say that? Damn, Amy. Did our plane go off course and land in feudal Britain?"

"Cicero—"

"You're a cold-hearted bitch. You swore to make these children your family," he fired back. "You promised Jayne on her deathbed!"

"Well, I was wrong. I'm sorry, but we can't do it."

His eyes blazed, but he spoke in an icy tone. "Where are they now?"

"Daisy and Galen are at the play school at church. Misty and Keenan are still at school. They'll be home in"—she glanced at the clock—"half an hour."

"Have you told them?"

Amy removed the last of the dishes from the dishwasher, then shrugged, not meeting Cicero's gaze.

"No. We waited for you to get here. We thought you could reassure them about living in foster homes."

"Reassure them. Right. They lost their mother,

and now this. There is no such thing as reassurance, Amy. Not in this case."

He finished with a stream of ugly language, then pivoted and banged his way out the door. Rose watched as he marched away from the Parnells' home. She spared Amy a disapproving look, then hurried after him.

She had to jog, and then all but run.

"Can you believe them?" he asked. "They're pregnant, so they want a redo on a promise to the dead woman who trusted them. Except for the baby. The baby is just a baby and a blood relation, so they'll keep her. Isn't Daisy lucky? Dammit, Rose, Jayne didn't make the arrangements for her children lightly. She talked to both Scott and Amy more than once. They knew what they were getting into. They promised Jayne. They promised her! How can they do this?"

"I don't know."

Rose was in shock herself. How do you make this kind of promise involving children and then go back on your word?

"Me, either. It's gonna tear those kids apart. I know they're a pain. I know that parenting those four is probably a whole lot more than Scott and Amy figured, but they had their chance to say no. They said yes. You don't get to change your mind about something that important."

Rose didn't know what to say to make him feel better. She had some experience with CPS. Caseworkers had an impossible job. They were usually incredibly overworked and burned out more frequently than just about any profession she knew of. She wasn't familiar with the foster system in Texas, but she couldn't imagine it being easy to place three children in any one home for an extended period of time.

But then, that wasn't going to be an issue, was it?

She'd gotten to know Hunt Cicero quite well over the past few weeks. He might bluster and protest and resist, but he wasn't going to let his sister's family be broken up, was he?

Rose knew it in her heart of hearts. Cicero wasn't going to walk away from these kids.

"It's true they are pains in the ass, but what kids those ages aren't? Not Misty, though. She is just as sweet as can be. Keenan and Galen are boys. Just normal little boys. And Daisy is their sister. Their sister! What in hell makes Amy and Scott think it's okay to pick one child over the others? Seriously? Because she's a"—he made finger quotes—"*blood relation?* That just totally pisses me off."

"So what are you going to do?" She knew he needed to think hard about this, but there really was only one solution.

"What can I do? I can't force them to be parents."

Rose didn't say anything.

Cicero raked his fingers through his hair. "I guess I can talk to the social worker, explain how important it is for them to stay together."

She responded carefully. "Yes, you can do that."

"I can cough up more money. Surely with enough money on the line the social worker could find a family to take all of them."

"Yes. Surely. Except for Daisy. The Parnells are going to keep Daisy."

He muttered another curse. "That's B.S."

"They're her legal guardians."

"Yeah, well, under false pretenses. If Jayne had known they were going to pull this nonsense only a few months after she died, she'd have made different arrangements."

"What arrangements? What other choice did she have?"

Silence reigned in the wake of that question, just as she expected. To Rose, the solution was obvious, but Cicero needed to find his way there himself. He'd get there, but it wouldn't be a quick or easy journey. He'd fight it before surrendering.

"I had some really great foster homes."

"That's good."

"Jayne and I got to stay together in three of them."

"I'm sure that was very comforting for you."

"It was."

"Keenan and Galen are young," Rose said.

"They'll probably have adoptive parents clamoring for them. Placing two young boys together probably won't be impossible."

"That leaves Misty the odd girl out. She's nine. Shy. Watchful. Responsible. She tries to be brave, but underneath, she's scared to death."

"Maybe someone who wants the boys will consider taking her, too, to be an extra pair of hands."

Cicero whipped his head around to glare at her.

"That's wrong. That's just wrong. She deserved better than this. They *all* deserve better. They deserve parents! Parents who love them and put them first, Rose. This is going to damage these children. A rejection like this one will affect them the rest of their lives. You don't just give children away!"

Rose inhaled a breath.

He closed his eyes. "You know I don't mean—Rose, I'm sorry. That was poorly done of me."

"I understand what you meant."

"Still, it was insensitive. I'm pissed off that people who promised Jayne something when she was dying, told her the one thing she cared about and needed to hear—that her kids would be okay and cared for—it was all lip service."

He shoved his hands into his pockets and his long-legged strides ate up the ground. They turned a corner, and Rose spied a neighborhood park halfway up the block. When she saw the group of young boys leaving the concrete basketball court, she fished in her back pocket for the change she'd stuck there earlier in the day. Cicero was mumbling to himself, so she just ran ahead without saying anything.

She approached the boys holding out a ten-dollar bill. "Does anyone want to rent me their basketball? You can pick it up later at the Parnells' house."

She quickly had a taker, and by the time Cicero entered the park, the boys were gone, and she stood dribbling the basketball at center court. One thing she'd figured out early in their relationship was that physical exertion helped him think. He had some serious thinking to do right now.

"Heads up."

She fired the ball at him. He caught it and took it to the basket. They took turns taking shots for about five minutes, and then Cicero started charging faster, jumping higher, dunking harder. She stepped back and let him work it out.

He ran. He jumped. He jigged and jagged at imaginary players. Shot lay-ups and practiced slam dunks. Soon sweat rolled down his face and his pace accelerated to nearly frenetic. He played hard for much longer than she had expected. The older children would be home from school by now.

Finally, he caught the ball and held it, then dropped his chin onto his chest. He drew in a series of deep breaths and exhaled in a heavy *whoosh*. Slowly, he turned his head and met Rose's gaze.

"Those poor kids. Life has dealt them a raw deal all around."

She nodded. "I know."

"The Parnells can't keep Daisy and dump the others. They're a package deal. A family. I can't let them be split up. I wouldn't be able to live with myself."

"No, you can't let them be split up."

"But I can't take them myself, either. I'm a bachelor. A loner. I'm a wanderer. I'm accustomed to picking up and going when the spirit moves me. You can't pick up and move four kids."

Sympathy washed over Rose. He was fighting so desperately.

"I don't know anything about childhood immunizations or potty training or oh, holy hell"—he met her gaze, a wild look of panic in his eyes—*"menstruation!"*

She smiled. "You'll learn, Hunter."

He held up his hand, palm out.

"That's just it. I don't need to learn that stuff. I don't want to learn it. Those kids need a parent, a father. I'm Uncle Skunk. Uncles don't get a period!"

"See!" she said, her smile going wider. "You already have a grasp of basic biology that you can teach them."

"Very funny." He dropped the basketball, bounced it once. Twice. "I don't know anything about being a father, Rose. I never had one."

"Then you're a perfect fit with those children. They've never had one, either."

"Scott was supposed to fill that role, not me," he said, continuing to let the basketball bounce. "He promised Jayne. I might lose track of time upon occasion, but I never go back on a promise. Look, maybe I'm getting ahead of myself. Maybe the authorities will be able to find a foster home that will keep them together. Foster homes get a bad rap. There are some truly wonderful people in the world who serve as foster families. I know that for a fact."

She wondered once again about the burn scars on his chest. She'd never asked about them. This probably wouldn't be the right time to bring them up. Or else it was exactly the right time to bring them up.

"I wish the Webers were younger. They'd grab these kids in a heartbeat."

"Were the Webers one of your foster families?"

"Yeah. The best. They gave me—" He broke off abruptly, giving his head a shake. "The foster system can do a decent job for kids. Sure there are some homes that slip through the cracks, but those aren't as common as people think. Out of the seven different homes I lived in, only one was seriously awful. And that wasn't the fault of the foster parents as much as it was the other kids in the home."

"Your scars. Were you burned by another foster child?"

He remained silent for a full dozen bounces of the ball. "Yeah. Kid was a serial killer in training, I'm sure. I was Keenan's age."

He let out a long, heartfelt sigh, then shot the ball toward the rim. When it whooshed through the net, he turned to her. "You just had to float that particular question right now, didn't you? Not too subtle there, Dr. Anderson."

She retrieved the ball and held it. "Ordinarily, I would say that you shouldn't make such a huge decision so quickly. But honestly, it's obvious what you are going to do."

"It is?"

"You love those children, Hunt. Those children love you. What choice do you have, really?"

"I don't have a choice. You're right. What does that mean for us? You and I are just getting started."

Only the force of her will kept Rose's smile fixed. It hadn't occurred to her until just now that his solution for the children might not include Eternity Springs.

"I've had experience with long distance relationships. They're tough to manage, but—"

"Long distance! I'll have to move out of the loft, but with four kids I'll darn sure want to stay within walking distance of the school."

"You won't return to Texas? You'll uproot them again?"

"I'm staying in Eternity Springs. I don't really have a choice. For one thing, I don't have a studio in Texas any longer, but more important than that, you are there. I'm not willing to give you up."

Wow. Okay.

Rose absorbed what he'd just said. He wasn't going to give her up.

It might not be the L *word, but it's more than I expected.*

"Now, if the prospect of the added baggage on my end scares you off, that's understandable," he continued. "But I'll warn you, I won't stop trying to convince you to reconsider."

His reassurance warmed her like the Caribbean sun. Attempting to lighten the moment, she teased, "Looking for an extra pair of babysitter hands?"

"An extra pair or twelve. You have lots of friends in town, and I'm no fool." His fleeting grin was a cross between boyish and sheepish, but then he grew serious.

"All kidding aside, *Bellissima*, I want to promise here and now that while I'll be eternally grateful for help, I won't abuse it. I've been on that side of the situation. I know what it's like to feel as though your good will and good intentions are being taken advantage of. I won't do that to you. At least, not intentionally. If I do, you call me on it."

He rubbed the back of his neck as his thoughts went a different direction.

"I wonder what sort of legal hoops we will need to jump through. I should probably call a lawyer. Wonder if I need a Texas attorney or one in Colorado."

"You've met Mac Timberlake, haven't you? Ali's husband?"

"Isn't he a judge?"

"He retired from the federal bench. He has a legal practice in Eternity Springs, and I'm sure he could point you in the right direction."

Cicero grimaced. "The prospect of legal bills is almost as much fun as doctor bills. What do you think—wait—that's Misty."

The nine-year-old walked into the park holding an apple in her right hand and a dog leash in her left. At the other end of the leash, a dachshund sniffed his way through the grass.

"Oh, no," Cicero muttered. "No. No. No. I might take four kids home with me, but I draw the line at dogs."

"What do you have against dogs?"

"Nothing. I like dogs." He narrowed his eyes and added, "I think she's crying."

Rose gave the girl a closer look, and when she spied the back of the hand carrying the red apple take a swipe at Misty's cheek, she knew that Cicero was right.

"I wonder what that's about."

"If Amy popped off and said something to her about kicking the kids out, I swear I won't be responsible for my actions."

Cicero tucked the basketball beneath an arm and started toward the girl.

"Hey, kid!"

Misty halted abruptly and looked up at Cicero, her eyes going round. "Uncle Hunk. What are you doing here?"

He ignored her question. "Are you okay? Why are you crying?"

"I'm okay." Her little chin came up. "I'm not crying, Uncle Hunk."

"You are too crying, and you have to quit calling me that," he groused. "What's wrong? Did Amy say something to you?"

The young girl frowned. "About what?"

"Well—about me. Didn't Amy tell you I was here?"

"No." Misty darted a curious look toward Rose. "I haven't been home yet. I walk Rooster every day after the bus drops me off. I earn ten dollars a week."

"What rooster?"

"Rooster!" Misty pointed toward the dachshund. "He's our next-door neighbor's dog."

"A dog named Rooster? What the—never mind." Cicero placed his hand on Rose's shoulder. "Do you remember Dr. Anderson from Eternity Springs?"

"Yes, of course. She put Galen's arm in a cast. Hello, Dr. Anderson."

Misty started to smile, but then she dropped her apple and brought her hand to her mouth. "Is something wrong with Galen?" she asked, her eyes anxious. "Is there a problem? Does his arm have cancer?"

"No, no, no," Rose hastened to assure her. "I'm not here as a doctor, but a friend. I've been visiting Bella Vita with your uncle."

"Oh." A world of relief hung in that single word. "Oh."

The pudgy little wiener dog waddled over toward Rose. She squatted down and scratched the dog behind the ears as Cicero said, "Back to my question. Why are you upset, Worm?"

She gave her shoulders a shrug, darted a look up at him, then returned her attention to the dog.

"It's nothing."

Cicero frowned down at her, then reached out and tipped her chin up until she met his gaze.

"I may not know much about ankle biters, but I *do* know women. Even young women. Nothing never means nothing. You haven't been home, so I'm guessing something happened at school. Do I need to go over there and knock some heads together?"

"Uncle Hunk!" she gasped. "No!"

"Well, I want to know—"

"It's private!" Misty exclaimed. "My personal

231

business. Can't a girl have a little privacy?"

That took Cicero aback. He shot a panicked look toward Rose.

"Private? Is she—she's not old enough—oh." His gaze turned pleading. "Rose," he begged.

Rose rolled her eyes.

"Go take Rooster for a walk and give me a minute to speak with Misty."

"Oh. Okay. That's a good idea."

Misty handed him the leash and he awkwardly patted her hand before making a fast retreat.

"What was that about?" Misty asked.

Matter-of-factly, Rose asked, "Has anyone spoken with you about getting your period?"

The girl nodded.

"Like a lot of men, Hunter is deathly afraid of that subject."

"He thinks I—oh." Comprehension dawned across her freckled dusted face. Her cheeks reddened, and she shook her head back and forth. "That's not it. I probably don't have to worry about that for a year or two. Mama told me. Two girls in my class say they get it, but I'm not sure they're telling the truth. One of them lies a lot anyway, and the other just goes along with what the first girl says."

"I don't want to invade your privacy, Misty, but your Uncle Hunt is worried about you. Is there anything we can tell him to ease his concern? You *did* look upset."

Misty glanced toward Cicero, then looked down at her feet. "It's all okay. Really. We will be fine. My mama told me we might have some rough patches, but that it would all work out in the end."

"You're having a rough patch now?"

Misty kicked at a yellow dandelion with the scuffed toe of her sneaker.

"It's an adjustment."

She'd repeated the sentence as if she'd heard others say it many times. Knowing the power of expectant silence, Rose waited.

"I don't want to go home. Scott and Amy have been fighting a lot and yesterday was especially bad because Keenan answered Scott's work cellphone and it was his boss and Scott got really, really mad. Then Galen ate too much candy and threw up on Scott's shoes and when Amy was cleaning it up, she threw up, too. And then she told him she's pregnant! They're going to have their own baby, and I just know that they won't want us anymore because we're too much trouble and we're not really their kids!"

Rose's heart broke for Misty and her siblings. Children were bright. They picked up on under-currents in a household more often than not. It wasn't her place to inform Misty of pending changes in her life, so she attempted to reassure.

"Honey, in my heart of hearts, I agree with your mother. It will work out for you all. And here's something else: You can trust your Uncle Hunk and you can depend on him."

Misty's lips twitched. "He doesn't like that nickname."

"Which is why it's so much fun to use." She held out her hand toward Misty. "Shall we go rescue Rooster from the Incredible Uncle Hunk?"

She glanced around the park for Cicero and saw that he had his cellphone to his ear, and was listening intently. When he started to talk in an animated manner waving his arms around, she reconsidered. "On second thought, they seem to be doing okay and there's something else I'd really love to do."

At Misty's curious look, she tilted her head toward the swing set. "I love to swing, but I'm a little embarrassed to be a grown-up and swinging by myself. Would you swing with me and give me an excuse to have fun while we wait for Hunter to finish his call?"

"I guess so."

Rose wasn't lying. She did love to swing. It brought out the child in her. She and Sage had spent a lot of time in parks while growing up. Throughout the world, the military base housing where they'd lived invariably had parks with swing sets. She and Sage would sit in swings side by side, and their father would take turns pushing them. More than once, she'd used this same excuse to swing with one of her patients in Davenport Park in Eternity Springs.

May in South Texas wasn't April in Paris, but it wasn't bad at all. Temperatures hovered in the low eighties with comfortable humidity, and the perfume of fresh mown grass drifted in the air. Pink Knock Out roses bloomed in abundance in beds around the park. Rose focused on a woman accompanied by a toddler and pushing a stroller as she set her swing moving. For a few minutes, she allowed herself to dream.

Cicero was going to accept the guardianship of four children. They were going to live in Eternity Springs. He said she mattered to him. What if—

A hand rested against her back and gave her a strong push. Hunter, she thought as she sailed toward the stars.

He's good at sending a woman to heaven.

They spent almost ten minutes swinging, and with every whoosh into the sky, Rose's hopes rose. In the last couple of months, her life path had taken an unexpected curve. She mattered to Hunt Cicero. Maybe, just maybe, she could matter to these motherless children, too.

Cicero was shell-shocked. Two days after arriving in Houston for a short visit with Jayne's children, he was leaving, heading back to Eternity Springs. He wasn't flying to Amarillo to pick up his car. Nope. He was driving a rented mom-mobile. An

SUV with an extra seat in the back and a car-top storage carrier packed full of all the worldly goods of four homeless children fixed to a luggage rack.

A luggage rack! It was a nightmare right out of the movies. He was no longer Cicero, glass artist and womanizer extraordinaire. He was Clark Griswold in *National Lampoon's Vacation.* All he lacked was Cousin Eddie.

What the hell am I doing?

It was a ten-hour drive to Amarillo and, factoring one stop every two hours, he had planned for them to arrive by eight o'clock tonight. Only they stopped four times the first hour. The first hour!

"We'll be lucky to make it home by the Fourth of July," he groused to Rose as she buckled Daisy into the car seat after yet another dirty diaper.

Thank God for Rose. He didn't know what he'd have done without her. Every time he got shaky about his decision to take the kids, she was there to offer a steadying hand. She showed extraordinary kindness and patience with the babbling horde, both individually and as a group—and she'd used her professional credentials to put Scott Parnell in his place when he questioned Cicero's suitability as a guardian.

The ass, Cicero mentally muttered for the thousandth time since informing the Parnells of his decision. He figured that the underlying reason for Scott's attitude was guilt. He didn't know how the man could sleep at night, breaking his promise to four children and a dead woman.

Cicero could understand how a person might get cold feet at the notion of taking responsibility for the half-pint demons, but once he made the commitment, he should follow through.

At dinner the previous evening, Scott had announced the move as Amy dished up spaghetti and meatballs. The kids had taken the news as well as could be expected, he'd thought. The live wire, Keenan, had asked if kids played T-ball in Eternity Springs. Misty then had asked Amy if she'd assume responsibility for the afternoon walk of Rooster. Galen had looked from his older sister to his brother and back to his sister again then started crying. Even the baby seemed to sense the tension in the air.

Cicero had seriously considered decking Scott Parnell with a roundhouse to the jaw. And Amy? Well, he'd give her some leeway due to her pregnancy and the fact that she was married to a prick, but those arguments only went so far. She'd broken a vow. Jayne was liable to find a way to haunt her.

"Uncle Skunk, he's touching me," Galen whined from the back seat. "Tell him to stop touching me."

"He got on my side. Tell him to stay on his own side. Are we there yet?"

Cicero curled his lip as he looked into the rearview mirror.

"Don't make me stop this car. If you make me stop this car, you'll be oh so sorry."

"Why is that, Uncle Hunk?"

"Because I'll take all of your DVDs and leave them by the side of the road."

"And who exactly is that punishing?" Rose mumbled.

"I know. But it sounds good."

The threat shut them up for all of thirty seconds. The kids argued about what movie to watch on the DVD player, but when they finally settled on *Frozen*, they quieted.

Cicero brooded. They were leaving Texas under tenuous legal circumstances. Officially, the Parnells remained the legal guardians of the horde and would for some time. Mac Timberlake had done what he could to facilitate the legal transfer of guardianship, but he'd cautioned Cicero that permanent arrangements would take some time and require jumping through some hoops. In the meantime, the children were officially "visiting" Colorado.

"I need to pee, Uncle Skunk."

If I don't pinch their heads off and bury them in shallow graves before we reach Dallas.

The three younger children finally fell asleep somewhere in north central Texas. In the far backseat, Misty appeared to be absorbed in her book, so Cicero thought it safe enough to attempt a quiet conversation with Rose.

"You are certainly getting more than you bargained for. I wouldn't blame you if you changed your mind and had me drop you at the nearest airport. Or rental car agency, for that matter. This is road trip torture, and we're only a little over halfway done for the day."

"I'm fine and you shouldn't view it as torture," Rose replied. "You should think of it as making memories for you and your family."

His family. The words, the idea, sank into his gut like a stone. He glanced into the rearview mirror to see that Misty had dozed off, too.

Softly, he said, "The family I didn't sign up for. I didn't want."

"I'm calling B.S. on that right now."

He looked over at her in surprise.

Rose shifted in her seat to face him and folded her arms. "I'm no psychologist, but it's clear to me after seeing you with Gabi and Flynn, with Mitch and the people on Bella Vita, and then with these kiddos, that you want family more than most. You make family everywhere you go."

"That's crazy," he protested. "I'm all about being footloose and carefree."

"Sure you are. That's why since we left Eternity Springs on vacation you've called one former foster mom to wish her happy birthday; called a different foster mother and father to wish them happy anniversary; you've attended a birthday party for someone you call *Mama;* you've scheduled a bachelor party for a friend you sometimes call *Bro;* and you're taking four children home to raise. That's only in the past two weeks. No telling what family related things you did the two weeks before that, or what you'll do in the two weeks upcoming."

Cicero scowled and punched the gas to get around an 18-wheeler.

"You have a point, but I've never looked at it that way before."

"I think because of Elizabeth, I've thought about the definition of family a lot. The genetic bond is important, but it's certainly not the only way to create a family. Family is what you make it, Hunt. From my perspective, you've done a fantastic job making yours."

"I'm afraid I've bitten off more than I can chew."

Rose glanced into the backseats.

"It won't be easy, but I suspect you'll find it the most rewarding thing you've ever done."

"I'm just thankful that the day care will have room for them by midsummer. Though, if the glass thing doesn't work out, I'm going to go into that racket. The price they get for child care makes my head spin. Of course, they'll earn every penny with these monsters. That reminds me, when we stop next time, help me remember to call the realtor, would you? She should have heard something from the homeowners by now."

He'd put out the word that he was looking for a rental in town, close to the school. Rose's sister had tipped him off to a suitable rental that might be available soon, and he was hoping to learn that the rent would be within his reach. In the meantime, Celeste had offered him a reduced rate for the same cottage at Angel's Rest where he'd stayed with the kids in February. She truly was an angel.

The urchins woke up and after what must have been the three thousandth potty stop of the day, they launched a new version of travel torture—they started singing. For ninety minutes, four voices belted out Disney tunes—and on a couple of songs, five voices since Rose chimed in—until finally, Cicero's ears and nerves could stand no more.

"Enough!" he roared. "That's enough. I want five minutes of quiet. I'm going crazy."

The kids went silent. For about twenty seconds.

Then Galen said, "I want to go crazy, Uncle Skunk. Can I go crazy, too?"

"Too!" Daisy squealed. "Too! Too! Too! Too!"

They stopped for dinner and a mental health break at the next burger joint he spied. The kids ate burgers, fries, and milkshakes and he had hopes that carbo-loading would put them to sleep. Instead, half an hour later, Keenan puked all over his brother, which started a chain reaction.

Since showers were needed and nerves were

fried, they stopped early for the night. That's when Cicero discovered yet another unhappy reality necessitated by the change in his circumstances. He needed to rent two rooms. Because the hellions were young and impressionable, they divided up into girls and boys.

Having four kids around was going to play hell with his sex life.

As he pulled Rose into the hallway for some privacy to kiss her good night, he observed, "I have one question. How did Jayne manage to get pregnant so many times?"

He entered his room with Rose's laughter ringing in his ears.

For the first time in more than two weeks, he slept alone. He didn't like it. He tossed and turned and learned that Galen talked in his sleep. A lot. And Keenan? Well, from this moment on the kid wasn't allowed to eat grilled onions if the two of them were sleeping in the same room.

Cicero awoke the next morning tired and cranky and facing another extraordinarily long day behind the wheel. The guttersnipes were perky and rambunctious and loud. Cicero's head pounded before they reached the city limits of the north central Texas town. In self-defense, he made two stops, the first at a branch of his bank, and the second at a dollar store. At the bank, he changed two twenties for ones. At the store, he refused to let the children go inside, but he effectively stopped the whining when he asked, "If you had to pick one favorite candy what would it be?"

Five minutes later, he returned to the car with pads of drawing paper, four packs of crayons, and the biggest bag of Hershey's KISSES the store sold. He got into the car, passed out the drawing supplies, then lowered his sunglasses, and threatened. "You can draw, you can watch a movie, you can sleep. No whining about him being on your side. No asking if we're there yet. For one solid, blessed hour, I want quiet. For every fifteen minutes of peace and quiet I get, you get a piece of candy and a dollar, *if* there are any left."

"Are you going to eat them all, Uncle Skunk?" Keenan asked.

"I'm not going to eat any of them. I'm a 3 MUSKETEERS–man. But every time one of you makes so much as a peep, I'm throwing a KISS and a buck out the window. When the bag is empty, it's empty. When the money's gone, it's gone."

"Really?" Galen asked.

"Really."

"You won't throw money out the window," Keenan accused.

"Just watch me."

He started the SUV, rolled down the window, tore open the plastic candy bag, and tossed four foil-wrapped KISSES onto the asphalt parking lot.

Misty gasped. "Uncle Hunter!"

"You littered!" Keenan accused.

"Don't make me do it again."

In the passenger seat, Rose snorted. Then she reached into the bag and swiped a handful of KISSES and murmured, "My emergency stash."

Cicero nodded to her, shifted the car into gear, and headed out of town. The scamps didn't learn real fast. In the first ten miles, he threw fifteen pieces of candy and seven dollars out of the window. Finally, though, they seemed to catch on and for a gloriously quiet half an hour, he heard only whispered comments. The hoodlums really did like their sugar fix.

They drew for a while, and watched another Disney DVD. For this first leg of the trip, the boys had the backseat and the girls the middle one. He pretended he didn't hear Daisy sing along to *The Lion King* directly behind him. You couldn't hold a two-year-old to the same candy standards as you did the older kids. All in all, he considered the idea a success because it bought him peace and quiet for a hundred miles.

He was feeling pretty good about things as they rolled through the Panhandle of Texas. Cotton fields lined either side of the road. He had the cruise control set, the Stones playing on the stereo loud enough to drown out the sound of the movie

Frozen coming—yet again—from the DVD player. Beside him, Rose read the romance novel that she'd purchased at the last gas station. He remembered a study he'd read in a magazine a while back that said how women who read romance novels had more and better sex than other women.

Works for me.

The flashing red lights came up behind him fast. Frowning, he glanced down at his speedometer. He was legal. Maybe they'd go around.

He tapped his brakes and pulled over toward the shoulder. The cop car kept coming, falling in behind him. He muttered a curse, and applied the brakes as Rose said, "There's a roadblock ahead."

"Wonderful," he replied. "Must be some sort of checkpoint. I wasn't speeding."

"What's going on, Uncle Hunk?" Misty asked.

"It looks like Dudley Do-Right is about to tell us."

Dudley and his partner, he corrected, seeing two highway patrolmen approach either side of the car. In front of them, another patrol car eased toward them. A flutter of unease rolled through Cicero. They were in the middle of nowhere, Texas. Something about this didn't feel one bit right. He rolled down his window.

The officer placed his hand on the grip of his sidearm. "I need your hands up where I can see them. Right now."

"Officer, what's this—"

"Now. Hands up!"

Cicero's chin dropped open in shock but he raised his hands, as the other officer said to Rose, "You, too, lady. Hands up."

"I want you out of the car," said the first officer. "You, too, ma'am."

In the backseats, children began to wail.

"Don't shoot Uncle Hunk," Misty cried.

"He didn't mean to litter!" Keenan added.

A brush or two with the law during his wild twenties had taught Cicero that the best way to handle a situation like this was to follow directions and keep his mouth shut. So when the trooper told him to place his hands flat against the car and spread his legs, he did it without protest.

As the officer frisked him, Cicero spied the piece of drawing paper propped in the window beside Keenan. In red crayon, it read:

Help!
I've been kid-naped.

Cicero banged his forehead against the mom-mobile. Hard.

Thirteen

"He did *what?*" Shannon O'Toole asked with a gasp in her voice as she handed Daisy a doll to hold. At Celeste's request, a large group of friends were gathering at the community center building three days after Rose's return to Eternity Springs, which had been a day later than planned, due to the events in the Texas Panhandle.

"Keenan put a sign in the car window saying he'd been kidnapped," Rose replied. "He'd seen it on TV and thought it would be a good idea to do it, too."

"Oh, my gosh. I'm torn between horror and laughter. What did Cicero do?"

"Before or after the trooper pulled his stun gun?" Rose dryly asked.

Shannon's chin dropped, but then she couldn't hold back the laughter as Rose gave her a blow-by-blow report of the event. "You can't blame the troopers. They were doing their job. But our circumstances were unusual to say the least, and it took some time to get everyone on the same page. The fact that Cicero had already contacted Mac Timberlake and gotten the ball rolling on a formal custody arrangement made everything so much simpler."

"Is that going to be involved?"

"Not really. The Parnells have provided the documentation he needs in order to enroll the kids in school or approve any medical treatment they need, but Child Protective Services in Texas will need to work with CPS in Colorado to get the details ironed out. He'll have a court appearance. It'll take a while."

The arrival of more of their friends interrupted any further conversation between Shannon and Rose. Everyone exchanged greetings, then Celeste stepped onto the dais at the front of the room.

"Good afternoon, my dears. Thank you all for coming. As you most likely have heard, we have four new pint-sized citizens to welcome to town. It's the Eternity Springs way for us to help, and after speaking with Cicero and Rose, I thought a bit of formal organization was in order. To recap the situation, these poor dears lost their mother in January and now our own Cicero has stepped up and brought them to live with him. I know we all want to help welcome these children to town. Cicero will be moving into the Garfields' house once school is out in June, and Brandy and the children are able to join Greg who is loving his new job in Connecticut, by the way. In the meantime, they're living in one of my cottages, and he has the basic necessities that he needs to provide their care. Of course, being a bachelor, he has little beyond those necessities. I thought it would be fun to throw a welcome party in June and shower these little ones and our friend Hunter with things they're going to need."

"That'll be fun," Sarah Murphy said, pulling up the calendar app on her phone. "Do you have a date picked out?"

"I have three. Let's see what works best for everyone, shall we?"

Once the date was agreed upon, Celeste brought up the next item on the agenda. "Hunter will enroll the oldest two of the group in school tomorrow, but Little Angels Day Care won't have room until mid-June, I'm afraid. He's going to need help with babysitting, especially for the younger two. I want to give him a list of people to call. If you're willing to volunteer, please add your name and number to the signup sheet I'm sending around. Include your usual availability."

Celeste passed around a clipboard, then turned to Rose.

"Did you have something you wanted to say to the group?"

"I do. Thank you, Celeste." Rose stood up and hugged the older woman. "I don't believe it takes a village to raise a child. It takes an angel. Thank God we have you."

Turning to face her friends, she added, "Thank God we have all of you."

She surveyed the room. Nic Callahan was signing her name to the babysitting roll. Hope Romano rocked her fussy eleven-month-old in her arms. Savannah Turner was hurrying to corral her newly crawling eight-month-old and Gabi Romano and her mother Maggie played a silent game of peek-a-boo with Sarah Murphy's Michael whose second birthday was coming up. Ali Timberlake held Sage's three-year-old, Racer, as Cat Davenport pulled a plastic cup full of dry Cheerios from her diaper bag to offer to her two-year-old Johnny.

A sudden lump formed in Rose's throat and she fought back tears. She shifted Daisy from one hip to the other. For the first time since she moved to Eternity Springs and these women began marrying and reproducing like rabbits, she felt like she belonged.

She continued. "Since none of you have asked me about my vacation with Hunt, I figure you must have made a collective agreement to respect my privacy."

"No, that's not it at all," Gabi said. "I've been keeping them up-to-date on developments. Mitch kept me apprised."

Rose laughed. "Why am I not surprised?"

Nic said, "We're your friends and we're happy to see you happy, Rose. Anything we can do to help you stay that way, we're glad to do."

"Absolutely," Sarah added. "If an apple a day keeps the doctor away, I figure an hour of baby-sitting now and again surely helps her to stay."

"Well, on Hunt's behalf, I can't thank you

enough. The man is pitifully overwhelmed, what with his regular work schedule and Whimsies opening later this week and now all that needs doing where the children are concerned. I'm doing what I can to help, but after being gone for more than two weeks, my clinic schedule is packed."

For the next half hour, the women talked and discussed and scheduled. Gabi quizzed Rose about her impressions of Bella Vita. In full mother-of-the-bride mode, Maggie not so subtly inquired about the status of Rose's love life by asking if Rose wanted her to save all of her notes on wedding vendors.

"You're getting way ahead of us there, Maggie."

"Nevertheless, I'll copy my file for you. I do have a soft spot in my heart for Cicero. I want him to be happy."

Rose considered the harried man who'd handed over Daisy along with a diaper bag empty of diapers—but filled with Keenan's baseball glove and cleats—this morning. "Once he learns of all this help you all are offering, he'll be ecstatic, I'm sure."

"While you're copying wedding vendor lists, would you mind making one for me?" Ali asked. "Just in case."

"Just in case?" Sarah repeated. "Are wedding bells gonna chime for the Timberlakes?"

"Maybe." Ali gave Sarah a crooked smile. "Chase is coming home over Memorial Day and bringing his girlfriend to meet us. A note in his voice gave me a heads-up. I won't be at all surprised if they're engaged."

"That's nice," Rose said. Then, seeing the wistful smile that Sarah and Ali shared, she added, "Isn't it?"

"Yes, it is," Sarah replied, giving a firm nod. "You want him to be happy, Ali."

"I do. I really do. It's just that Mac and I had hoped he'd satisfy his wanderlust and come home and settle down. With a local girl."

With Lori Murphy, Rose thought, recalling that Sarah's daughter and Ali's son had been sweethearts for a while. Their life paths had taken them in different directions, and they'd parted friends. Now Chase Timberlake made his living doing sports adventure photography all over the world. Lori Murphy was in vet school at Colorado State.

"How long has he been dating this girl?"

"Around eight months, I believe," Ali responded. "Maybe a little longer. He talked about bringing her home at Thanksgiving, but they got a last minute assignment. They work together. They've both been in Chile for the past month."

"I'll bet you're looking forward to seeing him," Rose said.

"Oh, I am. It's been entirely too long. We get to see the other two kids every six weeks or so, but my wanderer doesn't stay in one place long enough for us to catch up to him. It leaves me with a hole in my heart."

"Kids can do that to you," Rose observed.

Sarah hitched her little Michael up on her hip, then gave Ali a one-armed hug. "Well, he's coming home in a couple of weeks, and he's bringing a maybe daughter-in-law with him. Perhaps you'll get that grandchild you've been wanting."

Grinning, Ali scooped Michael from his mother's arms. "If not, you and Sage are doing a fine job of filling that particular hole in my heart. Oh, Mikey"—Ali gave his chubby cheek a smooch—"you feel so good in my arms."

Rose clutched Daisy's twenty-some pounds a little tighter. She knew the feeling. Her arms were fuller than they'd been in what felt like forever.

Cicero didn't share her point of view.

"I'm trying not to take that comment personally," he grumbled into the phone later that evening after she'd repeated the sentiment to him. "I feel like I've been replaced by a snot machine."

Sitting in the window seat of her attic apartment at Angel's Rest, she stared across the grounds of the estate toward the lighted windows of the cottage where Cicero and his new family lay tucked in their beds.

Grinning, she said, "Stop whining."

"I'm serious. We have to find some time to be alone together. How about I sneak out and up to your room right now?"

"No, Hunt. You cannot leave those children alone in the cabin."

"I've done it before. Misty can—"

"No. Nine is too young. You are lucky nothing bad happened. Anyway, it's late. I worked a double shift today, and I have the early shift tomorrow."

"I miss you," he complained, a hint of a whine in his voice.

His words warmed her like brandy on a February night. "I miss you, too."

His voice dropped to a low, needy rumble. "What time do you get off work tomorrow?"

"Two o'clock."

"Oh yeah?"

She heard a rustling of paper, then he said, "Huh. Tuesday afternoons are tough. Looks like Maggie Romano is a possibility. Think it's too late to call her tonight?"

"For what?"

"Babysitting. She's on the list. Available until three p.m. I'd like more time, of course, but I can do good work under pressure. It could tide us over until—when is your day off?"

"Friday."

He groaned. "Friday is bad. We have the soft

opening of Whimsies. But you could come over after the shop closes. You could sleep over."

"We've had this discussion. I'm not sleeping over."

"But—"

"Good night, Hunt. Sweet dreams."

"*Bella Rosa*," he protested.

The sound of her name on his lips was lovely music by which to fall asleep.

Days passed, and they slowly established a bit of a routine. Cicero got the older children off to school and dropped the younger two with the volunteer babysitters of the day. Having a constantly changing group of playmates who weren't his siblings allowed Galen to thrive. Daisy proved to be different. As the days went on, she grew anxious, fussy, and extra clingy. Cicero fretted and asked Rose to give the little girl a thorough medical checkup.

Recognizing that what ailed the two-year-old was the lack of stability in her life, Rose took action. She proposed a solution to bridge the gap until day-care slots opened up. "I'll switch to evening shifts until school is out," she told Cicero as she lay naked in his arms during a stolen half hour in the bed of his studio loft apartment. "I'll keep Daisy and Galen in the mornings."

He rolled up onto his elbow, resting his head against his hand, and frowned down at her.

"That'd be great. Except—what about you and me? We won't ever have time alone."

"Welcome to parenthood, Uncle Hunk."

"This really sucks." He flopped back on the bed. "We have all the responsibility, but we didn't get the playtime that created it."

"Oh, hush. You've had plenty of playtime."

"Not lately."

"Absence makes the heart grow fonder."

"My heart isn't the organ that's giving me grief."

She picked up her phone from the bedside table and checked the time. "I still have twenty minutes. It's too bad you're not up for another—"

He was on her in seconds—and she was ten minutes late to work.

For the next week, Rose reveled in motherhood. As Racer Rafferty's aunt, she was no stranger to babysitting, but this was different. These children —all four of them—had already made a place for themselves in her heart. Little Daisy with her chubby cheeks and shy disposition. Galen, who teetered between boyhood and babyhood. Keenan, the oh-so-live wire. And Misty, the quiet, thought-ful, still-waters-run-deep sort of girl. A part of Rose knew she should protect herself. The relationship with Cicero was still new, and experience had taught her that her heart could be shredded when she least expected it. But life was so good now, so fulfilling.

For the first time in a very long time, Dr. Rose Anderson was well and truly happy.

In hindsight, she wasn't the least bit surprised when that happiness came crashing down on top of her.

"What's the matter with Rose, Uncle Hunk?" Misty asked on the eve of Memorial Day weekend as they sat down to a supper of beans and weenies and broccoli that nobody would eat.

"What?" Cicero asked. "What do you mean? Did something happen?"

"That's what I'm asking you."

He looked at her blankly.

"For heaven's sake, Uncle Hunt. Don't you notice anything?" Misty rolled her eyes in disgust. "Rose isn't acting right."

"What do you mean she's not acting right?"

"Uh, *duh*. You really are clueless, aren't you?"

"Hey. Watch your mouth."

She sniffed huffily. "You should watch your girlfriend closer. She didn't go to Galen's T-ball practice yesterday and she left Daisy with Mrs. Rafferty so that she could go running. Today, her eyes were swollen as if she'd been crying."

Cicero speared a hunk of hot dog with his fork and chewed it slowly, considering Misty's comments. He hadn't noticed Rose having swollen eyes. Wouldn't he notice something like that? "It's springtime. She probably has allergies."

"Sure." Misty gave an exaggerated roll of her eyes.

"She's spent all her spare time with you guys. She's due a little time to herself."

"Right."

Keenan glanced up from his plate. "I saw her cry."

"What? When?"

"Yesterday. Daisy called her Mama, and Dr. Rose told her not to call her that, then she burst into tears. Daisy started crying, too."

Huh. Absently, Cicero spooned a stalk of broccoli onto his plate. He didn't like broccoli, didn't know how it had ended up in his refrigerator, and he didn't really want to eat it. But he had to set an example, didn't he? Ranch dressing might make it more palatable.

He grabbed the Ranch bottle from the fridge, then squirted some on his plate. He speared the broccoli with his fork, swirled it in salad dressing, and ate it. Now that he thought about it, Rose had acted a bit distant the past week or so. Last night when she'd begged off stopping by the cottage for a glass of wine after her shift, claiming to be tired. And she'd canceled the "lunch" he'd gone to great lengths to arrange for them after they'd gone an entire week without managing to have sex.

Something was wrong. He'd been too busy to see it.

He had a flash of memory of their fight on the

island, when she'd declared she wasn't a doormat. Had he been treating her that way? Was this his fault?

He rose from the table and carried his plate to the sink. He rinsed it, loaded it into the dish-washer, and tried to recall their interactions during recent days. Yes, she'd skipped the T-ball game, but she'd gone kite flying with them. She'd seemed perfectly fine day before yesterday when he got tied up with work and called because he was going to be late. She'd flat-out told him not to worry, that she'd find a sitter. She hadn't bothered to scold him at all.

Yes. Something was definitely wrong.

He glanced at the clock on the microwave. Her shift wasn't over for a couple of hours yet. "What sort of homework do you have tonight, Keenan?"

"I don't have none."

"You don't have any."

"That's what I said," Keenan replied, his eyes going round with exasperation.

"You have homework every night. What is it? Math? Reading?"

The boy scowled, but he eventually admitted, "Math."

"Go do it now."

"My mommy didn't make me do my home-work."

"I'm not your mommy. Misty, what about you?"

"I did my homework after school."

Of course she had.

"I want homework. Can I have homework?" Galen asked.

"Yeah. Get the broom and sweep the kitchen floor."

"What?"

"This is your home. Sweeping is work."

The kid lit up like a July Fourth sparkler, and as he scampered to find the broom, Cicero lifted Daisy out of the high chair. Her chubby little legs kicked and she chortled. Cicero's grin died as his nose wrinkled. "Oh, geez. Another dirty diaper, Squirt?"

He looked from the baby to Misty. "Worm? Sweetheart?"

"Nope. Your turn."

She returned her attention to her book—*Old Yeller*, he noted. Great. He'd have another crying female to deal with before long.

Sighing, he carted the toddler into the bedroom and plopped her down on the changing table Celeste had provided. He was getting pretty good at the diaper changing thing, but this particular one had gone nuclear, and it took him some time to get her cleaned up.

He was fighting her chubby little legs into a romper when Misty joined him. He started to ask if the dog was dead yet, but she had interest rather than tears in her eyes, so he deduced the answer to the question before she asked, "So what do you think is wrong with Rose?"

"I don't know, but I'm going to ask her."

"You are?"

"Yep. When Captain Arithmetic finishes his homework, I thought we'd walk over to the ice cream shop and take some to her."

Misty slumped with obvious relief.

"I'll check on Keenan."

"Do not do his homework for him!"

Half an hour later, they stood in the ice cream shop choosing flavors. The kids picked theirs quickly. They took some time debating what flavor to choose for Rose. Finally, they settled on strawberry—because, Galen insisted, she had a pink name.

Keenan pointed out that some roses were yellow so maybe they should get her a dip of lemon chiffon and another of vanilla for white roses. "And then we should all get three dips so that it's fair."

"Forget it, Boyo." Cicero ruffled Keenan's hair. "Life isn't fair."

"I know. If it was fair, Mommy wouldn't have died." The matter-of-fact way he said it gave Cicero's heart a twist.

Cicero brooded as they walked the rest of the way to the clinic. For a man who knew a whole lot about women, he apparently didn't know very much about women. How had he missed Rose's recent distance toward him and the hellions?

Why had it taken a nine-year-old to call his attention to trouble with his love life?

Because he was swimming as hard as he could manage just to keep his head above water, that's why.

He held Daisy in his arms and brought up the rear as Keenan pushed open the clinic door. He and Galen rushed inside. Misty offered, "I'll hold Daisy while you talk to Dr. Rose."

He considered a moment, then nodded. "Thanks."

Keenan rushed up to the desk where a receptionist checked in the patients and declared, "We brought Dr. Rose ice cream. Three scoops! But in a cup because Uncle Hunk said the dips would slip and fall off the cone if Dr. Rose had a patient and couldn't eat it right away."

The middle-aged receptionist whom Cicero knew also worked part-time at the local sandwich shop smiled at Keenan. "That's very smart of your Uncle Hunk. I'm afraid Dr. Rose isn't here right now. Are you here just to visit or does one of you need to see a doctor? Dr. Sage is covering for Dr. Rose this evening."

"Really?" Cicero frowned. She hadn't said anything to him about having the night off. He wondered what had come up. Even as he framed a question to ask, an inner door swung open and Sage Rafferty strode into the waiting room wearing a white coat and carrying a tablet computer.

"Lena, what is the password for—" Spying the demons, she broke off. "Hello, kiddos. Is someone not feeling well?"

"We brought ice cream for Doctor Rose," Keenan said.

"Three scoops," Galen added.

Sage's lips twitched. "If my sister eats three scoops of ice cream then she'll be the one with a tummy ache." Glancing up at Cicero, she said, "I guess I misunderstood. She's making a run into Gunnison for supplies for our clinic—though it's really an excuse to eat Mexican food for supper. I thought you were going with her."

That bit of news sparked his temper.

"No. Though we talked about going." Just yesterday. He'd told her that he'd been craving Mexican food. "When did this trip come up?"

"This morning."

Sage's brow creased, but before she could say more, Keenan piped up. "Can I eat Doctor Rose's ice cream since she's not here?"

"No," Cicero replied, a little more sharply than necessary. He scooped the paper dish out of the boy's hands. "I don't need any bellyaches tonight. I guess Rose and I got our wires crossed. C'mon, brats. Who wants to play a round of Putt-Putt on the way home?"

"Me! Me!" shouted the boys, dashing toward the door.

Cicero handed Sage the ice cream. "Here, you

have this. Isn't calcium good for expectant mothers? If you see your sister, tell her—"

"Yes?"

"Never mind. C'mon, Misty. We need to catch up with the hooligans before they decide to rob the liquor store on the way to miniature golf."

A few minutes later, when he set Daisy down in order to pull out his wallet and pay for the game, he absently rubbed his hand across his chest. Damned if this wasn't the strangest sensation, one he'd not experienced in what seemed like forever.

He felt like such a loser. Rose had hurt his feelings.

Fourteen

Weary from the drive and the burden of her worries, Rose chose not to deliver the clinic supplies upon her return to Eternity Springs. Instead, she set her alarm for half an hour earlier than usual, which would give her enough time to run by the clinic before picking up Daisy and Galen from Cicero. She hadn't expected to toss and turn all night, but she should have. She really hadn't been sleeping well at all.

When the alarm sounded, she ignored it for fifteen minutes, then dragged herself out of bed. She had to rush, including skipping her morning coffee, and as a result, she was a little frazzled and quite grumpy when she carried the first of three cardboard boxes into the clinic.

Discovering Sage there, lying in wait and wearing a scolding expression, didn't cheer her up one bit. Once her sister opened her mouth, Rose got downright cranky.

Sage demanded, "What's wrong with you?"

"Excuse me?"

"I hope I can. Are you consciously trying to sabotage your relationship with Cicero?"

Rose momentarily went still, then tried to recover with a breezy, "I don't know what you're talking about."

Sage spat a word that would have earned her son, Racer, a spanking had he said it. "You haven't acted like yourself for the past two weeks. This isn't like you. Something is going on. What is it, Rose? Did Cicero cheat on you or something?"

"What? No!"

"I didn't think so. It's obvious that he's in love with you."

Rose closed her eyes, her heart aching, as Sage recapped his visit to the clinic the previous night. "Maybe you didn't come out and tell an outright lie, but you darn sure misled him and me. That's not like you, sister. I want you to tell me just what the heck is going on."

In the face of her sister's direct command, Rose could no longer keep the news or her fears to herself.

"I have a lump in my breast," she said.

For an instant, Sage's countenance reflected a sister's natural concern and consternation, but then she shifted into physician mode, firing off a series of medical questions for which Rose had few good answers.

"What do you mean, you don't know?" Sage demanded.

"I haven't had a biopsy."

A frown line creased the bridge of Sage's nose. "What did the ultrasound show?"

When Rose didn't immediately respond, she said, "Honey?"

"I haven't had an ultrasound, either. I haven't seen my doctor."

"And you found this lump two weeks ago?"

"Ten days."

"Rosemary Jean Anderson! What in the world are you thinking?"

"That I'll get around to it when I'm ready. It's my body, my decision."

"That's bullshit," Sage shot back, her voice vibrating with anger. "You aren't alone this time, Rosemary. You have people who love you."

Sage couldn't understand. She had someone who loved her.

"Hunt has never said those words to me."

"I'm not talking about Hunt Cicero, though I do believe he loves you. I'm talking about me. About Colt. About Racer. We're your family and we definitely love you and we're not going to run out on you if times get tough."

Rose gritted her teeth. "No, I'll be the one running. Moving, anyway."

"What are you talking about?" Sage snapped, shaking her head. "Moving? Move where? Why?"

It would destroy her to leave, but if the cancer was back, she'd do it. Why stay here? Why watch the people she loved deal with her cancer? It would be as bad as the disease itself. Not to mention the fact that the small town clinic was merely that—a small town clinic.

"If the cancer is back, if it's spread, I won't be able to stay in Eternity Springs. We're equipped to deal with many medical issues here in this clinic, but cancer treatment isn't one of them. You can't argue with that."

"I don't care if you move to the moon for treatment, I'll be at your side."

"But your family, your life, is here. You're pregnant, for heaven's sake."

"Airplanes do exist, you know. And guess what? Celeste can fly on them, Nic and Sarah can, and Ali and Cat. Savannah. Hope. Maggie. Shoot, I think I'll buy Moon Airline stock today."

Rose didn't respond.

"What is the matter with you?" Sage roared. "You know better. You can't ignore this. Waiting kills people!"

Provoked, Rose shot back. "I'm afraid to find

out, all right? We're doctors. We know all the realities, all the statistics. But as a patient, it sucks, Sage. Because at the end of the day, in this, that's what I am—a patient in denial."

Blinking rapidly, Rose tried to keep the tears from falling. "I don't want to know, Sage, but not knowing is making me crazy. I'm scared to death to face this monster again!"

The anger drained from Sage's face. She reached for her sister and wrapped her in her arms. Rose clutched her in return, and sheltered by the loving embrace, allowed the tears to flow.

"I know you're afraid," Sage soothed. "I'm afraid, too. It's totally rational."

"Fate is such a vicious bitch. Just when I begin to hope and dream again. When I begin to think that maybe, just maybe, I might get my own happy ending, it kicks me in the teeth. Oh, Sage, I'm angry. Bone deep furious. Not just for me, either, but for Hunt and the kids."

"He won't desert you like Brandon did. He's not a scumbag."

"I know that. But I can't put them all through another bout of cancer. Those kids just lost their mother! They're just beginning to heal. I can't rip open that wound. It's better I stop this now before we all get in too deep."

Sage grabbed a tissue from a nearby box and wiped tears from her sister's cheeks. "I think that ship already has sailed. I won't make a call on what's between you and Cicero, but those children are already in your heart and you're in theirs. So, let's do what's best for those kiddos."

Sage made it all sound so damn easy.

It wasn't.

"We need to start with an exam," Sage continued, her tone brooking no argument. "We can do this a variety of ways. We can do a preliminary exam and sonogram here right now, we can call Lynda Rydzell and ask her to work you in, or we can call your oncologist in Denver and take his first available appointment."

Rose drew in a deep, shuddering breath. How much easier her burden seemed now, having shared it with her sister. And yet, she still wasn't ready to face a diagnosis.

"I'll call Lynda."

"Do you have your phone on you?"

"No. I'll call her later."

Sage gave her a look. "I have her number. We'll call now."

Ten minutes later, Rose had appointments with her regular doctor in Gunnison for an exam and possible biopsy later that afternoon. Once she disconnected the phone call, Sage said, "Colt is out of town himself today, but I'll call Nic and see if she'll watch Racer for me."

"No," Rose said. "Don't do that."

"You're not going on this appointment alone."

"No, I won't. I'll ask Hunt to go with me. If I'm

going to face this monster, I might as well do it. The drive will give us the chance to talk things over."

"What about the kids? I'm happy to babysit."

"With Colt away? Five kids and you pregnant? Not a good idea, Sage. If we do a biopsy, Lynda said she'd rush the results. I'll stay overnight to get them." Rose considered a moment, then said, "Celeste is already scheduled to watch the children after school. I'll ask if she's able to watch them overnight if need be. If not, I'll go down the list. Someone will step up. I'm sure."

"You let me know if they don't." Sage reached for her sister and gave her another hard hug. "We will deal with this. Whatever happens, we will deal."

"Okay." Rose glanced at her watch and said, "I need to run. Hunt will be needing to get to work."

"You let me know if he can't go with you, okay?"

"I will."

Rose meant it when she said it, but when she stopped by the cottage to pick up Daisy and Galen for the morning, she found that Cicero had already left for the studio. Celeste and the two youngest children waited for her.

"Hunter knocked on the kitchen door early this morning," Celeste said. "He needed to get to work early and asked if I could watch the children until you arrived."

Relief at the reprieve washed over Rose. She didn't want to face Cicero. Not yet. Not until she knew something one way or another. Sage's heart was in the right place, and she appreciated her caring and concern, but now that she was away from it, she really wanted to do this thing by herself.

She'd gone through cancer alone last time and she'd beaten it. As precedents went, that wasn't a bad one to follow.

"He was in a bear of a mood," Celeste continued. "Dealing with creative types can be challenging, can't it? But oh, so exciting, too. There's nothing like a creative fire to stoke the passions, don't you agree?"

"It does keep life interesting," Rose replied as she gathered little Daisy into her arms and held her tight.

For the next few hours, Rose did her best to soak in the simple joys of the morning and forget about the afternoon's impending storm clouds. She took Daisy and Galen on a walk, read to them, and baked chocolate chip cookies with Galen while Daisy napped. She packed picnic lunches and spread a blanket in the rose garden, and after they munched on peanut butter and jelly sandwiches, carrot sticks, and sliced apples, they lay on their backs and found shapes in the clouds.

She dropped the pair off at Maggie Romano's bed-and-breakfast with a heavy heart. How would she bear to walk away from these little guys? How would she survive walking away from Cicero?

If the cancer had returned, if this was a new cancer, she'd fight it hard, just like she'd fought the first time.

Her body might survive, but what about her heart?

Cicero wanted to tell Gabi he didn't give a flip about dreamweavers or whimsies or anything else to do with stocking the retail shop, but he bit back the words. It wasn't fair of him to take his bad mood out on his partner. Gabi had worked her ass off to get the doors open at Whimsies—and with sales better than expected before the official grand opening, she deserved praise. Just because Rose's recent attitude and actions had shoved a particularly sharp thorn into his paw didn't mean he had leave to bite Gabi's head off.

Though if he heard one more word about wedding playlist selections he swore his head would explode.

"Hey, Cicero?" Gabi called. "It's almost three o'clock and I worked right through lunch. I'm starving. I'm going to make a sandwich run. Do you want something from the Blue Moose? Today's specials are roast beef or chicken salad."

Lying on his back beneath the leaky bathroom sink, he gave his wrench a twist. "Beef."

"Be back in a bit."

The jangle of bells on the front door signaled her departure. Alone in the shop, when the wrench slipped and he barked his knuckles, he didn't think twice about letting loose with a stream of inventive curses. While blood pooled and pain throbbed, he asked himself why the hell was he playing plumber when he should be blowing glass? His time could be much better spent. He had three commissioned pieces due by the end of the month in addition to the Albritton albatross hanging around his neck. With all the turmoil surrounding the kids, he'd not come near to re-creating the creativity of the island.

Instead, he lay flat on his back fighting a rusted hunk of metal and brooding about the woman in his life.

Emotion churned in his gut like a bad egg salad sandwich. He was disgusted with himself. He'd gone out of his way to avoid Rose this morning rather than confront her. He'd run off and sulked and nursed his little baby feelings instead of facing her like a man. How chicken was that?

"You're losing it, Cicero," he grumbled, wiping his bloody knuckles on his jeans before tackling the stubborn bolt once again. He put extra torque into the effort to loosen the bolt. Finally, it gave.

He wished his temper would give, too. It was counterproductive.

He replaced the washer, and as he tightened the

bolt, he heard the door bells jangle again. "Did you forget your wallet?"

"It's me," Misty called, then moved to stand in the bathroom doorway. "The new sign out front looks really good."

"Thanks. What are you doing out of school?"

"We had early release today."

"Did I know that?"

"Yes. It's on the calendar on the refrigerator, and I told you before you left this morning."

"Oh." He set aside his wrench and scooted out from beneath the sink. Grabbing for the towel hanging from a ring above him, he wiped his hands and asked, "Where's your brother?"

"A birthday party. I told you that, too."

"Oh." He did remember that now. "And you have piano lessons, don't you? Why are you here instead of there?"

"I want to talk to you about something."

A note in her voice sounded a warning. This wasn't going to be a casual conversation. He closed his eyes and fought back a wave of frustration. He didn't want or need more drama.

Since when does it matter what I want or need?

He bit back a sigh and rolled to his feet. Misty wore jeans and a red T-shirt with the Whimsies logo on the front. He'd designed the logo, but Gabi must have ordered the shirts. The graphic looked darn good—though he didn't know how he felt about his nine-year-old niece advertising

274

"Come Play With Fire" across her chest. He twisted the spigot on the sink and eyed the plumbing closely. So far so good.

Turning around, he smiled at his niece. "Let's hear it."

Her shoulders lifted as she filled her lungs with air. Misty was obviously nervous. His trepidation rose. If this were Keenan, he'd brace himself for a report of a broken window or dog bite—Keenan being the one to use the teeth. But with Misty—did this have something to do with Rose? Had she found out what bee was in the doctor's bonnet?

"I gave a report in school today."

He wondered if she knew she was wringing her hands.

"Okay. Did you blow it? It's not the end of the world, I hope you realize. I know that you're very smart and want to grow up and go to college, but you shouldn't put so much pressure on yourself. Not at your age, anyway. One bad grade every now and then won't derail you."

"I didn't blow it. I got an A plus."

Cicero folded his arms, tilted his head, and studied her. "Okay, then what's the problem?"

"Not a problem. I would like to present it to you, and I'd like you to promise not to interrupt until I'm done."

Hmm. Something told him he wasn't going to like this.

"Okay."

She licked her lips and began. "My report was on the benefits of owning a dog."

Oh, crap.

"Misty, we've been down this road before."

"You promised you wouldn't interrupt!" she snapped.

He sighed heavily, but she'd trapped him admirably, so he propped a shoulder against the doorjamb and admitted to being cornered. The girl had her facts down. He learned that petting a dog lowered blood pressure, and that kids who have dogs miss fewer days of school due to sickness. She explained that owning a dog teaches responsibility, and that children who have dogs have better self-esteem. "Dog owners recover faster from heart attacks and have higher survival rates, too!"

That was probably her best point of the bunch, considering that he was playing father to the dervishes of destruction.

He lost track of the number of points in her presentation, but he sensed she was winding down. He had words of praise for her report ready, along with the well-practiced refusal to add a dog to their family when she threw him an unexpected loop.

"I'm not asking that we adopt a dog, Uncle Hunk." She recited the handful of unassailable reasons against the idea that he repeated whenever the question arose. "It's a big commitment. Pets can be expensive. Now is not the time."

Warily, he considered his response. He would not be outsmarted by a nine-year-old.

"That was an excellent report, Misty. I'm not surprised your teacher gave you an A plus. Gabi has gone for sandwiches. Do you want me to call her and ask her to bring something for you?"

"No, thank you. Our new house has a fenced yard."

Well, hell. He'd tried.

"Dr. Nic gave a talk at school earlier this week. She said that there is a big need for temporary foster homes for dogs. This summer, when we are out of school and in the new house, I thought it would be a good way for us to be good citizens and thank Eternity Springs for being so nice to us by providing a temporary foster home for a dog."

Oh, you're good.

"And, we can learn how hard it is to take care of a dog. Once we see it for ourselves, we can quit bugging you so much about wanting a puppy."

Very, very good.

"Worm, as time goes on, you and I are going to tangle horns over and over. Sometimes, you'll get your way. Other times, you'll have me wrapped around your finger so tight that I won't be able to tell you no. But every so often, you'll reach for something that you won't have a gnat of a chance getting me to agree to."

He hated crushing her spirit, but better nip this one in the bud.

"Just so you know, this is one of those gnat times. As long as you are living with me, we won't have a dog. Period. Give it up."

"Are you allergic?" she asked in a little voice.

He considered his answer, then settled for bald honesty. "No, Misty. Bottom line is I won't have a dog. Let it go."

The rapid blinking of her eyes signaled the threat of tears, but she bravely lifted her chin. Cicero saw her mother in her then, and his heart gave a twist of pain. Despite it, he was in no danger of melting. Not about this.

Both he and Misty turned toward a sound in the back room of the shop. Gabi set a pair of brown paper bags on the table in the break room.

"Soup's on," she said, meeting his gaze. "Hey Misty. I bought cookies to go with our sandwiches. Do you want one?"

"No thanks, Ms. Gabi. I'm leaving. I have to get to my piano lesson."

"Be careful crossing the street," Cicero told her.

The look the girl gave him before she left silently declared that this subject wasn't closed. When they were alone in the break room, Gabi asked, "So what do you have against dogs?"

"I don't have anything against dogs. I like dogs. I just won't own one." He unwrapped the sandwich she handed him and snagged a bag of chips. "So, Legs, are we selling the T-shirts she was wearing or are they strictly promotional?"

An intelligent woman, Gabriella went along with the change of subject. An hour and a half later, she declared their work at Whimsies done. "Thank you so much for all your help, Cicero. I think we're officially ready for our grand opening."

"Good, because I'm ten minutes late picking up the ankle biters. I don't want to abuse your mother's hospitality."

"She won't care if you're late. She's in heaven doing the grandmother thing, and she's taken your kids under her wings like her own."

Cicero knew it was true, so he took the extra time before heading to Maggie's to stop by the studio and grab the mail he had ready to send. He saved it for Daisy because dropping envelopes into the mail slots at the post office was one of her favorite things. He lifted the stack from his desk, then turned to leave. A woman's sharp voice stopped him in his tracks.

"Cicero!" Sage Rafferty exclaimed, anger flashing in her eyes. "I couldn't believe it when I looked out of the gallery window and saw you walk into your studio. Why are you here? Why didn't you go to Gunnison with Rose?"

"You've got it wrong. She had her Mexican food in Gunnison yesterday remember, and I wasn't invited to go with her."

"Not yesterday. Today. She was supposed to go to Gunnison this afternoon."

"Why? Does she have a guy there on the side now?"

Sage held up her hand, palm out. "She didn't tell you, did she? I swear I want to wring her neck. She promised!"

"Promised what?"

"No way would I have stayed here if I'd known you wouldn't be with her for the exam. Why does she think she has to face this alone?"

"Face what alone? What exam?"

"You know what? Rose isn't my patient. She's my sister. I'm not bound to any confidentiality agreement."

"Dammit, Sage. What are you talking about?"

"Rose thinks her cancer has come back."

Fifteen

Rose sat in her room at the B and B trying to convince herself that she honestly was absorbed in the PBS program about volcanoes. She did find geothermic forces of nature interesting. It wasn't like she had *Real Housewives of Eternity Springs* on TV.

A smile flickered on her lips, the first in hours. If somebody decided to produce that particular show, she'd darn well watch it. It'd be a hit with the female demographic, without a doubt. The men in town were to-die-for hot.

"To die for," she muttered aloud. "Great word choice there, Dr. Anderson."

She lifted the ice pack away from her breast and decided she'd iced it enough. The radiologist who'd performed the core needle biopsy had been gentle, quick, and efficient. Soreness and bruising appeared to be minimal. She almost wished the procedure had caused her significant pain since she desperately needed something to distract her from her thoughts right now.

She could call Sage. That would certainly provide a distraction.

Rose had kept her sister updated throughout the day by text messages, but by around three o'clock, Sage had apparently decided that texts weren't good enough. She'd started calling. And calling. And calling. Finally, Rose had sent a text explaining that she simply wasn't up to talking, but that she'd phone tomorrow immediately upon receiving her test results. She'd also asked Sage to get someone to cover for her with the kids in the morning.

The kids. Her heart twisted at the thought of them. She'd wanted so badly to provide some stability for the little loves. They'd faced one blow after another. It wasn't fair. And here she'd begun to think that maybe—just maybe—she'd found the family she'd hoped for. Found the man—

Her thoughts turned to Cicero. Thinking about him was almost as difficult as wondering about her test results. No, that wasn't true. She couldn't think about one without thinking about the other. It hadn't escaped her notice that he hadn't attempted to call her today. Nor had he texted.

He must be wrapped up in his work, which was no surprise, really, what with the retail shop's grand opening around the corner. She wondered if he'd noticed that she hadn't called today, either. He'd be home with the kids by now. Maybe he—

Her cellphone rang and she checked the number. Cicero.

"Speak of the devil," she murmured.

She yearned to answer the call, to hear his voice and to pour out her fears. She literally sat on her hand to keep from reaching for the phone. It rang six times before going to voicemail. She waited to hear the ping that indicated a new message. Instead, the phone rang again. It rang every five minutes for the next half an hour, until finally she shut it off, and returned her attention to the erupting volcano on TV.

Ten minutes later, she startled when her room phone rang. For the space of two rings, she stared at the old-fashioned phone on the bedside table. She hadn't told Sage where she'd be staying. Had she guessed?

More likely it was the front desk letting her know that the pizza she'd ordered for supper had arrived. Rose seldom ate pizza, and never had both Mexican food and pizza in the same week, but tonight she'd decided to indulge herself. Cautiously, she picked up the handset. "Hello?"

Her innkeeper said, "Dr. Anderson, a gorgeous bouquet of flowers just arrived for you. Would you like to come downstairs and get it, or should I send the deliveryman up with it?"

Flowers? Who could have sent her flowers? No one knew where she was staying. Well, except for Lynda Rydzell. Rose had mentioned where she'd reserved a room during her appointment.

Lynda. Oh. Wow. Had she received the lab results? Were they bad and this was her way of expressing sympathy?

Don't be stupid, Rose. Yes, the lab was doing a rush on her results out of professional courtesy, but it was beyond ridiculous to think along those lines. It was much more likely that Sage had guessed where she'd stay the night and tracked her down with an apology for the phone harassment. "If you'd send them up, I'd appreciate it."

"Will do," the innkeeper said.

Rose pulled a robe on over her sleep shirt and dug bills for a tip out of her purse. At the sound of a knock, she opened the door. The bouquet was big and bright and cheerful. But when she shifted her gaze from the flowers to the deliveryman, her smile froze.

"Hunt!"

"I'd like to wring your neck." He shoved the flowers at her and strode into her room.

Rose stood in the open doorway, holding the flowers, her mouth gaping open like a two-pound trout.

He prowled his way to the center of the room, then stopped and whirled around. His jaw was set, his eyes hot with anger, accusation, and maybe, a little bit of fear. "I need you to explain something to me, Dr. Anderson," he snapped. "How did you and I go from 'you matter' to 'you aren't important enough to share the big stuff with'?"

She'd hurt him. It was there in the drawn line of his mouth and in the way he folded his arms.

Surprised, she asked, "How did you find me?"

In a half rage, he answered, "Sure as hell not from the directions you gave me, or because I checked in to the bed-and-breakfast with you. Not because I drove here with you, or shared this day with you."

Guilt steamrollered through her. She set down the flowers. "Hunt—"

He held up his hand. "No. I'm talking. I wasn't important enough to talk to before. You have to wait your turn."

"That's not true!"

"Isn't it?" he exploded, throwing his arms out at his sides. "You shut me out, Rose. You didn't trust me. Why not? You know what I think? I think it's because you have no faith in me, that's why. One man treats you like a jerk so that means all of us are asses, right?"

284

She closed her eyes and she heard a catch in her voice when she said, "No, Hunt. That's not it at all."

"I tell you what," he continued, as though she hadn't spoken. "I've had two women in my life totally piss me off. One was the foster mother in the foster home from hell when she ignored the fact that we were living with a young psychopath, and the other was Amy Parnell when she threw away my kids. You have managed to take my pissed-offedness to an entirely new level. You want to know why?"

He wasn't looking for an answer, she knew, so she didn't try. She just kept her mouth shut.

"You left me and the kids out of it. That says that we aren't part of the equation at all. I guess I'm an idiot because I really thought we were. You still have a sister who loves you and what do you do? You treat her like pond scum. Sage was a mess when I saw her! She's worried sick, and here she is pregnant. Do you know how lucky you are, Rosemary? Your sister is still alive. Your sister loves you, and you shut her out."

He doesn't understand.

Like a flashbang grenade, Rose's temper exploded. "I don't mean to hurt anyone. But right now, for a change, for a little while, life needs to be about me. It needs to be about me! Don't you understand? I'm a doctor. I love being a doctor. I love to spend my days taking care of other people, my patients and now Misty and Keenan and Galen and Daisy. I love doing that more than you can begin to understand.

"I also take care of Sage. I'm the big sister. That's what big sisters do. And even though you are the most independent man I've ever met, sometimes I take care of you, too. And I'm not talking about sex, either. I'm talking about emotional support. I'm happy to give it. It's what I do, who I am. It's what I need to do."

She struck a nerve. His anger seemed to dissipate.

"*Bellissima*," he began—

"No! It's still my turn. Let me finish." She balled her hands into fists at her side, shaking with rage. Trembling in fear. "I need you to hear this. I need you to understand. Today, I needed to be selfish. I'm hanging on by a thread because I'm waiting to hear results that can go one way or another. There is no in between! Don't you get it? I'm doing the best I can and today I needed to do what I needed, not what other people needed me to do.

"Maybe that's not nice. Maybe it's not fair. But neither is cancer. I just don't have it in me to be strong for you and my sister right now. I'm too scared to be strong!"

He strode toward her with open arms, dragged her against him, and held her tight.

"Okay. It's okay. I'm sorry. You're right."

"I'm scared, Hunter. This time I'm really scared. I have so much to lose now. The thought of it weakens me. I'm not strong enough."

"Then lean on me. It's my turn to be strong and offer support."

His arms felt like heaven, and she sank against him.

"I love you, Rose."

His head dipped and he spoke softly, but with conviction, against her ear. "I'm talking love with a capital *L*. You need to know that saying it is a big hairy deal for me. I've never said those words to another woman."

He drew back, tilted her chin up so that she met his gaze. "I love you. I am here for you."

She couldn't stop the tears from overflowing. "Oh, Hunt, I love you, too. That's why I'm so frightened. I have so much to lose. It wasn't like that last time. Last time when I got sick, I was estranged from my sister. Brandon and I were only going through the motions. The stakes weren't as high."

"Don't say that."

"It's true. Facing my own mortality showed me that I needed to fix the relationships in my life. I came to Sage and found Eternity Springs. I found family and friends. I found children to mother. I found you. It's been so wonderful."

He stroked the back of her head as she spoke into his shoulder. He didn't respond, simply held her and listened. It was exactly what she needed, and the words continued to pour out.

"I have been so blessed in my rebirth. I have faith and that sustains me. What breaks my heart is the thought of putting you and the kids through cancer mere months after losing your Jayne. I don't want to do that to you. Can you understand? I love you all so much and I don't want to cause you more pain. I can't bear the thought."

She broke, tears flowing like a river as she cried. She was hardly aware when he picked her up and carried her to the padded wooden rocking chair that sat in the corner. He rocked her back and forth, murmuring soothing sounds, saying, "I understand, sweetheart. It's okay. You cry it out. Get it all out. You've earned a good cry."

He handed her tissues from the box on a nearby table, and from time to time kissed away the tears from her cheeks. How long he held her, rocked her, she didn't know, but eventually, she cried herself empty. Exhausted, she cried herself to sleep.

She awoke some time later spooned against him in the big four-poster bed. She moved her thumb across his knuckles. He pressed another kiss against her temple and his deep voice softly asked, "Better?"

Her throat felt raw, so she simply nodded.

"I'm sorry I railed at you, *Bella Rosa.* I want to do whatever you need me to do. You tell me what that is."

Rose thought about it a few moments, though she really didn't need to think about it at all. "Just love me."

He rolled her onto her back and rose up over her. His warm brown eyes stared into her soul as he vowed, "I do, Rosemary. I do."

Then he lowered his mouth to hers and proceeded to show her just how much.

Cicero lay sated and spent with Rose tucked up against him sleeping peacefully. Fatigue dragged at him, but sleep remained elusive. His thoughts spun; his stomach churned. Icy fingers of fear clawed at his heart. Had he been alone, he'd have howled his anguish at the moon.

He loved her. He was in love with her.

The reality of it blew him away.

He couldn't pinpoint when it had happened. It could have been the moment he first saw her at the Valentine's Day dance. It may have been the compilation of all of the little moments between then and now. It might have been in that split second earlier today when he realized he might lose her.

He couldn't bear the thought that he might lose her. He'd just found her. He hadn't known it, but he'd been looking for her all of his life. All these years, all the women, how could he have been so blind to his heart's desire?

He didn't want the bachelor lifestyle. He

wanted a home and a family. He wanted a wife and children. He wanted Rose and Misty and Keenan and Galen and Daisy. Finally, he recognized his true heart's desire. Please, God, he prayed. Don't let it be too late.

Cancer was the devil.

A huge lump of dread hung in his throat. Silently, he lectured himself about the power of positive thinking. He reminded himself that infection had killed Jayne, not cancer. He even tried to tell himself that fate wouldn't be that unkind to the urchins as to steal another mother away from them.

Except, he didn't believe the lie. Fate was a cruel bitch. Fate treated kids like dirt all the time. Like that day when his mom had promised to take him to watch the Cardinals play.

He's never been to a professional baseball game before. He is beyond excited as he vaults from the school bus and rushes down the street to the duplex where he's lived with his mom for the past seven months. Seven months clean—a record for her.

He's almost begun to believe in it. In her.

Pike doesn't meet him at the door, but he's not concerned. Mom isn't due home from work yet, so his dog will be in the backyard. He glances at the clock. He has twenty minutes to throw a ball with Pike before he needs to leave for the hardware store. He's officially too young to have a job, but the owner pays him in cash to sweep the floor, clean the bathrooms, and stock the shelves. He's saved fifteen dollars to buy a ball cap and peanuts and a soft drink. Gotta be sure not to forget his ball glove. They have tickets in right field. Maybe he'll catch a fly ball.

Hey, a guy can hope, can't he?

He hurries to his room and changes into his work clothes. Then he heads to the kitchen in search of an after-school snack.

The glass pipe sitting on the kitchen table stops him cold.

In a Colorado bed-and-breakfast over two decades later, Cicero clutched Rose a little tighter and banished the memory to the vault with the rest. Grimly, he told himself that he'd been down this road before; that he knew to take it one step at a time, one day at a time. He had strong, broad shoulders that Rose could lean on. He didn't want to fight this battle again. He sure as hell didn't want the children to face it again, but if that's the hand fate dealt them, well—

They would be there for her. *He* would be there for her. Period.

Though it would shred his heart beyond repair.

Hope is the thing with feathers.
That perches in the soul
And sings the tune without the words
And never stops at all.

What a crock. Hope is for fools.

No wonder that the work he'd done for the Albritton was so pedestrian. It was difficult for an artist to make magic when the subject was nothing but an illusion. Cicero didn't hope. Not anymore.

He finally drifted off to sleep, though he stirred often throughout the night, aware that Rose, too, tossed and turned. They awoke early the next morning and with a late afternoon doctor appointment, had time to kill.

After calling to check on the kids, and allowing Sage to vent some of her frustration with Rose, they swore off any more talk about test results and played tourist, checking out the Gunnison Pioneer Museum. They ate Mexican food for lunch, then walked to the ice cream shop for a cone afterward.

Cicero relayed a story Gabi had told him about catching her widowed mom dressed like a biker babe and making out with her handyman in that shop a couple years ago. The story got a sincere laugh out of Rose, which he considered a victory, because as the hours ticked by, they both grew more tense.

Finally, half an hour before her appointment, Rose addressed the elephant in the room.

"One of the worst parts of my job is delivering bad news. It's true that over time you're able to thicken your skin, but it's never easy. I admire oncologists and other professionals who do this day in, day out. I'm afraid I need a heavy percentage of well-baby checkups to balance delivering pathology report results."

"You have a compassionate heart, *Dolcezza*."

She let out a shaky breath. "I have a terrified heart."

He laced his fingers through hers, then brought her hand to his mouth and kissed her knuckles. "Flynn likes to say that Gabriella has a valiant heart. It's a good word for you, too. Did you ever watch classic TV westerns?"

Her mouth twisted with a grin. "That's a strange conversational turn."

"Jayne absolutely loved them. It made buying gifts for her easier because I could always give her DVDs. The only problem was that she made me watch them with her. Last night, while I watched you sleep, I thought that you are like one of those great cowboy heroes. I kept hearing the theme song from one of the series running through my head."

She gave him a wry look.

"You have a peculiar way of thinking, Hunt Cicero."

"Brave, courageous, and bold—that's you. You have a core set of values that you live by. You have integrity. You take pride in your work. You're tough, but fair. You are a source of inspiration to me and to the rapscallions and to everyone who knows you. You make me want to be better than I am, Rose. Thank you for that."

He could tell that his little speech had stolen hers, so he decided to lighten the moment. "Now what you need is the outfit."

Bemused, she said, "A cowboy hat?"

"Nah. A saloon girl outfit. With feathers."

Feathers. Cicero frowned as a thought—an idea —hung just beyond his reach. Then Rose laughed and distracted him, and he offered her a warm, loving smile.

"All right, Marshal Dillon," she said. "Shall we go see what Dr. Rydzell has to report?"

"Let's do it."

When her name was called in the physician's office, she surprised him by tugging him along. He hoped she didn't notice how clammy his hand was, and as they took seats in a conference room, he wished he'd brought along a bottle of water. *Or a bottle of bourbon.*

They waited five interminable minutes for the door to open. Cicero couldn't help but flash back to similar waits with Jayne, and his heart thundered.

On the opposite side of the door, he heard paper rattle. His gaze locked on the doorknob. As it began to turn, Rose gripped his hand hard and whispered a soft prayer.

The doctor entered the room with a smile on her face. "No cancer," she said, conveying the most important information first.

Cicero released the breath he'd been holding. *I really like the doctors in Colorado.*

Sixteen

Memorial Day weekend kicked off the official tourist season in Eternity Springs, and this year the festivities included an old-fashioned picnic on the Angel's Rest estate. A barbershop quartet provided entertainment along with a trio of skits performed by the summer theater group. Local merchants displayed their wares in booths along the perimeter of the picnic grounds.

Rose manned a first-aid tent conveniently placed between the Whimsies booth and that of Vistas Art Gallery, and across from the food booths, which included sweets from Sarah Murphy's bakery shop Fresh and pizza right out of the ovens at Ali Timberlake's Yellow Kitchen.

Rose watched with sympathetic amusement as Ali checked her watch for what must have been the two-dozenth time in the past twenty minutes.

"Ali, settle down," Sarah called out. She didn't see her husband approaching her from behind, their toddler son in his arms, their young adult daughter walking at his side. "You are going to get watch-checking elbow, and Rose here will have an ice pack on you when Chase arrives. That's not how you want to meet your daughter-in-law to-be, is it?"

At Sarah's words, Lori briefly froze. The look

that flashed across her face wasn't hurt or shock or even surprise. The closest description Rose could come up with was haunted.

That's curious, she thought.

Ali didn't notice the Murphys' arrival. She was looking at her watch again. "He said he'd be here an hour and a half ago. I can't help but worry. I know it's ridiculous. He travels all over the world and goes to the wildest of places and I seldom fret."

"Seldom?" Sarah questioned dryly.

"Perhaps occasionally is a more appropriate— why, look who's here!" she broke off, a wide smile dawning. "Lori!"

Sarah whirled around, smiled wide, and threw her arms around her daughter. A vet school student, Lori didn't get home often, and Rose knew that Sarah had been almost as anxious as Ali to see her child.

Lori Murphy had matured into a lovely young woman. She had her father's height and gorgeous green eyes, and her mother's dark hair, fair complexion, and curves. She was the product of Cam and Sarah's high school romance; her little brother, their reunion baby.

Rose wondered if the flash of emotion that had crossed Lori's face meant she harbored some regret for the ending of her own high school romance with Ali's son Chase a few years back.

Ten minutes later after the young man arrived,

she decided that yes, it probably had. Of course, Lori's reaction paled in comparison to the look on Chase's mother's face when she got a look at her son's new girlfriend.

Lana Wilkerson had to be at least ten years older than Chase. Rose's physician's gaze noted the lines around Lana's eyes.

At least ten. Probably more like fourteen.

Petite like Sarah, Lana had blond hair and a vivacious way about her. A producer for the television show on which Chase worked as a still photographer, she was put together in that way of wealthy women that Rose had always admired but seldom managed to achieve—the perfect haircut and highlights. Classic and understated jewelry. Expensive bag.

How was it that some women could casually toss a sweater around their shoulders and look perfect, while when she did it, she looked unkempt?

Chase introduced his lady with pride and a bit of a strut. The men in town appeared appropriately impressed that Chase had landed a trophy. Although, even as she thought it, Rose wondered if the word trophy was appropriate when referring to a woman who was with a younger man.

The women in town had another name for her, one that wasn't nearly so attractive. Ali Timberlake uttered it first after Chase and his lady wandered away to take in the sights of Eternity Springs.

"My baby is going marry a cougar!" Ali wailed.

Rose wondered if anyone else had noticed the flash of emotion in Chase's eyes when he'd introduced Lana to Lori. The two young people weren't indifferent to each other. Something lingered there for both of them. No wonder their mothers got a wistful look in their eyes whenever the subject of the Chase and Lori romance came up.

Rose relayed her observations to Cicero on Monday evening as they gathered up supplies for the after-school outing they'd planned with the children. Word was the fishing had been particularly good up at the Timberlakes' private fishing spot above Heartache Falls, and they planned to celebrate the successful grand opening weekend of Whimsies by catching their supper.

"Ali tried," Rose said as she tucked a jar of peanut butter into her picnic basket. "She put on a good front. I know her well, though, so I could tell that she wasn't happy. It was hard enough when it was only a meet-the-parents weekend, but when he turned it into a traditional Eternity Springs wedding proposal, I know she's worried."

"What's a traditional Eternity Springs wedding proposal?"

"One that's over-the-top romantic."

"You mean a cheesy public spectacle?"

She thought of Jack Davenport's parasailing with Cat. "No, more like special, private spectacles. Chase took his Lana rock-climbing on Sunday, and proposed halfway up the cliff face of Murphy Mountain."

Cicero arched a brow.

"That's romantic?"

"To them, apparently. Personally, I look at climbing and think of broken bones rather than romance."

"That's something I'll have to remember."

She shot him an abashed look. "Wait. Don't think that I was hinting or something. This was simply a discussion about my friend and her twenty-something son dating a woman close to my age."

Cicero's slow grin made her toes tingle. He pulled her into his arms. "You thinking about ditching me for a boy toy, *Bellissima*?"

His teasing made her melt. She ran her finger along the neckline of his collar and turned a one syllable word into three when she drawled, "We-ell, there is something to be said for stamina."

He snorted.

"You saying there's a problem with my staying power, Dr. Anderson?"

"Not at all. Just something to watch for during, you know, checkups."

"Good thing you're my doctor. Your prescriptions are wonder drugs."

"Oh yeah? Which one do you like best?"

He nibbled at her earlobe.

"Difficult question. Your doctor's bag of tricks keeps expanding. I do think naked yoga has improved both my dexterity and stamina, don't you?"

Keenan's young voice intruded into the moment.

"Would you two please stop the smoochy stuff?" he complained from where he stood in the kitchen doorway.

Laughing, Cicero released her, though he gave her butt a slap as she walked away.

With the summer season upon them, Rose and Cicero both knew that this would be their last full day away for quite a while. Plus, Cicero's move away from the cottage and into the house next week would make their stolen late night moments more difficult to achieve. He'd tried to convince her to move in with them, but Rose was having none of it. That wasn't the proper message to send or example to set for the children.

Which brought her thoughts back to the look in Cicero's eyes when she'd talked about Chase Timberlake's marriage proposal. They had talked around the subject of marriage a time or two, and he'd said enough for her to sense that he wasn't opposed to the idea. She tried not to think about it. After all, she'd waited seven years on Brandon, hadn't she? She never wanted to *wait* again.

If it happened, it happened.

If not—well—she had more today than she'd ever had before, so she refused to fret about it. The worries of the last few weeks had reminded her how important it was to live her days with joy and contentment and, most especially, love.

The viewing area at Heartache Falls was crowded with summer tourists. They stopped for a few moments so that the kids could ooh and aah, and make use of the facilities, but since fishing was the real appeal of the outing, Cicero warned them they had only five minutes to sightsee.

After explaining that he didn't need to use the restroom because boys could pee anywhere, Keenan quickly gathered a small pile of rocks to use in that age-old pastime—throwing them over a cliff. Galen joined him at the safety railing, and soon Cicero participated, too. When Misty joined in, Rose leaned against the SUV with a sleepy Daisy in her arms and watched the action with joy.

"You have a lovely family," an older gentleman said as he approached the car with Oklahoma plates in the parking spot next to theirs.

"Thank you," Rose said, laying claim. "I do."

Just then Cicero threw back his head and laughed at something Galen had said. When the three children turned and raced toward her, calling her name, Rose's heart swelled with happiness. She sent up a quick prayer of thanksgiving, then buckled Daisy into her car seat.

"It's like herding cats," Cicero said once he finally got both boys into the car. They continued on their way, and in a few short minutes, she pointed out the gate leading to the Timberlakes' property.

"Any chance young Chase and his kitty cat will join us?"

Rose smirked at the appellation.

"The other Timberlake kids are home, too. Ali mentioned that the whole Timberlake family planned to visit Mesa Verde today. We'll have the fishing hole to ourselves."

"Good." Cicero reached for her hand. "I was hoping that today would be a Cicero family outing, away from the tourist hordes. Not that I'm opposed to tourist hordes, mind you. Whimsies did bang-up business over the weekend, and your sister sold three of my pieces from the gallery."

"That's wonderful," Rose said, answering to both the information he'd shared and the fact that he'd included her in his family. Never mind that he was the only member of it actually named Cicero.

"It's a nice way to start. I'm feeling downright positive about this summer."

"Me, too."

Rose guided them to the wildflower-carpeted meadow with a creek running through the center of it. The children were thrilled when Cicero pointed out a bald eagle sailing against the blue sky high above them. Rose was pleased not to see any wildlife in the meadow. When she'd stopped into Cam Murphy's sporting goods store to buy salmon eggs for bait the previous day, he'd told her that he'd seen a cougar in this meadow on a previous visit—and he'd been talking about the four-legged variety.

The kids bailed from the car like the wild animals they were. Cicero handed out fishing poles, and led the boys toward the creek. There, much joy commenced when they dug worms from a white Styrofoam cup and handed them to their uncle to slide onto their hooks.

"Yeew!" Galen cried.

"Cool!" said Keenan. "I want to squish the worm. Can I squish the worm, Uncle Skunk?"

Galen immediately said, "Me, too!"

"Maybe later. Misty, do you need some help?"

"No, thank you. I'm all set." She held up the jar of bright pink salmon eggs, preferring not to "murder living, wiggling animals."

"All right, then. Let's go dunk our hooks."

Rose helped Daisy with her cartoon character fishing pole, and as luck would have it and to the boys' great dismay, she pulled the first fish from the stream. Keenan scored next. While Cicero showed the older boy how to remove the hook from the trout's mouth, the younger brother ate half a jar of salmon eggs. Misty howled a protest, and Cicero declared it was time to drag out the snacks Rose had packed.

They ate peanut butter crackers and fruit, with canned fruit punch for the kids and a nice red wine for the adults. After lunch, the fishermen went back to work while Rose stretched out on the quilt beside Daisy and read her a story until the little girl fell asleep. Relaxed and happy, Rose drifted off too.

She awoke to an itchy nose, giggles, and murmured conversation. Her eyes fluttered open to discover Keenan and Galen kneeling on either side of her, dandelions in their hands, and devilish expressions on their faces.

"Were you two tickling my nose?"

The giggles swelled into chortles of laughter.

"Come with us, Dr. Rose. It's your turn to catch a fish."

She sat up, then glanced down at Daisy, who continued to nap. "Maybe after Daisy wakes up."

"I'll watch her," Misty volunteered.

Sensitive to the amount of time Misty was asked to watch over her siblings, Rose said, "That's okay. I'll fish later."

Cicero winked at Misty while Keenan took hold of one of Rose's hands and Galen the other. "You hafta fish now, Dr. Rose. You hafta!"

"I think Daisy's slept long enough," Cicero said. He bent and scooped the little girl up into his arms. "Go with them, *Bellissima*."

The boys tugged her up onto her feet. Keenan said, "We have your fishing pole all baited and ready."

"With worms or eggs?"

A bit of a panicked look crossed Keenan and Galen's faces, and they looked toward Cicero. He winked at them and said, "Neither. We used a combination of stinker and rascal bait."

Warily, she arched a brow.

"Rascal bait, hmm? I don't believe I've ever heard of rascal bait before."

"Uncle Skunk says he hopes it'll work real good today. It's the perfect day for rascal bait."

They pulled her toward the creek where she saw a second quilt spread upon the ground and a champagne bucket and two flutes. *And chocolate-covered strawberries?*

"Well, now," she said. "This is certainly roughing it."

"Your hook is already baited and in the water and everything."

"That's too bad. I wanted to see what a rascal looks like when he's on the hook."

"Sit down, Dr. Rose," Keenan said. "Hurry!"

Rose wanted to laugh. She couldn't recall the last time she'd seen anybody so obviously up to something. She thought she knew what. She'd overheard boys arguing over a rubber snake earlier that week. If she had to guess, she'd find it hanging from the end of her hook when she pulled the line from the water.

"Here's your pole!" Galen exclaimed.

Rose glanced up at Cicero, who wore an anticipatory expression himself. Really, boys never did grow up, did they? She took a seat on the quilt and tucked her legs beneath her. "Those strawberries sure look good."

"After you fish," Keenan declared. "Hurry, Dr. Rose."

Cicero sat beside her, leaned casually back on his elbows and stretched out his long legs toward the bank of the creek. "Go ahead, Rose. Reel us in."

Us? A crazy idea flittered through her mind. *Us?* He wouldn't—she gave him a sidelong glance. He watched the protected pool in the frothing creek intently and with an uncommon stillness.

Rose reached for the fishing pole and immediately sensed a resistance against her line. She caught her breath as hope flared and her heart pounded. Champagne. Strawberries.

Children.

Cicero.

Rose slowly turned the fishing reel until she caught sight of a rainbow of bright colors on the end of the line. It was a fish. "A rainbow trout?"

"Be careful now, Dr. Rose," Keenan cautioned. "Don't break it."

A glass trout fashioned in the colors of the rainbow. A fishing lure was hooked through the trout's mouth. It was a fishing lure like none she'd ever seen before.

From the center of it dangled a gold ring with a diamond solitaire.

"Oh," Rose said, freezing in place.

Cicero reached out and grabbed the line, pulling it safely over land. Meeting Rose's gaze, he said, "You've hooked us, *Sirena Bellissima.* Will you keep us?"

"Uncle Skunk! You're supposed to say will you marry us!"

Never taking his stare off of Rose, he said, "Give me a chance, heathen. Rosemary, I love you. Will you be my wife? Will you be a mother to these children? Will you be our family?"

"Yes!" she said fiercely, joy bubbling through her like the froth on the creek. "Yes, Hunt Cicero, I will marry you. I will be your wife and a mother to these children. I love them. I love you."

The kids cheered, and Cicero visibly relaxed. He snagged the fishing pole from out of her hand and carefully set it down. Then he leaned forward and kissed her firmly and sweetly. Releasing her lips, he declared, "Pile on."

The kids swarmed her, and they all exchanged hugs and kisses until Cicero pushed them away. "Enough. Leave us alone for a few minutes. You'll find cookies from Fresh in the picnic basket. Go get 'em."

With cheers, the children dashed back toward the other quilt and the basketful of treats. Rose watched them go with a full heart. When she turned back to Cicero, words died upon her lips. He held the ring he'd retrieved from the fishhook in his right hand. His left was extended, silently asking for hers. Emotion clogged her throat, and she blinked back happy tears as she placed her hand in his. "It's a beautiful ring, Hunt."

"I'm glad you like it. I've been saving it for years. The diamond is of excellent quality. I thought if you don't care for the setting or want something other than yellow gold, we can have the rock reset."

Oh.

Trying to keep it light, she asked, "You bought it for someone else?"

He scowled at her.

"Of course not. I'm not so big a heel as to give you a ring I bought for another woman. You talked to me about fate that day in Gunnison. Here's my take on it. This ring was meant for you. I knew I was falling in love with you the night of Gabi's engagement party when you walked downstairs wearing that emerald dress. You were my *Sirena Bellissima.*"

"Beautiful mermaid," she murmured.

"Yes, beautiful mermaid. That's why it's appropriate that I give you a gift from the sea. I found the ring my first year in the Caribbean, when I swam in a lagoon of an uninhabited island. It sparkled and caught my eye."

"Seriously? You found it?"

"I found it. It's a big ocean out there, Rose, but I found it." He slipped the ring upon her finger. "And thank God, I found you."

Their lips met and clung, until Keenan's voice intruded. "Put that back, Galen! You've already had three cookies. You need to save that one for Uncle Skunk and Doctor Mom!"

Rose jerked her head back. Shakily, she repeated, "Doctor Mom?"

"Jayne was Mama to them. Misty suggested the name for you. I think it's a great one for them to use, don't you?"

Doctor Mom.

"I can't think of anything I'd like better."

Seventeen

Cicero rolled crystals of color into hot glass on the marver, shaping the teardrop meant to be part of the chandelier the studio was making for a hotel in Boca Raton. He whistled along to Poison's "Fallen Angel," which was blaring from the studio speakers as he worked—and added a little flair to his movements for the benefit of the tourists watching from the bleachers. When he finished, he would turn down the music and chat up the visitors. People liked a show and he was glad to give it, especially since Gabi had pointed out the correlation between his interaction with guests and an increase in retail sales. Nevertheless, he'd be glad to turn that particular bit of the business over to Mitch. His apprentice had arrived in Eternity Springs late last week for his promised summer visit, and he was a natural at charming the visitors.

In its first month of operation, Whimsies already had hit a home run, and the tourist season was just getting kicked off. Locals assured him they still had ten strong weeks ahead of them. On one hand, he couldn't be more pleased. On the other hand, he cursed his timing roundly.

Between his work, her work, and responsibilities to the hoodlums, he and Rose were the proverbial ships passing in the night—only nights had little to do with anything since she still refused to move in with him or even to sleep over. Payback, Flynn had told him, for laughing at his similar predicament.

Ten minutes later, he placed the teardrop in the annealer, peeled off his gloves, then played to the crowd until he spied a bright-eyed Misty hovering in the doorway. She wore her hair in pigtails, a jumper he didn't recognize, and a smile filled with teeth straight enough to give him hope of avoiding braces. After gently ushering the visitors from the studio toward the retail shop, he greeted the girl.

"What's up, Worm?"

Her voice shook with excitement. "I got it, Uncle Hunk!"

"You did! That's wonderful!" He wracked his brains. *Got what?*

"It's just the backup part—it's called under-study—but Mrs. Hendricks says that Laura Simpkins is going on a family vacation and has to miss the last two nights of the play so I'll definitely get on stage those nights and maybe more."

Now he remembered. Summer theater.

"Congratulations, Worm. I'm happy for you. What's the play again? *Little Orphan Annie?*"

"No. They're doing *Annie* now. It runs until the Fourth of July. We're doing *Sound of Music.*"

"That's right. The hills are alive and everything." He reached out, and playfully tugged a pigtail. "Proud of you, Misty."

She beamed. "Thank you."

"What role will you play?"

"Brigitta! Isn't that a beautiful name?"

"It sure is." Cicero grinned at his niece. She'd sure come out of her shell in recent weeks. Rose's influence, he was sure. That and the fact that time seemed to be working its magic on her grief. "You know what? I say we go out for pizza to celebrate."

"Really? Cool!"

He thought through the logistics for a moment, then pulled out his phone to call Rose. It rang before he could make his call, and recognizing the number, he frowned. "You should go tell Gabi about the play. See if she and Flynn want to meet us for supper. Mitch, too."

She started to turn away, then paused.

"Do you think they'd come to watch?"

"I'll bet they'll be in front row. Right next to me and Doctor Mom."

"Okay."

Cicero watched the happy girl scurry toward the retail shop, and then he turned the lock on the studio door and answered the phone.

"Hello, Amy. What can I do for you?"

"Hello, Cicero. How is everyone in Eternity Springs? Are the children out of school yet?"

He gritted his teeth and counted to five. He found it ridiculously difficult to speak pleasantly to this woman, but he couldn't afford to pop off to her. Not until after the last of the legal issues involving the kids were smoothed out, anyway. He and the Parnells needed to work as a team when dealing with the bureaucracies of two states. He couldn't afford to say what he wanted to say.

"Everyone is fine. This is the first week of summer vacation for the kids."

"That's wonderful."

Yeah, easy for you to say. You're not the one scrambling to find day care and activities late in the day when so many of the programs are full.

"Are you still staying at the cottage beside the creek?"

"No. We moved into the new place earlier this week."

"That's nice."

That's nice. That's wonderful. Why is she calling?

"How is Daisy?"

Cicero did another five-count of teeth gritting.

"All of the children are doing well. Misty just landed a role in summer theater. Keenan scored two runs in T-ball last night. Galen has a new best friend who is taking him camping tonight, and Daisy got a haircut yesterday."

"You cut her hair!"

"No, I took her to a salon to have it done. It looks cute."

He saw no reason to mention the chewing gum incident that necessitated the trip.

"Oh. Well. Hair grows back. She has her father's hair, you know. His was the same strawberry-blond color, and she has a cowlick in the exact same place as he did."

Cicero's heart softened a little. He knew that Amy had loved her brother. She'd lost a sibling, too. Grief can make a person say and do crazy things. He needed to remember that and cut her some slack.

"It's a gorgeous color. She'll grow up to be a heartbreaker someday."

"Yes. Now, I should explain why I'm calling. Scott and I are traveling up your way. He has a conference in Colorado Springs. We remembered that dude ranch near your little town when we picked the children up after our ski trip last winter. They have a four-day program. If it's all right with you, we'd like to take the children there after Scott's meeting next week."

Well now, she'd managed to totally surprise him with this one.

"All of the children?"

"Yes. The place is called Storm Mountain Ranch."

Cicero knew it well. Flynn owned a section of land that had once been part of the ranch. He and Gabi were building a new home there.

The possibilities of a few days sans children made him downright giddy. He'd get a reprieve from changing diapers and cooking supper. He could work on his own schedule. He could sleep in.

Rose could sleep over.

Yet, he hesitated. Would an excursion like this only confuse the little monsters? They were settling in well to Eternity Springs, and he didn't want anything to disrupt that or cause them any feelings of insecurity. Cicero rubbed the back of his neck. They'd have a blast at the dude ranch. Heaven knows he couldn't steal the time away to take them. It was a long weekend, just a long weekend with their aunt and uncle.

"I'm familiar with Storm Mountain Ranch. The folks who run it do a great job. The kids would love it."

"Good, then. We'll plan on it."

They synched their calendars, and Cicero ended the call with a grin on his face. This was a good sign. As angry as he was with Scott and Amy over their abandonment of the children, they still were family. He needed to remember that. A person couldn't have too much family. He needed to do his part to make the situation work.

The fact that the Parnells still wanted to be involved was a positive development. *And, if this visit goes well, maybe I can hit them up to babysit so we can honeymoon.*

He chose his words carefully when he told them about Amy's call, and the proposed visit to Storm Mountain Ranch. Confusion wasn't a problem. The wild animals went wilder, and fired questions like a string of Black Cat firecrackers. Would they really ride horses? Would the cowboys be real? Would they sleep in a bunkhouse? Would they be tourists like all the new people in town?

He told Keenan and Galen that yes, he'd buy them cowboy hats to wear and they could choose what color. He also promised Misty that she could absolutely return to town for rehearsal for her play.

"I'll drive up and get you myself," he assured her.

The magic moment came as they left the pizza joint, and Keenan spied something that caused him to shout with delight and dart toward the base of an aspen tree. He scooped a feather up off the ground and said, "Look! It's an eagle feather!"

Cicero didn't think so, but he wasn't about to steal the boy's thunder. "Cool."

"It's my lucky feather. I hoped and hoped and hoped that I'd get to be a real cowboy someday. Now I get to ride a horse and sleep in a bunkhouse and wear a hat. And I have a feather for it!"

Hope. Feather. Knee-high cowboys.

Cicero turned to look at Gabi, Mitch, and Rose. "I need to go to the studio. Now."

Rose switched off the bedside lamp in Galen and Keenan's room, and tried to avoid the creaky spot in the wood floor as she walked softly toward the door. The two slept peacefully—finally—and she wanted it to stay that way. Between excitement over the upcoming trip and the fact that they still were adjusting to their new home, getting them to settle down tonight had been a tougher task than usual—especially with Cicero at the studio.

When she'd seen that creative fire flare in his eyes, she'd known what to expect. She'd sent him off to work with a smile and full knowledge that this was what she'd signed up for when she agreed to marry him. Or, in Keenan's vernacular, when she agreed to marry them. Despite the long day and her aching feet, she couldn't be happier. She had a family. Finally, she had a family of her own.

She checked on Daisy and reassured herself that the child continued to sleep soundly. A light was on in Misty's room, and her door was cracked open, so Rose rapped softly and said, "Misty, are you still awake? May I come in?"

"Sure."

Rose expected to find the girl curled up in bed with a book. Instead, she sat in her window seat with her arms wrapped around her knees.

"Is everything okay, sweetheart?"

"Yes. Everything is wonderful. This was just the most special day. I don't want it to end."

"I love days like that." Rose crossed the room to the window seat and peered outside over Misty's shoulder. The yard was large for a house in the center of town and boasted two tall fir trees and a cottonwood with a low-hanging branch perfect for a tree swing. Tonight, light from a three-quarter moon bathed the yard in a silvered glow. "I'm so happy you got the part in the play."

"Oh, me, too. The music in *Sound of Music* is so awesome. I'll have four speaking lines plus I have a short solo in 'Do-Re-Mi.' That's a little scary. I hope I don't blow it. I have promise, but I'm not as good a singer as Laura Simpkins. She sings like an angel. I need to work on my breathing and pay closer attention to my projection."

Rose stopped herself from rolling her eyes.

"Mrs. Hendricks told you that?"

"Yes. I'm worried about it. I need voice lessons, but Mrs. Hendricks has no time in her schedule right now."

Carla Hendricks directed the summer theater, the music programs at the school, and the choir at St. Stephen's. She'd been a music major in college, and her claim to fame was the fact that she'd once been a singer on a float in the Rose Parade. The woman's heart was in the right place, but she did enjoy being the big choral fish in Eternity Springs's little music pond.

"Well, I don't know about Laura Simpkins, but I do know you have a lovely voice. I daresay I've heard a much broader section of your abilities than Mrs. Hendricks has—after listening to you on our car trip from Texas to Colorado."

"I was just singing for fun, then. I should always pay attention to my breathing."

"I'm sure you'll learn what you need to learn for the play. That's what rehearsals are for. But if you're worried about it, you could ask Mrs. Blessing for her opinion. I'm sure she would help you."

"Is she a singer?"

"Honey, from my experience, Celeste can do just about everything. Wait until you hear her voice—talk about singing like an angel."

"If she wouldn't mind helping me, I would love it."

"She loves helping people. She says she believes she was led to Eternity Springs for that purpose. Heaven knows, we needed her. She has worked miracles in this town."

Misty turned her face back toward the window. "I need a miracle."

Frowning, Rose asked, "Is there a problem we don't know about?"

"No. Uncle Hunk knows. He just doesn't care."

"Now, Misty," she chastised. "Your uncle is one of the most caring men I've ever met. What is this about?"

"This house. It's perfect. I don't see why we have to move again in just a few months."

Hmm. Has she hit the wall as far as moving is concerned? Is that what this is about? A security issue of some sort?

Rose really needed to talk to Cicero about counseling for these children.

"This house has good bones, and it's fine for a rental, but I think your uncle has his eye on buying the property next to Whimsies. He's trying to get all of our financial ducks in a row."

"I like that place, but this one is better."

"You think?"

"Yes."

"Why?"

"Just because."

Misty kept her eyes on the moonlit yard.

"Don't you think that house will suit our family better than this one? It's bigger. Each of you can have your own room. As Galen and Keenan grow older, we will all be happy about that."

"If we could stay here, I wouldn't mind sharing a room with Daisy."

"What's so special about this house?"

"Look what's in the backyard!"

Rose gazed out the window, expecting to see an animal of some sort. She'd noticed today that the deer had obviously gotten to the roses in the front yard. She'd have to ask Celeste what the landscape team at Angel's Rest used to keep them from the rose garden there.

"I don't see anything, Misty."

"There's a fence! It's a big yard with a fence. The other house doesn't have a fence."

"Yes. It is a pretty fence, I admit. I've always wanted to live in a house with a white picket fence."

"And a dog," Misty said, yearning in her voice.

Without thinking, Rose agreed.

"A fluffy one. Not too big. Not too small."

Misty turned her gaze away from the window, hope shining in her big blue eyes. "Do you want a dog, too, Doctor Mom? This house has a doggy door in the kitchen!"

Oh. That's what this is about. How dense can you be, Rose?

Aware that she needed to tread carefully, she said, "With the long hours I work and the places I've lived, it's never been practical for me to have a dog."

"But would you like to have one?"

"Misty, have you talked to your uncle about getting a dog?"

"About a million times." Her sigh held the weight of the world in it. "That's why I need a miracle. He won't even consider it. I don't know why. He said he's not allergic or anything. He just says nope, out of the question."

Rose had noticed Cicero's reticence about dogs, but they'd never discussed the subject.

"It seems like everybody in town has dogs but us," Misty continued. "I understand why we couldn't have one before. Mama was sick and we moved around a lot. But it's different now. We have a yard and fence and a doggie door! I told myself to quit hoping because it would never happen, but then today—today was just the best day. One of my dreams came true. It made me get my hopes up again."

"You should never quit hoping." Rose instinctively reached out and stroked Misty's hair. "Hope feeds our strength, and keeps us standing tall in the face of adversity. You are such a special girl, Misty. You are brave and loving and so strong."

"I'm not strong." Her lower lip trembled. "I'm really not. Everybody thinks I am, but I'm not."

"I say you are. I'm a doctor. I know about these things. I've seen you be strong."

"Really?"

"Really."

It was true. In so many ways, in these past few

months, Misty had been the glue that held this little family together while Amy Parnell and her husband floundered and Cicero stumbled around.

"I hoped that Mama wouldn't die. But she did. I loved her so much. Sometimes after the other kids went to bed she'd let me sneak out into the living room and we'd make popcorn and watch the shopping channel on TV. We'd pretend to buy whatever we wanted. It was so much fun. She was fun. Even when she was sick, we could do that. I miss her."

"I know about that sort of heartache. I was a little older than you when my own mother died. I still miss her."

"Your mom died, too?" Misty's eyes went round. "I didn't know that."

Rose nodded.

"I had a little sister to watch out for and a dad who was often clueless."

"Like Uncle Hunk."

"I didn't say that." Rose winked at the girl, then continued. "For a while after I lost Mom, I was filled with hopelessness. And you know what happened then?"

Misty shook her head.

"Nothing good. I walked around with a black cloud hanging over my head. I had a negative attitude, so bad things happened. It took me a long time to find my hope again. You are so much smarter than me, Misty. Life has given you some hard knocks, but you're still standing. You're still dreaming. You're still hoping. You hold on to that. Let those hopes and dreams continue to feed your soul and you'll stay strong. You'll stay positive. When you think positively, good things happen."

"Like getting a dog?"

Rose made a mental note to talk to Cicero and find out what his issue was with dogs. "I make no promises there, sweetheart. But I'll tell you this much. I hope so."

Misty offered a tremulous smile, then wrapped her arms around Rose's waist and hugged her.

"I'm so glad you are going to marry us."

"Me, too, Misty. Me, too."

She tucked the girl into bed, made her promise not to read too long, and gently pulled the door shut behind her. Turning toward the stairs, she stopped abruptly at the sight of Cicero sitting on the floor. He sat with his legs outstretched and crossed at the ankles, his back against the wall, his face tilted up, eyes shut, his expression filled with regret. *Oh, Hunter.* He looked as if the weight of the world rested on his shoulders. "Problems at the studio?"

"No. That went well. Great, in fact. A new design for the Albritton. I think this one is it."

He made no effort to move, so Rose sat down beside him. He reached for her hand and laced their fingers. "I was eleven. Jayne was back with her dad. I'd been with my mom about four or five months when she got high and landed in jail. My caseworker placed me with Jason and Christina Brotherton. They'd married older in life, thought they might want to adopt an older kid. They were great. Really, really great. My first week there, they brought home a puppy. A wheaten terrier. They asked if I'd mind if he slept in my room."

He fell silent, but Rose could tell that he'd only begun his story. Obviously, he'd overheard her conversation with Misty.

"They wanted to adopt me. Nobody ever wanted to adopt an eleven-year-old kid. Mom said she'd sign over her parental rights. They started proceedings. I was happy. Damn, I was happy. Pike slept in my bed."

"The dog's name was Pike?"

He nodded. "He was a stray. Like me. They found him on Pike Road."

"What happened?"

"Mom got sober. She got paroled. Changed her mind about me. I was so torn up. I wanted to go back to her—but I didn't. I loved the Brothertons. I wanted to be Hunt Brotherton. I heard them one night—Jason and Christina. They decided to fight for me. They'd decided to do it. Then the next day my mom knocked on the back door and begged them. She swore she'd stay off the stuff. She meant it, too. I know she did. She got a job and managed to rent a house. A house with a yard. The Brothertons let me go, and sent Pike with me. We had over a year. Sixteen really great months before she got high and left the gate open. Pike got out and was hit by a car."

"Oh, Hunt."

"I never lived with her again."

"You weren't returned to the Brothertons?"

"They got transferred to Japan. They adopted a seven-year-old girl. We email."

"Of course you do. They're one of your families."

He turned his head and stared at her with eyes fierce and intense. "I wanted one family, Rose. A nuclear family. She took me away from people who loved me, people who I loved, and basically, killed my dog. I look at dogs, and I think about loss. Losing Pike destroyed me. When it comes to dogs, I'm still that brokenhearted boy. I know how much Misty wants a dog. Maybe I'll get there one day, but I'm not there yet."

"That's the saddest story, Hunt. I totally understand why you feel the way you do."

One corner of his mouth lifted in a sad and crooked grin. "I totally hear the 'but' coming."

She squeezed his hand and mimicking the gesture he so often used, lifted it to her lips for a kiss.

"Not a 'but.' A 'maybe something to think about.' "

"That's the same thing as a 'but.' "

"You told me you'd finished your Albritton

entry. Now that you've mastered Emily Dickinson's feathered hope, I wonder if it's time you moved on to another poet."

"You've lost me."

"Alfred, Lord Tennyson."

When he made a circular motion with his hand, she quoted:

> " 'I feel it, when I sorrow most;
> 'Tis better to have loved and lost
> Than never to have loved at all.' "

"Rose—" he began, a protest in his voice.

"I wonder if that little boy's broken heart might finally heal if the man with one nuclear family—and a dozen extended ones—watched his daughter fall in love. Just saying."

Eighteen

With his hands shoved into his pockets, Cicero slowly circled the sculpture he'd removed from the annealer a short time ago. Three feet high, four feet wide, free-form, and perfectly balanced. He'd fashioned the work in shades of the sunrise —yellow, orange, rose, and gold. It was both delicate and substantial. Airy, but consequential. Definitely a statement piece. Some of the best work he'd ever done, he thought.

Now he needed a name for it. Something creative, but not too descriptive because the free-form nature of the work was intended for individual interpretation. He was drawing a blank. He'd put the women in his life to work on it. Maybe stop in at yoga one morning and ask the Ladies Who Lotus to help come up with something. In the past, he'd never much cared about naming his art. For him, the work was important, not the marketing of it. In this instance, he understood and accepted that the name for the work was part of the art.

"Oh wow," said Rose as she entered the studio. "That's it, isn't it? That's the Albritton piece? It's the most gorgeous thing I've ever seen."

He gave his fiancée a thorough once-over. She was dressed for their evening date in a classic black dress and pearls. "You should look in a mirror. You're a masterpiece."

She barely spared him a glance, so intrigued was she by the sculpture.

"Don't be silly. It's like it's dancing. Or—no—it looks like it's floating." She recited the Emily Dickinson poem and said, "I can see it, Hunt. I can't put into words exactly why it fits, but it fits."

Her praise warmed him more than he would have imagined. "Thank you."

"I can't wait to see what you do with Alfred." She glanced at him, then did a double take. "Oh my gosh. You're wearing a suit."

"Didn't you say you wanted to dress up tonight?"

"I did. I just—wow, Hunter. You totally *are* Uncle Hunk."

He gave a snort. "Speaking of the royal pains, Galen called me today."

"He did? Who got hurt?"

"Nobody, believe it or not. He wanted to tell me that the cowboy who drives the chuck wagon is called Cookie. Then Keenan got on the phone to tell me that his horse was named King, but everyone called him Exxon because he had so much gas."

"I can hear the giggles now. What about the girls? Did you talk to them?"

"Misty had a piece of news to pass along. It seems the Parnells are getting a dog. A puppy."

Rose cut him a look.

"Seriously? I thought dogs were an issue with them. Misty wanted one when the kids lived with them."

"Yeah, that's what I thought, too. Guess Misty's been driving the guilt wagon there, too." He returned his gaze to the Albritton piece and thought about Pike.

Lord Tennyson, my ass.

His fiancée interrupted his reverie. "What about Daisy? Did she say if she liked her hayride?"

"I didn't talk to her. Amy didn't put her on the phone."

At this, Rose nibbled her bottom lip and frowned.

"What's the matter?" he asked.

"I don't know. Nothing, probably." She brushed a speck of lint from the lapel of his charcoal-gray suit jacket. "Did Amy strike you as a little, well, possessive when she held Daisy?"

"No." Cicero waved away her concern. "I thought she looked a little guilty, which she darned well should, considering."

He slipped his arm through hers and said, "How about we declare a moratorium on kid talk for the night. They'll be home tomorrow and they'll eat up all of our free time and energy. I'd like for tonight to be about you and me. Deal?"

"Deal."

They walked to dinner at Ali's Yellow Kitchen where they dawdled over Tuscan chicken and a lovely Chianti. After their meal, they strolled over to Murphy's to listen to live music on the new outdoor patio Shannon had opened for the tourist season. They returned to the house, where he poured after-dinner brandies and they sat snuggled up together in the front porch swing.

Cicero stroked his thumb up and down her bare arm and announced, "Your sister flagged me down as I walked past Vistas this afternoon."

"Oh?"

"Supposedly she wanted to tell me that she sold one of my pieces in the gallery today. That was just an excuse. She really wanted to chew me out."

Rose pulled a little away from him. "About the Albritton? I told you that you should have tipped her off about the nomination before news got around the art world."

"Yeah, well, apparently, she's going to hold that against me for a very long time." He pulled her back against him. "I still say that that Sage should understand and respect the creative muse better than anyone. However, that's not why she gave me grief. I got to hear about our wedding instead."

"Our wedding?"

"I'm supposed to ditch any ideas I've entertained about eloping. You've never been married, and you deserve a wedding with all the bells and whistles."

Rose rolled her eyes. "Did you tell her I was the one who suggested we head for the courthouse?"

"And throw you under the bus? No way. I'm smarter than that. I told her that she was absolutely right. I explained that we've decided to wait until fall to get married. I didn't tell her that's as far as we've gotten with the discussion." He frowned. "I don't think she likes me."

"She loves you. If she didn't like you, she'd ignore you rather than yell at you."

"Okay, then. I guess that makes me feel better. So, *Bellissima*, let's talk weddings. Do you want a wedding? Like the one you were supposed to have? White dress, church, and a cake that's four stories tall?"

"I want you and the kids."

"That's not what I asked you. I don't want you to give up on the perfect wedding if that's what you want."

Locusts buzzed in the trees and she could smell the lemony perfume of the heritage rose in the yard. She lifted her head to a starry sky and watched the stars, swinging back and forth until she finally spoke.

"There was a time when I did want the dream wedding with all of the bells and whistles, as you said. I think that's likely something most women think about at some point in their lives. But I've learned that it doesn't matter if the dress is white lace or if the cake is slathered in buttercream icing and the bridal bouquet is white roses. What matters is the man who is standing there giving me his heart and his name and his children. Our wedding can be in a church, in a courthouse, or next to Angel Creek. All I want is to marry you. The how doesn't matter to me. It's the why. We're getting married because we love each other and we'll make a family with the children. That's what will make a perfect wedding."

Cicero's smile was sweetly endearing as he drew her in for a kiss. "I think you're perfect, my Rose."

"You aren't so bad yourself."

They took full advantage of the children's absence by making love outdoors, on the staircase, and in the shower before finally making it to his bed. They enjoyed a lovely, romantic weekend—one he hated to see end. Kids certainly put a kink in a man's love life. October and the white gown and Rose's wedding couldn't get here soon enough.

Yet, by midafternoon on Sunday when the Parnells were due back with the little monsters, both he and Rose waited anxiously for their arrival.

"They're like mold in the bathroom shower," he observed as he watched from their bedroom window as the Parnells' car pulled into the drive-way. "Grows on you when you aren't looking."

"You do have a way with words," Rose said as they walked downstairs.

Outside, doors slammed and feet pounded. The marauding multitude burst into the house with raised voices and overstuffed backpacks and grins as wide as the Grand Canyon.

Amy paused in the doorway with Daisy in her arms. Scott brought up the rear. Just as Cicero untangled himself from Keenan's chocolate-smeared embrace, he saw the two adults share an enigmatic look. Detecting some unknown under-current, his radar engaged. What the heck was going on here?

He pasted a friendly smile on his face. "Come

on in, folks. What can I get you to drink? Tea? Water? A beer?"

"Since I'm driving, iced tea is fine," Scott said, returning Cicero's smile. "Thanks."

"Just water for me," Amy added.

Since the Parnells had an early morning flight out of Gunnison the following day, Cicero had invited them to dinner before making the two-hour drive to their hotel near the airport. He'd figured since they were making the effort to mend their relationship with the kids, he should do his part to help.

Now though, after seeing that look, he wished they'd kicked the kids out at the curb and headed on their way. Something put him on high trouble alert.

Cicero grilled steaks and potatoes and Rose made a salad. The still excited kids kept conversation flowing as they all sat down to eat. The dude ranch trip had apparently erased any resentment they'd harbored against Scott and Amy for making them move. That was a good thing, he told himself, trying to shed his unease. The Parnells were family. Family mattered. He was glad to see them so happy.

And Houston was a long way from Eternity Springs, so he and Rose wouldn't have to put up with them often.

Cicero poured a Napa cabernet that paired well with the rib eyes he served. He didn't think twice about serving it to Amy. It was only when he caught sight of Rose's frown that he made the mental connection between her pregnancy and alcohol.

She noticed his hesitation, lifted her glass, and gave her head a sad shake. "Any reason I had to avoid alcohol no longer exists."

She'd miscarried?

"I'm sorry."

"Thank you." Amy changed the subject by saying, "This salad dressing is spectacular, Rose. Is that a hint of ginger I taste?"

Rose flashed a look filled with wariness toward Cicero, then said, "Yes. It's a favorite of mine. The owner of a local restaurant gave me the recipe. The Yellow Kitchen serves the most delicious food. You should try it sometime when you come to visit the children."

Scott and Amy's gazes met and in the process of cutting a bite of steak, Cicero went still. He felt as if he stood at the end of a cliff.

"Yes," Scott said, finally.

Cicero's tension eased. A bit.

The rest of the meal dragged by, the chattering of the children providing cover for the under-current of tension flowing from the adults. The boys yammered on about horses and cowboy rope tricks. Misty rather defiantly talked about the puppy due home from the breeder by the Fourth of July. Despite the hit to his appetite caused by the stress, Cicero ate every last piece of his steak. Some primal instinct made him want to eat red meat before the battle.

Because he had the distinct feeling that a battle lay before them. Rose sensed it, too, judging by the wary little looks she sent his way. She served apple pie for dessert, and he kept a sharp eye on the children's plates.

The minute they finished, he said, "Okay, heathens. You smell like billy goats. It's time to hit the showers and get ready for bed. Thank your Aunt Amy and Uncle Scott for the trip."

"Oh, Uncle Hunk," Keenan protested. "I don't need a bath."

"Some things never change, do they?" Amy said with a laugh. She stood and swooped Daisy up out of the high chair. "Come here, peanut. Why don't I help with baths, Rose, while you do the dishes?"

Rose's smile went brittle. "How sweet of you to offer, but it's Hunt's turn for the dishes." She held out her arms and said, "Her eyes are getting that droopy look. I'll take her now."

Amy's obvious reluctance to hand over the toddler made Cicero go quiet.

"Say good night, children," he said.

"You sound like Captain Von Trapp," Misty said. Giggling, she made an exaggerated wave with her hand and sang, "So long. Farewell." She gave first Scott, then Amy a hug saying, "Thanks so much for everything. I can't wait to see him in person."

"Him?" Rose asked, her arms still outstretched for Daisy.

"The puppy." Misty shared a look of joy with Amy and added, "And guess what? I get to pick out his name."

That's it, Cicero thought. Enough. Taking control of his household, he plucked Daisy out of Amy's arms and handed her over to Rose, saying, "Thanks for the help with baths, honey. Kids? Upstairs. Now. Amy, Scott, please join me in the living room."

He marched into the room without waiting for them and went directly to his desk. When they walked in hand in hand, he gestured toward a manila folder and extended a pen toward them. "Since the paperwork I sent a couple weeks ago seems to have gone astray, I asked my attorney to make another copy of everything. You can sign them while you're here. My next-door-neighbor is a notary and—"

"We received the paperwork," Scott said. "I planned to speak with you about it this evening."

"No time like the present."

Amy tilted her head toward the staircase where the children lingered. "Kiddos, we'll probably be gone when you finish your baths. Give us good-bye hugs."

One by one, the older children hugged the

Parnells and thanked them again before going upstairs with Rose. Cicero didn't miss Amy's soft "See you soon" to Misty, and once the children were gone, he abruptly turned on his heel and marched toward the front door. "Let's do this out on the front porch. Little pitchers and all."

Once the door shut behind them, he whirled on them. "What the hell is this? What sort of crap are you trying to pull now?"

Scott sucked air into his lungs, then exhaled in a rush. "Amy and I have reconsidered. We've decided not to relinquish our guardianship."

"If you think I'm going to let you steal Daisy away from her sister and brothers, just forget it. I'll be damned before—"

"No!" Amy interrupted. "Not just Daisy. You were right before. It's wrong to split them up. We see that now. We want all of the children."

Shocked, Cicero went silent. For a split second, he thought of how much easier life would be. No diapers. No babysitters. No tattling or whining or hitting. No chaos.

He loved the chaos.

"You can't have them," he snapped back.

No way were they taking his kids.

Scott said, "Actually, yes, we can. Our court hearing isn't for another week. We are still their legal guardians."

"When it's convenient for you, that is. I'll go to Texas and tell the judge the truth. You didn't want them. You threw them away. You sent them home with me."

"We requested help of a family friend while Amy soldiered through illness with a difficult, and ultimately unsuccessful pregnancy."

They were words right out of a lawyer's mouth.

"That's bullshit."

"That's the way it is."

Amy said, "Look, Cicero, we know you love them and that they love you. As long as you work with us, we are not going to keep them away from you. We sincerely appreciate how you stepped up when we needed help with them."

"As long as I work with you? I didn't 'help.' I accepted responsibility. Responsibility you shirked. Don't try to rewrite history, here. If I hadn't taken them, you were going to dump them on social services. That's what you wanted to do! Do you have the first clue what that's like? Thank God I did. I knew I damned well couldn't let it happen. Jayne would have been devastated to know that you put her kids into the foster care system."

Amy's face fell as his words struck a nerve. "No. We never would have gone through with that. We weren't thinking straight. I was so ill. Trying so hard to hold on to my baby. It was a difficult time for us. I needed—"

"You needed!" Cicero exploded. He pointed toward the staircase. "What about them? They had just lost their mother. You should have put their needs first."

Scott took hold of his wife's hand. "We did— we *are* doing—what we think is best for everyone. Jayne asked that Amy and me be parents to her children, not you. We are prepared to do that."

"Now, maybe. What about six weeks from now? I won't allow this."

Amy sighed.

"Cicero, you can't stop it. You can only make it more difficult for the children."

"Me make life difficult for them? Me? Don't try that B.S. on me. They're settled here. They're happy here."

"They've been here six weeks. An extended vacation."

"What was this weekend? A test run? An audition? Were you trying to see if you really wanted them or not?"

The flash of guilt on Amy's face made him want to hit something.

Someone. Okay, he wanted to hit Scott.

"Look, Cicero, we're not going to argue any more about this. Our original intention was to talk to you tonight about a convenient time to bring the kids to Houston. However, Misty is so excited about her play that we are willing to allow them to stay through July. Our school district begins classes on August tenth, so we'll come back up to watch her performance and leave here on August first. That's enough time to get them home and ready and settled before school starts."

They already are home.

"Don't do this." He balled his fists at his sides. "This is crazy. It's not right for you or for them. Look, I'm sorry you lost your baby. I can only imagine how difficult that is for you. But you can't replace one child with another. You can't—"

"You don't do this!" Amy snapped back. "Don't you dare presume. You don't know anything, Hunt Cicero. I lost my baby and my best friend in a short time span. Before that, I lost my brother! Yes, Scott and I were too quick to ask you for help with the children. But people make mistakes. We recognized ours and we intend to rectify it. We love Misty and Keenan and Galen and Daisy. When we told Jayne we'd take care of them, we meant it."

He read the sincerity in her words and expression, but he didn't believe it. How could he? "I know what it's like to be bounced around from home to home. It's not good. It's not healthy. Children need to feel safe and secure. They need to be able to count on you to be there."

Scott took a step forward. "Cicero, we are here because they can count on us."

"Have you told them about this?"

"No. We thought it best to leave that up to you. You'll know when the time is right."

"The time will never be right. You know what?

340

I don't care what you want or what guilt you're trying to assuage. The kids aren't leaving. Period. I'll fight you for them."

"You'll be wasting your time. Wasting your money. We've looked into it. You have no legal right to them, Cicero." Scott turned toward his wife. "Let's go, honey. Thank you for dinner. Thank you for taking such good care of the children. Amy, let's go."

"I want to say one more good-bye to the children."

She disappeared inside leaving Cicero and Scott standing alone.

"You don't want these kids," Cicero accused, his tone soft.

"I'll do anything for Amy."

Three interminable minutes ticked by in silence before she returned. With a subdued "Good night, Cicero," the Parnells took their leave.

He stood alone on his porch, anger and frustration and fear churning inside him. The screen door creaked. He looked around to see Rose—his lovely, beloved Rose—watching him with tears rolling down her cheeks, her eyes stricken with grief.

"Doctor Mom," he murmured, and opened his arms.

She fled into them and he held her tight, shut his eyes, and fought back despair. "We will fight this, *Bellissima*. I won't let them take our family away."

She nodded. "I'm going to call Mac Timberlake." Knuckling away her tears, she leaned up and kissed his cheek before heading back into the house.

Cicero shoved his fingers through his hair and attempted to control his thoughts. His gaze fell on the porch swing. Just a couple of days had passed since he and Rose sat there talking about their wedding. She wanted this family. She wanted this chaos. It was her version of perfect, everything she'd ever wanted.

Anger ripped through him. How dare those people come back and turn the children's world on its axis? Rose's world. His world.

Damned if that was going to happen. He'd fight until his last breath.

You have no legal right—

Just like the Brothertons.

Anguish, fear, and fury swept through him. He knew better than anyone the cost of legal rights.

Dammit, history wasn't going to repeat itself.

"I won't let them take it away from her. From us."

The screen door creaked a second time, and Misty rushed onto the porch. She held a smartphone in her hand, one he didn't recognize. "Look, Uncle Hunk. Look what Aunt Amy gave me. It's so we can call her and talk to her any time we want. And look, she's loaded it with pictures of the puppy! Isn't he the cutest thing ever? Uncle Hunk, won't you please let me—"

"Dammit, Misty," he snapped, not looking at the phone. "You are not getting a dog. Shut up about a damned dog!"

She pulled back as though he had slapped her. Cicero turned and walked off the porch into the dark, lonely night.

When Rose arrived at Mac Timberlake's law office at ten the following morning for the meeting they'd scheduled last night, Cicero sat on the front stoop, waiting. Rose took one look at her fiancé's tired eyes and wondered if he'd managed more than two hours sleep.

"Hey," he said as she walked up.

"Hey, yourself." She leaned over and kissed his cheek. "How are you doing?"

"Just peachy. You?"

"About the same. You have the kids all settled?"

"Yes. It's a stroke of good luck that Lori Murphy wanted to earn some money while on her school break. Having a full-time babysitter is a godsend." His mouth twisted in a crooked smile as he added, "I okayed a field trip to Nic Callahan's clinic to see the kittens that were born earlier this week."

"Isn't one of them allergic to cats?"

"Galen and Misty, both. I've been assured that they'll be okay as long as they don't try to hold one."

"Trying to make up for biting Misty's head off last night?"

"Am I that transparent?" He shook his head. "I shouldn't have yelled at her, but her dog obsession was just about the last thing I needed at the moment."

"She'll get over it," Rose predicted. "Kids are resilient. She'll forgive you."

"Resilient." He shook his head. "I don't know how resilient they'll be when this all breaks loose."

"Each day as it comes, right?"

"Right."

Rose gave his hand a squeeze of support as Mac Timberlake strode up the steps. "Good morning, you two. Sorry I'm running late. I made a couple of calls to Texas researching this situation, and it took longer than I anticipated."

He unlocked the door and ushered them inside and up a flight of stairs to his second floor office. Once inside, he asked them both to sit. "Cicero, I need you to repeat the story from the beginning. Go all the way back to when you first met your sister. Be as detailed as possible."

With interruptions for Mac's questions, the telling took almost forty-five minutes. Mac filled up a yellow legal pad with notes. When he finally set down his pen and leaned back in his chair, Rose saw little encouragement in his expression. She wasn't surprised.

"Articulate what you want," the former federal judge said. "Give me the bottom line."

"I want the kids," Cicero declared. His jaw was hard, and his eyes fierce.

"Why?" Mac pressed. "You are going to have to be specific and direct."

"Well, lots of reasons. I think—"

"Bottom line it," Mac repeated.

"I want—them to be happy."

"Excellent goal. Now, every decision we make needs to have that purpose at its root. Don't forget it. Tattoo it on your forehead if you must."

"Okay."

"So in order for those kids to be happy, what needs to happen?"

"They need to be loved and live in a stable home."

"You don't trust Amy and Scott Parnell to provide that."

"No!" Cicero shot to his feet and began to pace Mac's office. "They don't really want Jayne's children. They want their own. Grief is running this bus. I know what it's like to be bounced around from home to home, from a relative to a foster situation. It destroys all sense of a child's security. You can't count on anything, plan on anything. You can't let down your guard because you know that as soon as you do, as soon as you start feeling safe, you'll get that phone call, have that talk, be on the road again.

The Parnells have broken trust once. They'll do it again."

Mac turned to Rose. "What is your bottom line, Rose?"

"Hunt makes a compelling argument. My bottom line is that I'll support him one hundred percent in whatever decision he makes."

"You're engaged to him. Are you ready and willing to take on four children who aren't related to you? To be a mother to them?"

"I am. I want that more than anything."

"Okay, then. Here's the reality." Mac tapped his pen against the yellow legal pad filled with his notes. "This is going to be tough. Really tough. If you sue for custody, I will fight for you, but you need to know going in that the odds are stacked against you. It will take more time than you think and a lot more money than you guess."

"More time?" Cicero returned to his seat. "We can't do it before August first? That's when they want to take them back to Texas."

Mac shook his head. "I'm sorry, no."

Rose asked, "Can we get a temporary order of some sort to keep them here until the bigger question is settled?"

"I will try, but again, your chances are slim."

"So you're telling me we are going to need a miracle."

Mac nodded, and Cicero spared Rose a grim look.

"At least we are in the right place," she said. "Eternity Springs does miracles."

"What can we do to improve our chances?" Cicero asked. "Is there anything we can do? What's our best course of action going forward?"

Rose added, "Do we tell the kids what's going on?"

Mac's brow furrowed in thought. "That's your call," he said. "But if you don't tell them, the Parnells might. How would that affect them? The court will want to interview them, too. Their wishes will be considered."

"I think we'd better give that some thought."

Cicero dragged his hand down his face, and his weariness grew even more pronounced. "I don't want to upset them, but I don't want them to hear it from someone else, either. Maybe don't say anything until we see if we're going to be able to stop the August first move." He looked at Rose. "What do you think?"

"When will we know about that?" she asked Mac.

"I'll make some more calls. It should be fairly soon, I'd think. Let me reiterate that it's a slim possibility. You need to be prepared for the alternative. One thing I would suggest is that you consider moving your wedding date forward."

"I agree," Rose said.

"You wouldn't mind?" Cicero asked.

"I told you before that the bells and whistles don't matter as long as I have you."

"And the kids. You said me *and* the kids. I want to give you a family, Rose."

"You are." She rested her hand atop his and squeezed it. "Those four children will always be part of our family. No matter what, they will be part of our lives. Amy said she wouldn't keep them from us."

"That's before we sue. Oh, hell." He rubbed his weary eyes. "It could get ugly, right, Mac?"

"Custody suits often do."

"If we lose, we could lose everything." His expression turned bleak. "We might never see them again."

"We won't let that happen," Rose said, meeting his gaze and holding it. "Remember Mac's admonition about the bottom line. The kids' happiness and security is our bottom line. That means you need to be in their lives. We can't do anything to jeopardize that."

"What are you saying, Rose? Give up?"

"No. I think filing a lawsuit is the right thing to do. It will be a fair test of the Parnells' seriousness where the children are concerned. But Hunt, if they fight back—if they prove this is what they want and not a just response to grief—then we need to be ready to let it go. The kids don't need to be in the middle of a nasty custody fight."

He dragged his hand down his face again. "This

time, I'm Jason Brotherton. It's the same damned nightmare all over again."

Rose took hold of his hand and squeezed it supportively.

"She makes a good point," Mac agreed. "We could concede on a custody fight and gain a visitation agreement you could live with."

Cicero thought it through, then shook his head. "We don't know their motives. I don't trust them. You don't just throw away kids, and then want them back when it's convenient. You don't rip apart their lives on a whim. What they did was unforgivable. The kids deserve better."

He looked at Rose. "You and I are better."

"But we can't ignore the reality," she said. "If it's going to put the kids in the middle of a huge custody battle that we can't win, then nobody wins. The kids suffer. I don't think you want that. We have to put them first in this, and hope for that miracle."

His struggle was obvious. He recognized the reality of the situation. He just didn't want to have to accept it. Eventually, however, he acceded that he must.

"Okay. That makes sense. So, we have a plan. We file for custody, but hold a fallback position of a liberal visitation agreement. Where do we start, Mac?"

"I'll draw up papers this morning and get them over to you to sign. Will you be at your studio?"

"No," Rose said. "We're going into Gunnison."

Cicero frowned in confusion.

"Do you have a doctor's appointment?"

"No." She wiggled the fingers of her left hand. Her engagement ring sparkled. "It's the closest marriage license office."

"We are not going to get married at the courthouse," Cicero said. "Sage would chew my left butt cheek completely off."

"No. We'll come home and get married in front of our friends and our family. On Saturday night."

"You're going to throw a wedding in five days' time?"

"No, silly." She playfully hit his arm. "Of course not. Celeste and my sister will do it."

Nineteen

After leaving Mac's office, Rose and Cicero took an hour to formulate a game plan for the next six weeks. With a strategy in mind, they called their family and close friends and requested they come for lunch and an important discussion at Cicero's studio. Right at noon, their guests began to gather. Celeste, Sage and her husband Colt, Shannon, the Murphys, Gabi and Flynn and Mitch.

"Please, grab something to eat," Rose said, gesturing to the salad and sandwiches she'd picked up from the Fox's Den. "We've had a situation develop. We are under some time constraints, and we decided it'd be easier to share the story with you all at once. Hunt?"

He gave them a rundown of the Parnells' visit and the decisions they'd made in the wake of it. As Rose had expected, all of their friends expressed their concern and support. Sage wrapped her arms around Rose in a hug, and when she cried a little, it took all of Rose's will to fight off tears of her own.

Being a Saturday in June, the local churches and Angel's Rest already had weddings booked. However, by the time they reached the wedding license office, their friends had come through.

"An outdoor wedding at the Davenports' place, I can picture," Cicero observed after she gave her verbal okay to the arrangements those friends had cobbled together. "Eagle's Way estate is spectacular. But a wedding night in a tent?"

"Not just a tent. A yurt—a spectacular yurt. Trust me. You'll love it."

He picked up her hand and kissed it.

"Hey, I'll be with you. Of course I'll love it."

They told the kids about the wedding that night at supper. Their excitement sparked her own and for the first time that day, Rose put aside her worries and allowed herself to enjoy the moment. She was a bride-to-be. For the next six weeks, she got to be mother to these children.

She owed it to herself, to Cicero, and to the kids to live every moment fully and with joy.

She'd have plenty of time to mourn what might have been later.

To her surprise, she slept soundly and awoke, not to an alarm, but to a warm body curled against her in her bed. "Hunt! What are you doing here?"

"I bribed Lori to show up early this morning. I need some stress relief. I thought I'd go to yoga."

"And on the way to Murphy's Pub you just happened to lose your direction and your clothes?"

"Something like that, yeah." He skimmed his lips along the sensitive skin of her neck. "My muscles are tight. I'm really stressed, *Sirena Bellissima*. Help me?"

She rolled over on top of him. "I suppose it's the least I can do."

Forty-five minutes later, she left him sleeping soundly in her bed while she went to yoga class, energized and excited to begin her day. The class flew by, as did her shift at the clinic. She returned to Angel's Rest and went up to her loft to change her clothes before the scheduled three o'clock wedding planning meeting and found a single, long-stemmed red rose lying on her pillow.

She floated down to the kitchen where Celeste sat at the table, a yellow legal pad before her, and a phone at her ear. "That's perfect, Savannah.

Yes, of course we will wait. Rose and I will have a glass of lemonade and a chat."

At home in Celeste's kitchen, Rose fixed two glasses of lemonade and set them on the table as Celeste ended the call and said, "Thank you, dear. Savannah's running about ten minutes late, which is good because I can use a little break. It's been such a busy day. A good busy. I understand you had some excitement this morning."

Had she and Hunt been too loud?

As heat stung Rose's cheeks, Celeste continued, "My guests came back from the clinic singing your praises. They said their daughter might have died had you not acted so swiftly this morning."

"What happened?" Sage asked as she swept into the kitchen.

"A previously undiagnosed food allergy. Acute respiratory distress. Sit down, Sage. You look exhausted." Rose stood and fixed her sister a glass of lemonade.

"I am exhausted. I'm pretty sure my belly doubled in size overnight. August can't get here soon enough."

As soon as the words left Sage's mouth, she shot Rose a stricken look.

"It's okay, Sage," Rose said. "I'd feel the same way if I were you. I remember how miserable I was during those last weeks of pregnancy."

"I like that you speak about it now. For so long—" Sage smiled and blinked back tears. "Oh, here I go again. I cry at everything these days. Enough of this. Let's talk weddings. Celeste, judging by that notepad, you've made progress today."

"I have!"

Rose dropped her gaze toward the legal pad where she saw notes about folding chairs and photographers. She much preferred those sorts of notes to the ones Mac had taken yesterday.

"I can't thank you both enough for your help."

Blue eyes twinkled as she sipped her lemonade.

"I'm thrilled to be part of your wedding, Rose. I love the destination wedding events that we have at Angel's Rest, but having two of our own tie the knot is an extra level of special. This is going to be such a lovely wedding. Now, let me tell you what we have arranged."

She went down her list, beginning with reception plans. "Both Maggie Romano and Sarah Murphy have offered to bake your wedding cake. It's your choice, though even Sarah said you should choose Maggie's famous Italian cream. Ali has suggested this catering menu." Celeste pulled a printed sheet from beneath her legal pad and handed it to Rose.

"They're all my favorites," Rose said.

"Yes, that's what she said," Celeste said. She worked her way down the list, completing the reception information and continuing on to the ceremony itself. "Now, we are short on officiants, but Reverend Harold from St. Anne's over in Creede has offered to substitute for Reverend Leak of St. Stephen's, so that he can scoot up to the Davenports' to perform your wedding. I have a list of readings for you and Hunter to review before your meeting with Reverend Leak tomorrow at eleven. You can make that?"

"Um, yes," Rose said. "Of course."

"He will go over your vows with you. Do you want to write your own or are you more traditional?"

"Traditional," Sage and Rose said simultaneously.

The sisters shared a smile, as Celeste continued.

"We have Galen and Keenan as co–ring bearers. Misty and Daisy will be flower girls. If you will give me the boys' sizes, we can order little suits for them over the Internet and have them here in two days. Since the girls had matching Easter dresses, we thought they could wear those, only with sashes that matched Sage's dress."

"Your dress?" Rose asked Sage.

"I'm your matron of honor, of course. Due to my condition, I'm limited in appropriate choices of a dress."

Rose's lips twitched.

"Of course."

"Will Flynn be Cicero's best man? Or maybe Mitch?"

"Honestly, we haven't discussed it."

Celeste clicked her tongue and wrote another note on her legal pad.

"By the end of today, please. We will need a number and names. Well, that brings us to flowers and your dress. What would you like to carry in your bouquet, Rose? The meadow is carpeted with a rainbow of wildflowers this week—alpine timothy, bog sedge, rushes, bistort, Colorado blue columbine, larkspur, gentian, geranium, Jacob's ladder, monkshood, catchfly, phlox, and blue-bells."

"I'd like to carry daisies and bluebells."

"Lovely choice. Bluebell is Misty's middle name, I understand. The girls will be pleased. So that takes us to the main attraction. Your wedding gown."

"I know. I think I'll have to take Thursday to rush into Denver and try to find a sample gown that fits or shop the secondhand shops. I'd go tomorrow, but Dr. Coulson can't cover for me and—"

Sage linked her arm with Rose's and said, "If you don't find what you are looking for now, we'll make Thursday a girls' day to Denver. In the meantime, we should be ready. Shall we step into the upstairs to your suite? We're set up there."

Set up for what? Rose wondered as she and Sage followed Celeste upstairs. She walked into her suite of rooms to find it transformed. Wedding gowns lined one whole wall, hung on three long clothing racks. Six full-length mirrors were positioned in a semicircle at the center of the room. Boxes filled with white satiny fabric sat at one end of the line of gowns.

"How in the world?" she asked.

Savannah Turner sat on a chair beside one of the boxes, a tape measure draped around her neck and a beaded bodice in her lap. "I'd forgotten what wonderful stuff the Patchwork Angels had squirreled away."

Founded by the late LaNelle Harrison, the Patchwork Angels Quilting Bee had made the most beautiful quilts from fabric and embellishments from wedding gowns donated to the group. After LaNelle's tragic death three years ago, membership in the bee had dwindled.

"Once the tourist season is over, we should see about holding regular meetings again. I've missed the group."

"Where did all these dresses come from?" Rose asked, drawn to the racks.

"We're hoping to save you from having to make a Denver trip. Gabi said when she shopped she saw very few sample gowns to buy right off the rack. When you look closely, you might recognize many of these dresses. They are ours—gowns worn by the women of Eternity Springs, your sister, your friends, even some of your patients—

offered for the honor of becoming your 'something borrowed.' My grandmother taught me to sew and I will do any alterations you might need. Or, if you want to start from scratch and keep the design fairly simple, we can piece together something from the quilting supplies."

"Oh," Rose breathed, taken aback.

"We'll do our best to make it as close to your dream dress as possible, honey," Sage said.

"I don't know what to say," Rose added. "A woman's wedding gown is one of her most prized possessions. How generous of everyone."

"Well, people love to have a chance to pay back some of your generosity." Celeste gave Rose's rear a little swat. "Now, don't just stand there. Shop! We still have a list a mile long of things to see to."

Rose did recognize many of the wedding gowns. Lots of romance happened in this pretty mountain valley. But one gown in particular attracted her eye. Designed to fit close to the body from chest to knee, then to flare out to the hem, the ivory silk dupioni "mermaid" silhouette suited her hour-glass body type perfectly. Strapless, with a fanned, seashell neckline and V-shaped back and a chapel train, the gown was lightly embellished with crystal beads.

In her mind's eye, she recalled the first time Cicero had looked at her and murmured, *Sirena Bellissima*. Beautiful mermaid, she silently translated as she lifted the dress off the rack. "This is gorgeous."

"The racks are full of gorgeous dresses," Savannah said. "I do love that one. I can't recall who wore it, though. Must have been before my time in Eternity Springs."

"Try it on," Celeste encouraged. She breezily took it from Rose's arms and carried it toward her bedroom where she spread the gown across Rose's bed. "Slip it on and holler and I'll come zip you up."

"Okay." Rose removed a strapless bra from her lingerie drawer, stripped, and changed her bra. Then she unzipped the wedding gown and prepared to step into it when she spied a big blue tag tied with a ribbon and pinned onto the lining of the dress. Curious, she read the handwritten note on the tag:

Pick me! Pick me! If you love this dress as much as I do, please choose it. You would be doing me a grand favor. Please don't ever tell my mom, but while I love the dress and will wear it if you don't bail me out, it's not the wedding gown of my dreams. I said yes to this dress because my mother loved it best, and I've regretted my emotional, spur-of-the-moment decision ever since.

I want you to love your gown, so no pressure. (Pick me!) But this dress suits you and I'll bet you look like a million bucks wearing it. (Pick me!) Try it on and see. (And then, pick me!)

You'll get me off the hook with my mom, and I'll get the do-over I've been wishing for. (Pick me!) Consider it your wedding gift to me. (Pick me!)

Love, Gabi

Rose laughed aloud, tried on Gabriella Romano's wedding gown, and fell in love.

On the sun-kissed morning of his wedding day, Cicero took overnight bags for the hoodlums to the Callahans' house, dropped Galen and Keenan at Lucca Romano's summer basketball camp at the school, and left Daisy with Savannah Turner who'd promised to see that all four kids got up to Eagle's Way in time to get dressed for the ceremony.

Then he went to the studio. He had a notion to make a gift for his bride on their wedding day.

"What are you doing here, mon?" Mitch asked as he sauntered into the studio. "It's your wedding day."

"That it is. And I need to make my bride a little surprise." He wanted something light and bright and happy. Something that would make her smile. A piece to commemorate the day.

He went to work, let his mind drift, pictured Rose as he had left her last night after walking her back to Angel's Rest, her mouth swollen from his kisses. He thought of making love to her as he crafted a flowing, pulsing form in bright red, the color of life and love and passion.

He lost himself in his work—and came close to being late for his own wedding.

Like a good best man should, Flynn pulled his ass away from the fire and got him to Eagle's Way with eight minutes to spare.

Sage glowed with that special luminescence that expectant mothers often display as she walked up the wildflower-dotted aisle. Galen dropped his ring bearer's pillow, then Keenan picked it up and wouldn't give it back. The brothers traded punches until they took their assigned seats. Misty smiled shyly as she held her sister's hand and helped her drop rose petals on her way up the aisle.

Then Rose appeared and took his breath away.

"*Sirena Bellissima*," he said, lifting her hand to his mouth for a kiss.

They exchanged their wedding vows in front of family and friends, and danced the night away to a live band. Where the hell Flynn came up with the stretch Jeep limo that spirited them away from Eagle's Way to the infamous yurt, he hadn't a clue. Nor did he worry about it once he got a look at the tent.

Round and as big as a house, it had a wood floor,

indoor plumbing—complete with a sunken tub—and a round bed roughly the size of the Starship *Enterprise.*

She took him to the stars and back as they made love until dawn.

The following day, they went home to the monsters. Rose settled in to the mother role with enthusiasm, and their home and family became one filled with laughter, love, and joy.

On July third, Mac called with the news that his request for temporary custody had been denied. During supper, Amy texted new puppy pictures to Misty and asked her to ask Cicero to call them at his earliest convenience.

Rose sent him a questioning look. He'd decided to wait to share Mac's news after the kids had gone to bed, but she must have seen something in his expression because she suddenly set down her fork, dabbed at her mouth with her cloth napkin—a new addition to his home since the wedding—and excused herself.

"I need to check on dessert."

"Dessert?" Galen repeated. "We're having dessert? What dessert? I want dessert."

"I didn't see her cook anything," Keenan said. "Did you see her cook anything, Misty?"

Busy yearning at the pictures on her phone, Misty didn't look up. "She didn't bake. She didn't bring anything home."

Cicero gave his wife five minutes, then walked

into the kitchen where he found her staring at little bowls filled with instant pudding sitting on a tray. He ran his finger around the lip of the mixing bowl and licked it.

"Banana, huh? Butterscotch is my favorite."

"In that case, buy butterscotch and make it yourself."

"Whoa, the honeymoon's over fast, is it?"

She closed her eyes. "I'm sorry. I just—you heard something, didn't you? Tell me. Just tell me."

"I was going to tell you after the kids went to bed. Mac called."

"We can't stop August first, can we?"

"No. I'm sorry. We rushed the wedding for no good reason."

"Stop it." Always the healer, Rose reached out and touched his forearm. "Our wedding was wonderful and it was exactly what it was supposed to be."

"If I win the Albritton, I'm going to buy us our very own yurt. And our very own adult dress-up box like the Timberlakes have. I really liked the harem costumes." He took her in his arms and held her tight. Against her hair, he murmured, "I'm so sorry, Rose. I wanted to give you the children you wanted."

"You have. They are mine, no matter where they live, with whom they live, or what they call Amy or any other woman in their lives, I am their

Doctor Mom. Being with you has taught me that my definition of family has been too narrow. My definition of motherhood has been too narrow. I want—"

"Are we going to get dessert or—" Keenan broke off. "Oh, geez. Are y'all slobbering on each other again?"

"Go away, Sprout. Now." Cicero nibbled at his wife's neck.

Galen entered the kitchen on his brother's heels.

"I want dessert. Can I have dessert?"

Laughing, Rose ducked away from Cicero. "Banana pudding for everyone who is in their seats by the time I count to five. One, two, three—"

The boys fled squealing with delight. Cicero stared at the empty doorway, distracted by a flash of memory. "My mother used to do that, count like that. She'd pick random numbers, though. Not three or five or ten. She'd say seventeen or forty-three or one thousand sixty-seven. Weird, isn't it, what you remember about being a kid?"

"It's a good memory for you."

"Yeah. Yeah, it is."

"We have three weeks left with these darlings. Let's go make some memories, shall we?"

Twenty

It was the best July of Rose's life.

She worked. She played. She lived. She loved. Oh, how she loved. She made heart-shaped waffles for breakfast and had peanut butter sandwich picnics beside Angel Creek on her lunch break. She cheered Keenan when Cicero taught him to ride a bike without training wheels. She dealt with her first ear infection on the other side of the stethoscope.

She signed her scripts Dr. R. Cicero.

And the days flew by.

Her attitude remained amazingly positive. She knew that she'd be blue after the children left for Texas, but she refused to ruin what time she had left with them. Unfortunately, her husband wasn't taking the impending change as well. He grew grumpier as each day passed. She suspected that the long hours he'd been keeping in the studio lay at the root of his bad attitude.

At ten minutes to seven on the thirtieth, she waved to Shannon when she entered the theater. Moments later, Sage waddled down the aisle to the front row seats Rose had saved for them. "You came!" Rose said. "I'm so glad. I wasn't sure you'd make it."

"I'm due in a week," Sage grumbled. "I'll

probably carry this baby for another year. And I didn't want to miss Misty's big night. Is she excited? Nervous? Over the moon thrilled?"

"All of the above."

"Where's Cicero?" Shannon asked.

Rose glanced back toward the entry, frowning. "I don't know. Still at the studio, I guess. I called him right before you arrived, but he didn't pick up."

"I'm sure he's on his way," Sage assured. "A photographer was there taking pictures of the Albritton piece today. Maybe that ran long."

"He's been working crazy hours." Rose tore her gaze away from the doorway. "Whimsies' success has been both a curse and a blessing. Gabi and Mitch are working nonstop just to keep the shelves filled, and new commissions are pouring in for Hunt since word of the Albritton has gotten around."

"I sold two more of his pieces this week," Sage said. "And, I talked him into letting me see the Albritton work again. It's fabulous. Simply spectacular. He's going to win the fellowship. I just know it. Has he decided on a name for it yet?"

"Not that I know of. I thought he intended to ask you for suggestions."

"He did. I'm haven't come up with anything so far."

"Me, either. I think once Hunt and I get past

this weekend, we'll be better able to think about what's coming up in September."

Shannon patted Rose's knee. "Any news from Texas?"

"They'll be here tomorrow."

Sage wrinkled her nose in disapproval. "The plan is still to spring news of the move on the kids after the play?"

Rose sighed, checked her watch, then scoped out the entrance once again. Where is he? "Yes. It's what we negotiated with the Parnells. I honestly think this approach is best. Misty has been so wrapped up this play. She's made a friend of Holly Montgomery, and she's just so happy. Keenan has new friends he's not going to want to leave. What good would it do to tell them too much ahead of time and let them brood? You and I know it's most often easiest to pull the bandage off fast."

Sage dipped her head and rested it on Rose's shoulder. "I'm sorry, sister."

"We'll be okay. Hey, I won't have time to be blue. I have a new niece ready to make her entrance to the world."

The lights flickered and an announcer asked guests to take their seats. Rose dialed Cicero's number again. Again, no answer. She glanced back toward the entrance and spied familiar faces entering the theater. Amy and Scott Parnell. Her stomach sank. A part of Rose had held out the hope that when the time came for talk to turn to action, they wouldn't show.

She blinked back tears. *Hunter, where are you?*

Cicero sneaked a peek at his watch. He had twenty minutes before he absolutely had to leave. "That should be good, don't you think?" he asked the photographer.

"Just a few more shots. The afternoon light in this room is simply fantastic. Your piece pulses in places and glimmers in others."

"My daughter's play starts at seven. I won't be late."

"Sure. Okay. I understand. I have a daughter, too. How old is she, your girl?"

"Almost ten. I have a two-year-old, too." Even as he claimed them, he wondered why he used the word "daughter" rather than "niece."

"Little girls sure are special. I'll wrap it up so you can get to your play. Want to be sure you get a seat."

"My wife is saving one for me, but it wouldn't do for me not to be there when the curtain rises."

Eight minutes later, he ushered the photographer out the front door. He flipped the lock behind him, then headed for his office where he had a bouquet of flowers waiting to take to Misty.

A dozen yellow roses were nestled in green tissue paper and tied with a yellow ribbon. He'd just picked them up when he heard the back door open and footsteps pound across the studio's wooden floor.

The cry and crash stopped his heart.

Rose watched Marta and Liesl and Friedrich and Brigitta and the others sing about their favorite things—and plotted murder. As soon as the play was over, she'd march over to the studio and use his hammer on his head. Or maybe stab him with his punty. Or shove him into the furnace. Or pinch his head off with those big pliers of his.

Or, she could tie him into a chair, lock him in a room, and force him to repeatedly watch the video of the look on Misty's face when she'd first walked out on stage and noticed the empty seat next to Rose.

How could you do this to her, Hunt?

It was one thing for him to forget her at a Caribbean island party; but something else entirely to disappoint Misty on the most special day of her nine-year-old life. What project was so important that he would let her down this way?

There isn't one.

Something was wrong. Something was terribly wrong. He wouldn't be a no-show if he could possibly have avoided it.

But a little part of her remembered that night on Bella Vita. She couldn't forget that the man was an artist. When it came to his work, her husband could be selfish and blind and temperamental with a capital *T*. He had been grouchy lately. Could this be his way of protecting himself from the pain of the children's departure? Make them so angry that they'll be glad to go? Sort of a one-sided separation anxiety?

Surreptitiously, she checked her pager. Nothing. Okay, then. If anything too serious had happened, someone would have paged her.

She tried to lose herself in the production, but her mind drifted. Minutes dragged by. When the final bows were taken, she wanted to rush from the theater to go searching for her husband. Instead, she waited for Misty at the stage door as planned and called him. This time her call went straight to voicemail. She thought a moment then sent Lori Murphy a text. "Do you know where Hunt is?"

"The studio," came the answer as the Parnells walked up, and Sage and Colt joined her. They had flowers to give Misty. Rose had never felt so empty-handed in her life.

When she exited the stage door minutes later, Misty's watery gaze swept over the waiting gathering. The hope in her eyes died.

"He didn't come, did he? I thought maybe he got stuck at the back, but he wasn't here at all. Why didn't he come to my play, Doctor Mom?"

"I don't know, honey. I'm anxious to find out

myself." Rose gave her hard hug. "Congratulations, Misty. You were the best Brigitta ever."

"We were here, sweetheart," Amy Parnell said, stepping forward, handing Misty a mixed flower bouquet and giving her a hug. "You were wonderful. We are so proud."

Shyly, the young girl said, "Thank you. I didn't think you'd be here until tomorrow."

Amy blinked fiercely. "We couldn't stay away. I didn't want to miss your debut."

"That's nice."

"C'mere, beautiful," Colt hugged Misty and Sage handed her flowers. "Congratulations."

Sage added, "You were fantastic."

"Thanks Uncle Colt. Thanks Auntie Sage."

Rose watched Scott's eyebrows lift at the girl's use of the words aunt and uncle. She said, "Amy and Scott Parnell, meet my sister and her husband, Sage and Colt Rafferty, and our friend, Shannon O'Toole."

Colt shook their hands. Sage kept her hands folded over her baby belly, her smile polite but not reaching her eyes. Shannon offered a cool hello.

Rose spoke to Misty. "Your uncle isn't answering his phone and Lori said in a text that he's at the studio. I want to walk over there and see what's up. Want to come with me?"

"Yes!"

The two-block walk took only minutes. As they

approached the front door, Rose noted the closed sign in the window. "Let's try the side door."

Misty suddenly broke into a run, leaving the adults bringing up the rear.

Cicero propped his tired legs up on the table in the storage room, took a long pull of his beer, and tried to remember the last time he'd been this tired. He drew a blank.

He felt like he'd been run over by a cement truck. Then a gravel hauler. And finished off by a trash truck.

He dropped his head back, closed his eyes, and tried his level best to dismiss all the negatives. He reminded himself to think of the positives. He got to sleep with Rose every night. It was only the end of July.

He didn't have a damned dog.

He tipped the longneck and savored the crisp, cold ale as the back door opened and a whirlwind burst into the room. Misty saw him, stopped short, her chest heaving. Her eyes bright with tears. She held flowers in her arms. Flowers from somebody else.

"Keenan is right!" she accused, her voice brimming with righteous anger. "You are Uncle Skunk! You broke your promise to come to my play!"

He heaved a heavy sigh. He'd hoped to be able to finish his beer before this happened. He took one more sip of beer, then spied not only his wife standing in the storeroom, but also the Raffertys and the very last people in the world he wanted to see—the Parnells.

Oh, joy.

He wasn't brave enough to meet Rose's gaze. He didn't give a damn about Amy and Scott. He focused his attention on the unavoidable.

"Hey, Worm. How was the play?"

"I can't believe you stayed here drinking beer rather than coming to my play."

"Misty, let me—"

She was having none of it. "It was just like the spelling bee. Mom drank too much and forgot about it. I guess you're both drunks."

"Hey!" Cicero pulled his feet off the table. "You don't talk about your mother that way, young lady."

"She was my mom and I can talk about her how I want. You're not the boss of me."

"Yeah, little girl, I am. For a couple more days, anyway, I am the boss of you and as long as you're living in my house, you will do as I say."

"Then I don't want to live in your house any-more!"

His emotions churning, Cicero lost control of his tongue. "Well, sweetheart, don't look now, but you're about to get your wish."

"Hunter . . ." Rose warned as he set his beer bottle on the table and stood.

"You're telling her like this?" Amy snapped, her eyes flashing with anger as she stepped forward. "That's not what we agreed, Cicero. This isn't how it's supposed to be. I spoke with a counselor about how to tell the children they're moving back to Texas and she said—"

Oh, hell.

"Amy!" Scott grabbed hold of his wife's arm and gave it a shake. "Watch what you're saying."

With any luck, Misty had been too wrapped up in her own emotions to notice either his slip or her aunt's, but one look at the girl showed him his run of luck hadn't changed.

"M-m-moving?" she repeated.

Cicero took three determined steps toward the girl and dropped to his knees in front of her.

"Worm, I didn't make it to the play tonight because as I was leaving for the theater, Lori showed up here with the kids. She was sick. Then the boys got sick. Daisy got sick. I'm so, so sorry I missed your play. It broke my heart to miss it, but sometimes life throws you a curve ball."

"Sick? Everyone's sick? Where are they? Are my brothers and sister okay?"

"They were throwing up. It was disgusting. I called Dr. Coulson and he gave me the skinny on what to do. They're all okay. They're asleep upstairs. I'm hoping Doctor Mom will go up and check on them."

From the corner of his eyes, he saw Rose

already moving toward the other room and the staircase to the loft where the younger kids slept. He breathed a sigh of relief.

Misty asked, "Why did Aunt Amy say we're moving to Texas?"

The question was a knife to his heart. "Worm, when your mother got sick, she wanted the very best for you. She believed that your Aunt Amy and Uncle Scott were those people. I thought the same thing, too. Remember, I hadn't met Doctor Mom, yet."

"They didn't want us," she said in a little voice.

Amy covered her mouth with her hands. Scott placed his hand on his wife's shoulder. Cicero noted their stricken expressions and for the first time, he felt a pang of empathy for them. "That's not true. They wanted you. They still want you. You guys are lucky because everyone wants you."

"It doesn't feel lucky."

Cicero reached out and gently tugged her pigtail. "Worm, here's the deal. I love you with all of my heart. I would crawl to the moon and back for you. I am going to do the very best I can for you. You were happy in Houston before. You'll be happy again and y'all can come visit when the weather's good and not have to be here when snow is six feet deep."

"I think they only want Daisy. They want a baby."

"No!" Cicero gave her shoulders a little shake.

"They want you all. Amy? Scott? Explain to Misty how all of the kids are equal in your eyes."

At that point, he heard Rose's horrified gasp and knew she'd seen the mess on the studio floor.

Rose knew immediately that the shards and fragments of broken glass lying beside the overturned display table was the Albritton piece. Horror filled her and acting instinctively, she gasped and turned back toward the storage room. "What happened, Hunt?"

"Keenan bumped into the table just right."

"It's the Albritton piece."

"Yeah."

"It's broken?" Sage's gasp was a repeat of Rose's own. "Oh, no. Oh, no! That piece was a masterpiece. Can you repair it?"

"It's shattered," Rose explained.

Sage covered her mouth with her hand. "Oh, Cicero. That's terrible."

Anger flashed through Rose as she pictured it. "That careless boy. I've told him dozens of times not to run indoors. He truly is a bull in a china closet and what he's done now—"

"Keenan broke your contest piece?" Misty asked in a squeak. "Is that why you're letting us go?"

From the corner of her eye, Rose saw Scott Parnell turn to Sage and ask, "What's the Albritton piece?"

While her sister explained the breadth of the disaster, Cicero met first Rose's gaze, then Misty's.

"No, don't blame him. It was an accident. An unfortunate accident. The boy needed the bathroom, fast. He was trying to get there."

Tears started rolling down Misty's cheeks. She walked over to Cicero and hugged him. "I'm so sorry, Uncle Hunk. I'm sorry I got mad. I didn't know."

Rose's heart broke and Cicero's voice sounded husky as he said, "I love you, Worm. And that's why everything is going to be okay."

"Can I do anything to help?" Misty asked.

"Yes. Actually, yes you can. Run over to the Trading Post and pick up a box of diapers and some wipes. I used all we have and Daisy is in a towel and duct tape right now. Have them put it on my tab."

"Okay, Uncle Hunk. I'll hurry." Misty turned toward the door, then hesitated. "Maybe—could duct tape fix the Albritton?"

"I'm afraid it's beyond duct tape, but don't worry." He winked at her. "We have the Super Glue that's gonna fix it just fine."

Rose had seen the shattered glass. Nothing could fix that piece. It was beyond repair. Her gaze swept over the Parnells who waited to steal away her children. Shattered, just like our family, she thought.

As though he'd heard her despair, Cicero shifted

his gaze her way. He winked at her, too. "Love and hope, *Bella Rosa.* Trust me. As bonding agents, they can't be beat."

At the end of the day from hell, fresh from a shower and wearing his favorite ratty sweatpants, Cicero joined his wife in the porch swing and tugged her close. "They're all asleep. Finally."

Rose idly trailed her finger up and down his fleece-clad thigh. "Did you get the boys to drink anymore water?"

"Yeah. I told 'em if they didn't finish the glass, that you were going to hook them up to a tube that pumped it into them directly. Through their peckers."

"Hunter!" She pulled away from him. "You did not!"

"I did," he said, grinning with satisfaction as he pulled her back into his arms where she belonged. "You should have seen the looks on their faces. Horror turned to disbelief pretty quick, but they both drained their drinks." He paused and his grin died. "It got their minds off their troubles, anyway."

They had planned to wait until tomorrow to tell the boys about the move, but Keenan had awakened while Cicero and Rose were giving Daisy a bath, and Misty spilled the beans to him. He'd taken the news poorly, certain he was being punished for having broken the Albritton sculpture. Cicero finally talked the boy out of that notion—at least, he thought he had—but it had taken some work.

"I don't like how Keenan is being so quiet. It's like his little live wire has shorted out."

"He'll recover and recharge," Rose said. "He's young. They've lived here a few months, not a few years."

Cicero pushed against the porch's decking to set the swing into motion.

"Good months."

"Yes, very good months." She snuggled closer against him and admitted, "My heart fell when I saw Amy in the back of the theater. A part of me had held out hope that they'd change their minds."

"Me, too."

The swing's chains creaked rhythmically as they sat in reflective silence for a time. Eventually, she said, "You know, Hunt, I don't have to live in Eternity Springs. Maybe we should think about moving closer to the kids."

Cicero frowned. He hadn't been expecting that one.

"Sage would shoot me dead. Then the rest of your friends would decapitate me and your patients would stick my head on a spike and stick it in the ground beside the city limits sign."

"Now, Hunt—"

"Seriously, *Bellissima*. You are needed here. I

don't care how many physicians work at the clinic, you are this town's doctor. You are the heart of Eternity Springs. We will visit the monsters, and the monsters will visit us as often as we like. That's the deal we have with Scott and Amy."

"I will miss them so much."

"I know. I will, too."

With a grouchy note in her voice, she said, "You have an awfully positive attitude about this entire evening."

"You wouldn't say that if you'd seen me adrift in a sea of vomit."

She pulled away out of his embrace and turned to face him. Light from the porch lamp cast a golden glow across her face, and illuminated the wonder in her expression as she asked, "So what happened? How did you get from there to here?"

"I think I hit bottom when I snapped at Misty for her crack about Jayne's drinking. That made me feel like such a dick. All night long, hell, all month long, I've felt so helpless. I've felt hopeless. Tonight, I stood in my studio with the best work I've ever done lying in a shattered mess at my feet, knowing I'm losing a chunk of my family—again. Feeling like I'd let you down."

"Let me down? No, Hunt."

"I gave you a family. I couldn't keep it from slipping away."

"They're going to Texas, not Timbuktu."

"I know. And I also—finally—understand

Dickinson. Because of you." For what might have been the millionth time, he quoted the verse:

> " 'Hope is the thing with feathers.
> That perches in the soul
> And sings the tune without the words
> And never stops at all.'

"Tonight, the minute those harsh words to Misty left my mouth, I looked over and you were there and I got it. It's Dickinson, but it's Tennyson, too. And, it's Dr. Seuss."

"Dr. Seuss!"

He leaned forward and captured her mouth in a firm, confident kiss.

" 'Don't cry because it's over. Smile because it happened.' But it's bigger than that. It's yoga in the morning and ice-cream cones on a summer night. It's pub debates over fantasy baseball, hiking an Alpine meadow, and learning to braid pigtails that match. It's sex on a beach on Bella Vita Isle. I wish I could better articulate it, but I'm not a writer, not a word person. But I *am* a glass artist. I can—I will—create it out of glass."

Halfway through his speech, her eyes filled with tears. "I think you said it very well, Hunt Cicero."

"Well, wait until you see it. It's gonna blow you away. Might even win the Albritton."

"I can't wait to see it."

"I can't wait to get to work on it. I already know what I'm going to call it."

"What?"

Grinning, he crooked his finger for her to lean toward him. When he had her ear, he whispered, "It's a surprise."

Then he nipped at her earlobe and nibbled his way down her neck, and soon finished off a truly challenging day playing with a different kind of fire.

On the first day of August, Rose watched the Parnells drive away with the children and bravely told herself she'd faced more difficult good-byes in her life. Elizabeth. Her father. Friends who'd lost their lives on the battlefields in Afghanistan. Today's good-bye wasn't permanent. In some ways, it made her life easier. Caring for four children certainly wasn't the easiest way to begin married life. Nevertheless, she couldn't recall the last time her arms felt this empty.

So she wrapped them around Cicero's waist.

"And I thought our drive from Houston was bad," he said, a little catch in his voice. "We didn't have a puppy along for the ride, too. I can't believe they didn't board the dog at home."

"They thought having the puppy along would keep the kiddos from being sad," she said, trying to keep the bitterness out of her tone. She only partially succeeded.

"They damn sure thought wrong about that, didn't they? Does it make me a bad person to feel superior because the kids didn't cry when they left Houston, but they're bawling when leaving Eternity Springs?"

"Not in my book." Rose didn't take her gaze off the Parnells' car as it approached the intersection at Spruce Street. Once it turned and drove out of sight, she'd go inside and begin cleaning up after breakfast. To her surprise, the vehicle sat. And sat. And sat at the intersection. She wondered if Galen was throwing a tantrum.

"Huh," Cicero said. "His backup lights have come on."

Rose realized he was right, as the SUV pulled into a driveway, then turned around. "They must have forgotten something."

She furrowed her brow, trying to think of what it might be. Trying to imagine what else they could squeeze into their car.

The Parnells' SUV turned into their driveway. The back door opened and Misty climbed out, her eyes red and rimmed with tears. She was carrying her dog.

"Honey, what did you forget?" asked Rose.

"Nothing. I didn't forget anything. I want to— it's just that—you and Uncle Hunk broke my heart."

Rose and Cicero shared a look.

"We broke your heart? What did we do, Worm?"

Tears poured down the little girl's face. "I love you."

"We love you, too," Rose said.

"I know. We know. You are going to be so lonely without us."

"Yeah, we are. Is that what's breaking your heart?"

"Yes!"

"Well, there's no need for that. We'll be okay. Doctor Mom and I have each other."

"You need more," she wailed.

"Worm . . ." Cicero said, at a loss.

"Here." She shoved the dog at her uncle. "You need him, Uncle Hunk. Aunt Amy and Uncle Scott said I could give him to you. He'll keep you and Doctor Mom company. You can take him on walks. He'll keep you company when Doctor Mom is at the clinic. When he's a little older, you can take him to the studio with you."

"A dog? You want to give us your dog?"

"I'll be busy in Texas. I'll have drama club and Girl Scouts and softball. I won't have time for a puppy. You take care of him for me, Uncle Hunk."

"But—but—"

"You love him for me. Okay? Send me pictures of how much he's grown." She shoved the dog into his arms. "And you pick out the perfect name for him. Okay? You'll do that?"

"I-I—no."

Rose's heart sank.

Hunter, no.

"We're going to pick out his name together." Cicero clutched the puppy against his chest and scratched him behind the ears. "You and I will text about it."

"You'll keep him?"

"We'll take care of him. He's your dog, Worm, but Doctor Mom and I will give him a home. He'll be here waiting for you when you come to visit."

"Good. That's good. I love you, Uncle Hunter. You, too, Doctor Mom."

When it became clear to Rose that Cicero couldn't speak without breaking down, she hugged Misty and said, "We love you, too, baby."

The car horn sounded. Misty looked toward it, then said, "I have to go now. Take good care of him."

Cicero cleared his throat. "Don't worry, Worm. He'll have a name before you guys hit the New Mexico border."

Misty gave them both one last hug, gave the puppy one final kiss, and hurried back to the car. This time, when the Parnells reached the intersection at Spruce Street, the car kept on going.

With a shaky smile on her face, Rose reached out and scratched the pup behind his ears. Cicero's eyes were closed and he cradled the pup against his chest.

"Are you okay?" Rose asked.

"Have you looked at this dog?" He looked at

her with watery brown eyes. "It's some sort of cosmic coincidence. He's a wheatie. A wheaten terrier. Just like my Pike."

Music blasted from speakers mounted high in the rafters of what had once been a church. Gabi had put together the classic rock playlist of songs about fire, and it had quickly become his favorite music to work to. As Cicero extended his long metal blowpipe into the white-hot crucible and gathered glass, he lost himself to the beat of Jimi Hendrix, Van Halen, Queen, U2, and Kiss.

Heat from the furnace burning at two thousand degrees fanned the flames of his passion for the image fully formed in his mind. The vision burned inside of him, suited to words like powerful, dangerous. Passionate. Raw. Earthy. Sexual.

He'd been working on the core of the piece for hours—or maybe days.

No, a lifetime.

He added color to the gather of glass, worked it, shaped it, added life with a steady, measured stream of air from his lungs. While the Boss sang of fire, Mitch interpreted Cicero's wordless gestures and returned the figure to the furnace to heat.

Cicero closed his eyes. Sitting at his workstation, he swayed to the pulse of the vision in his mind as much as that of the music pounding through the studio. At the edge of his awareness, he noted a sound—a stirring—in his studio, but he refused to be distracted. The fire within him burned hot and fast and consuming.

He cut his hand through the air. Mitch returned the heated piece to him. He took the jacks and stretched the glass. Fierce, strong, shatterproof. Now, to add the ballet.

Using tools long mastered and vision newly birthed, he spun his glass into a form airy and graceful and magical. Eternal.

Hunter Cicero played with fire for a living and today, he paid homage to the gift of his talent.

And when it was done, when he placed his work into the annealer, he acknowledged the triumph singing in his blood. Although he wouldn't see the final colors until it cooled, he knew. Keenan had done him a favor.

This piece was superior to anything else he'd ever done. Simple, graceful, delicate. Striking and strong. A cosmos of color surrounding a vibrant, brilliant red and gold center. A steady heart. A generous soul. It would be his pièce de résistance.

Without looking toward the observation bleachers, he grabbed water from the fridge beside the annealer. He twisted off the lid and lifted the bottle to his lips. As cold water soothed his throat, the applause began softly. One pair of hands. Rose, he knew. Now, more. Gabi. Mitch.

And others.

Cicero turned around and the bottle slipped from his hand.

The children. Their children. Daisy sitting on his wife's lap in the front row, the other three sitting beside her, still as church mice but for the clapping of their hands. Their eyes were bright. Their smiles bright as the sun.

"What—" he croaked out.

Rose stood and handed Daisy off to Misty, who in turn handed the dog over to Keenan. Rose stepped forward, coming to him with her arms outstretched.

"They got as far as Amarillo. Amy said she'd never seen such love as what Misty showed you by giving you her dog. She'd never realized that you aren't simply Uncle Skunk to the boys, but their father."

Cicero closed his eyes and swallowed hard.

Rose continued. "She said that she'd promised Jayne that her children would have a mother and father who loved them. That was her promise to your sister. She sees now that they have that with us. She and Scott don't have to feel guilty. They've kept their promise to Jayne. They've signed Mac's papers, Hunter."

"The children are ours?"

"The children are ours. We have our family."

His breath exhaled in a rush. He took her into his arms, buried his face against her head, and fought back tears.

Clearing his throat, he added, "And a dog, too."

Epilogue

The California Coast

Two dozen round tables set with white tablecloths dotted the manicured green lawn of a private home with a breathtaking view of the Pacific Ocean. But as the sun began to sink into the sapphire sea, painting the sky in luscious shades of crimson, orange, and gold, Rose couldn't stop looking at her husband. If he looked any hotter, she'd burst into fire.

The tuxedo fit him like a dream. She'd thought him the most gorgeous man she'd ever seen in his suit, but wearing a tux—wow. He must have felt the power of her gaze because he interrupted his conversation with Colt and Flynn and gave her a slow, smoldering smile.

"My dragon," she murmured as two of their guests returned to their table following a trip to the ladies' room.

Sage wore green, and looked amazingly slim for a woman who'd given birth just a little over a month ago. Celeste glimmered in her golden gown. Fresh from the first leg of an extended honeymoon spent on Bella Vita Isle, Gabi sported the tall, tanned tropical goddess look in island batik.

"It's almost time," Gabi said to Cicero. "Are you nervous?"

"A little," he admitted. "I find speaking in front of a crowd intimidating."

"Don't worry," Shannon said, arranging the skirts of her sapphire gown. "None of the women will be listening to what you say."

"True," Gabi agreed. "They'll be too busy looking at you."

He scolded the women with a look and took a sip of water as Celeste opened up her purse. "Before the announcement, I have a little gift for you and Rose, Hunter."

She set two small boxes on the table wrapped in white paper and gold ribbon.

"Celeste," Cicero chided. "This wasn't necessary. This isn't a gift occasion. The fact that you and so many of our friends and family are sharing this moment with us is gift enough."

"Oh, hush, mon, and open the present," Mitch said.

Rose didn't have to open the box. She knew what she'd find inside. Sure enough, tucked inside and lying against gold satin was an Angel's Rest blazon, one of the pendants Eternity Springs's angel gave to those whom she deemed had embraced love's healing grace. It was a treasure Rose had coveted for a long time.

"Thank you, my friend," she said, leaning over to press a kiss against Celeste's rosy cheek.

Just as the president of the Albritton Foundation stepped up to the podium, Celeste said, "May God bless you and your family, dearest Rose, as you have blessed our town with your healing hands."

"Good evening, ladies and gentlemen," boomed the president's voice across the estate's sprawling lawn. "Welcome to the biennial Albritton Foundation fellowship award dinner. I hope you all had the opportunity to view the work of our finalists on display inside. We are certainly thrilled to have art of such beauty, breadth, and variety to illustrate our theme for the year."

He spoke for a few more minutes, then introduced the three finalists. As Cicero made his way to the front accompanied by thunderous applause, Rose's heart swelled with love, and tears of joy overflowed her eyes.

The tears didn't abate when moments later, the foundation president announced this year's grand prizewinner, the masterpiece in glass entitled Rose's Bloom.

Center Point Large Print
600 Brooks Road / PO Box 1
Thorndike, ME 04986-0001 USA

(207) 568-3717

US & Canada:
1 800 929-9108
www.centerpointlargeprint.com